They are the Merricks,
two brothers and a sister, restless, daring, proud.
English by birth, they came to Scotland
with their father to occupy McClairen lands.
And there each would find a love as wild and glorious
as the Highland isle they claimed as their own.
Ashton, the eldest son, is the passionate one.
Raine, the second son, is the reckless one.
Fia is the only daughter. This is her story. . . .

The Ravishing One

D1007879

"IS THIS SOME NEW FORM OF WITCHERY?" THOMAS DEMANDED.

"A torment dreamed up in that complicated little mind of yours? Because it is unnecessary. There is nothing you can do to make me want you more and to make that wanting more unbearable."

"But you are bigger, far stronger than I," Fia pointed out.

"I am weaker than a day-old kitten where you are concerned, madam. I am undone by you. I could no more force myself on you than I could fly."

"Even if I tempted you, teased you, brought you within an inch of what you want?"

He shook his head. "Would you have blood, Fia? Blood I would gladly give, if you would but cease these games and leave me in peace."

"I cannot."

"Then we are transfixed here, for I cannot leave you." His smile was infinitely sad.

"What do you want?" she asked softly.

"I want you to bid me to stay," he commanded. "But bid me to stay knowing that I will have you beneath me on your back."

He said not a word about affection, but she was a woman, not a maiden. Her marriage bed had had no affection in it. She knew now its presence because she'd known well its absence. He needn't say the words for them to be true.

"Please," she managed to say, "stay."

Dell Books by Connie Brockway

A DANGEROUS MAN

AS YOU DESIRE

ALL THROUGH THE NIGHT

MY DEAREST ENEMY

MCCLAIREN'S ISLE: THE PASSIONATE ONE

MCCLAIREN'S ISLE: THE RECKLESS ONE

MCCLAIREN'S ISLE: THE RAVISHING ONE

McClairen's Isle

The Ravishing One

Connie Brockway

A DELL BOOK

Published by
Dell Publishing
a division of
Random House, Inc.
1540 Broadway
New York, New York 10036

This novel is a work of fiction. Names, characters, places, and incidents either are the product of the author's imagination or are used fictitiously. Any resemblance to actual persons, living or dead, events, or locales is entirely coincidental.

If you purchased this book without a cover you should be aware that this book is stolen property. It was reported as "unsold and destroyed" to the publisher and neither the author nor the publisher has received any payment for this "stripped book."

Front cover art by Alan Ayers
Back cover art by Lisa Faulkenstern
Insert photo © IT STOCK INT'L / Index Stock Imagery / PNI

Dell® is a registered trademark of Random House, Inc., and the colophon is a trademark of Random House, Inc.

ISBN: 0-440-22630-9

Printed in the United States of America

Published simultaneously in Canada

July 2000

10 9 8 7 6 5 4 3 2 1

OPM

For my wise, witty, savvy father.
You were my very first hero, Dad,
and you still could give
lessons in "hero."

Acknowledgments

After writing a certain number of books, I find I keep thanking the same people. I am not about to stop now. I'd like to think this is because we've formed friendships and relationships that simply improve with age. In fact, as Carr would say, I insist on it. Because I know for a fact that the following people, whose talent, generosity, and encouragement have aided, nurtured, and sometimes, quite frankly, wrenched me from the fire, get better with each passing year.

So thank you Damaris Rowland, my wonderful agent, and Maggie Crawford, my insightful and talented editor. Thank you Susan Kay Law, Geralyn Dawson, and Christina Dodd, a triumvirate of wonderfully gifted writers who are always willing to put their talents at my disposal. Thank you Michelle Miller, for years of primo friendship, and Grace Pedalino, for whatever it is you do. And finally, all my love to you David and Rachel, lights of my life, joy of my existence. You are, all of you, truly the very best.

Prologue

*S*ome said Lady Fia Merrick was born bad, others that she'd only been raised to it. Whatever the case, it was generally agreed that she could not end up being anything but bad.

After all, her notorious father, Ronald Merrick, Earl of Carr, had killed her mother, his wife. Not that the little girl had any notion of this. She only knew that one day she had a doting mother and two brothers and then she did not.

No one came to explain. For the next several days her nurse arrived in a distracted, frightened, and silent state and then, one morning, after a tearful and furtive kiss she, too, disappeared.

Oh, people came. Meals appeared, someone aided Fia with dressing and undressing, and a long series of interchangeable faces arrived daily to mind her. This task usually fell to a maid-of-all-work no more than a decade older than Fia. The exhausted, frightened girls would set her down in whatever corner of the castle they were working and hiss at her not to move or speak while they went about their chores.

So Fia, by nature reticent, became more so. She cautiously followed, and silently watched, becoming a black-haired little shadow following in the footsteps of her servants. When she was noticed at all, it was with surprise and alarm and suspicion. As she was daughter of the Demon Earl, the servants considered Fia's silence unnatural, never realizing that they themselves had inspired it with their unspoken threats to abandon her should she ever make herself a bother. Because it was Fia's greatest fear that someday she would wake and find herself utterly alone. The wretched staff was too frightened of her father—and later of her—to adopt her into their circle, the other guests at the castle had no interest in the small doll-like creature, and her brothers were not allowed to see her.

Where other children learned their letters and numbers and were indoctrinated into the ways of their class by instructors, siblings, parents, and friends, Fia was uniquely alone. She knew nothing except that which she gleaned through observation. By six years of age Fia had learned to take her education where she found it. Instead of a classroom with books and paper and ink, her school was the castle-cum-gaming-hell known as Wanton's Blush.

There had been a time when Wanton's Blush was a

proud and unassailable island fortress belonging to an equally proud and unassailable line of Scots, the McClairens. For three hundred years the castle had stood as Maiden's Blush.

Then, one year in the early reign of George II, Ronald Merrick was chased out of England by a pack of creditors and found himself at Maiden's Blush, the guest of Ian McClairen, a man as honest and open-hearted as Merrick was devious and selfish.

Now, Ronald Merrick may not have had money, but he did have charm aplenty and he used it to hide his true nature from his hosts. Gloriously handsome and urbane, he easily won over the score of Scottish ladies then living at the castle, the most important being Janet McClairen, Ian's favored young cousin.

Seeing a plum ripe for his plucking, Ronald married the girl. For years after, he lived off the genial munificence of his Scottish hosts, feeding on their hospitality, gaining their confidence, and learning, to their everlasting regret, of their secret Jacobite loyalty.

After the Jacobites were routed at Culloden, Ronald testified against his wife's family, achieving two goals in doing so: the first being the executions of the McClairen men; the second being Maiden's Blush and the island on which it stood, a gift of a grateful monarch.

For years Janet refused to believe what she knew in her heart, that her husband had betrayed her people and that their blood had paid the price of turning Maiden's Blush into a sumptuous, decadent palace, rechristened Wanton's Blush.

When Janet could no longer hide the truth from

herself she confronted Carr. And he, with no more guilt than he'd felt upon betraying the McClairens, pitched her from the island's cliffs, claiming her death a terrible "accident."

In truth, murder came so easily to Carr, and the rewards from it were so substantial, that twice more he wed and killed wealthy heiresses. At which point his once-grateful sovereign heard of Carr's new habit and forthwith unofficially banished Carr to Scotland on penalty of death should he ever return to London and flaunt his ill-gotten gains.

For the first time Carr knew desolation. London had been the motive for his murders, his triumphant return to London the single goal to which he'd aspired.

But desolation shriveled and became the black seed of a tenacious resolve. He would return to London in splendor and power. He turned Wanton's Blush into a gaming hell and made a career of collecting debts both monetary and otherwise, blackmailing, pressuring, and slowly accumulating enough wealth and power so that no one dared gainsay him his objective. The people he collected at Wanton's Blush were the powerful, the wealthy, and the decadent.

And thus these were Fia's tutors.

Indeed, she would have reached adulthood without even the most rudimentary academic skills had not, in the beginning of her seventh year, a disfigured, hunched Scotswoman with a black veil draped over half her face presented herself at the kitchen door. She came seeking employment, asking only for room and board in return for caring for Carr's three children. Thus for the first time in two years Carr was reminded of his children's existence.

Carr's aversion to ugliness warred briefly with his greed, and greed—as was ever the case with Carr—won. The woman, Gunna, was hired. To Ash and Raine, well on their way to becoming the hell-spawned reprobates the locals deemed them, the old woman was a curiosity to be tolerated, ignored, and finally reluctantly respected. But to Fia, the ugly old woman was a revelation.

Gunna not only taught Fia the rudiments of reading and writing, but all her vast knowledge of Scottish lore and folk wisdom. But most important, Gunna, unfailingly honest in her acceptance of her own deformity and her own weaknesses as well as strengths, taught Fia to be honest with herself, to never turn from a truth, no matter how painful.

Gunna's broken appearance had separated her from her fellow man just as Fia's exalted status and otherworldly calm had set her apart. Perhaps 'twas the natural affinity of opposites, perhaps some sense of unspoken kinship, but the girl and the twisted old woman forged a deep, abiding bond.

Unfortunately the same providence that had supplied Fia with a caring counselor also drew her father's attention to her.

For in being reminded of his daughter, Carr noted how pretty she was. If she kept the promise of her childish beauty, one day she would be a prize. It would be a waste not to spend the necessary time cultivating her, ensuring she was a willing accomplice in the future

Carr envisioned for her—that future being in London, wed to power. He could not browbeat, belittle, or deride her as he did her brothers, for they were simply cubs to be driven from the pride, *his* pride, but she . . . Instead, Carr set about wooing his child.

Fia never stood a chance.

Wise though she was, she'd never learned to withstand loneliness. Gunna was a teacher and counselor and custodian. Carr offered something Fia had never known, a flattering companion.

He began to ask for Fia, to command her presence after dinner, to display her on his arm at milder entertainments—always careful to remind her that her manner and her purity must remain unimpeachable. And Fia, for so long ignored and overlooked, drank up his attention like parched earth drinks the rain.

Carr became Fia's confidant, her adviser, and her witty guide in the ways of the ton. And she became his familiar, eagerly accepting whatever he said as truth, his opinions as gospel. And all the while, he molded and shaped her to become his creation.

His whispers taught her whom to emulate and whom to despise. She learned her famous smile from an ancient French courtesan, her graceful, liquid walk from a Russian ballerina, the art of banter from a Hungarian princess. But when she was not following her father's amused suggestions, practicing the wiles he insisted she would someday need, mastering the arts of seduction, she retreated behind a smooth, watchful mask, and that, her stillness and unassailable self-containment, was uniquely and specifically her own.

On one hand, her sense of self was bloated by her father's constant flattery. On the other hand, the hard core of watchfulness and honesty central to her character whispered skeptically. In the end she saw far more than Carr wanted her to see.

One day a young man named Thomas Donne came to Wanton's Blush. He was purportedly a Scotsman cast off by his clan for his cowardly refusal to fight for Bonny Prince Charlie. He did not look cowardly to Fia. He looked magnificent.

It was not only that he was tall and dark-haired with gray eyes and a suave manner—handsome, urbane young men were endemic to Wanton's Blush. No, it was his character that set him apart. He was as different from the other guests as Carr insisted that he and Fia were.

Oh, he gamed and drank and lounged and trifled with various women, but Fia had the distinct impression that none of it meant anything to Thomas Donne, that it was simply a way to pass time until . . . Until what?

His eyes were as watchful as Fia's own and his hands as still. His manner was courtly; his bearing was impeccable. But most important, he treated the fifteen-year-old Fia with consideration. When he gazed at her, he was not gauging the depth of her décolletage or counting the gems adorning her person, he was looking at her. And he spoke to her. Simple conversations without innuendo. He asked her questions about what she liked, what she did not, whom she'd read, what she thought.

Fia fell in love. From a font of self-containment she became a nervous, adolescent girl. Not that anyone at the castle—most especially Thomas Donne—noticed. To them she appeared as cool and serene as ever.

Love made Fia vulnerable and miserable. When Donne next came to Wanton's Blush she noted his attentions to a young woman named Rhiannon Russell whom her brother Ash had brought to the castle. She was consumed by jealousy. So much so, that when Donne escorted Rhiannon into the garden on a cold, blustery day, she followed.

She crouched, trembling with self-loathing, on the far side of the stone wall, preparing to hear him make love to the woman. Instead she heard words that would change her life.

"This isn't simply a nasty family," Thomas said. "It's evil. Carr *killed* his first wife and then killed the next two. No one says it, especially those dependent on him for their gambling. Who would dare? But in London everyone knows, accepts it as fact—including the king."

The wind took the next words.

"—what your guardian is, Miss Russell! He left his sons to rot in God knows what form of hell rather than spend any of his precious money to ransom them."

More lost words, but by that time Fia could not tell if 'twas the rushing in her ears or that of the wind that shred them.

"His brother raped a nun! He is as bad as his sire. They all are. Fia is nothing more than Carr's whore, groomed to fetch the largest marriage settlement possible!"

She'd staggered to her feet and fled to the castle, her mind whirling, intent on one thing. Finding proof. Though she did not need it. All of her suspicions had finally found a voice. *His* voice.

In Carr's library, hidden in the mantel cache she'd seen her father opening, she found a thick packet of material. She did not find proof Carr had murdered her mother but she found other things, horrible things, more than enough to substantiate Thomas Donne's claim that the Merricks were a cursed family.

She forced herself to face the truth. She was the daughter of an evil man. Evil blood ran in her veins. Carr had cosseted, pampered, and groomed her to be sold to the highest bidder. And he'd made her complicit in his plan.

Overnight Fia changed. A weaker girl might have continued on in the role fate and blood had chosen for her. But Fia was not weak. The hard core of her hardened further. When Donne left a few days later after betraying her brother Ash and nearly costing him Rhiannon Russell's love, Fia noted it with newly born cynicism but no surprise.

She set about making her own plans, keeping her own counsel. She did not create an open breach with Carr but subtly challenged and derided him when she could. Perhaps deep within she'd hoped to see some evidence that her perfidy hurt Carr. It didn't. It only amused him. He'd used her from the beginning.

She vowed she would be used no more. Not by Carr. Not by anyone.

She'd intended to wait longer to realize her plans but when her brother Raine secretly returned to Wanton's Blush set upon an ill-fated course, she found she could not stand by and watch his destruction. Unbeknownst to Carr, she accepted a couple's precipitous invitation to journey with them and be their guest in London.

It was a desperate move. Carr would pursue her, if not himself then through any of a hundred agents, and drag her back. Once more, providence interceded. While Fia fled, Wanton's Blush burned and Carr, trapped inside retrieving his blackmail material, was seriously injured.

By the time he'd recovered, Fia had already accomplished her goal. Having taken society by storm, she'd culled from her herd of suitors a wealthy Scot, a lowland widower decades her elder, Gregory MacFarlane, and eloped with him to Scotland. MacFarlane was a bluff, unimaginative man who in wedding an English earl's daughter had achieved his lifelong ambition to gain entry to the upper echelons of English society.

Fia's intention in wedding him was just as cold and clear and simple. She needed only to wait until her husband died, at which time she, as his widow—as his *Scottish* widow—would inherit his estate. Finally she would be independent. And in the meantime, she was out from under Carr's thumb.

Things might have gone according to Fia's plan here out except for one simple matter. Upon arriving at MacFarlane's home in the lowlands Fia discovered that Gregory had neglected to tell her that he had two children.

And thus, two heirs.

Once more life had handed Fia a two-edged sword.

If Gunna's arrival in her life had been a revelation, MacFarlane's children were an epiphany. Each day something new, something astounding, confronted Fia. A few days after their arrival she discovered something that so confounded her that she could not help but question Gregory about it at breakfast.

"The tutor is teaching the girl Latin," Fia told him.

"Oh? Oh, yes," Gregory responded absently, chipping away at his hard-boiled egg. "He said the chit had a knack for languages."

"You mean you *knew* about it?" The notion that anyone would pay someone to instruct a *girl* dumbfounded her.

"Oh, yes. Rather resourceful of me, getting the education of both me brats for the price of one, eh?" Gregory continued eating as though he'd said nothing untoward, which only gave credence to Fia's growing suspicion that she had no real concept of what the world, the world outside Wanton's Blush, considered . . . normal.

"You mean Cora is being educated in the same disciplines as her brother?"

"Yes. Let's see . . . history, geography, and mathematics. I believe the fellow wants to throw in a smattering of philosophy, too." Gregory popped a bit of biscuit in his mouth.

"I see," she murmured. But she didn't. *"Why?"*

"Why?" Gregory paused in spreading soft cheese on his bread. "Because. Because that's what one does. One educates one's children. Just as your father had you educated and my father had me educated. I can't see that it did either of us any lasting harm and it keeps them occupied, but if you rather they didn't—"

"No! No, of course you are right," she said.

An idea occurred to her. She pondered it a moment. Then, in a voice that shook with fear that her plot might be discovered and she herself exposed as the half-bred monster posing at humanity that she was, she said, "I suppose that it is my duty as their . . . their stepmother to sit in on their lessons and make sure they are . . . they are properly attending them?"

"If you wish," Gregory responded calmly. "Do try the creamed haddock, m'dear. It's delicious."

He studied her as he chewed, a frown slowly forming on his face. "Tell me, Lady Fia, do you have a particular *modiste* you utilize? Because upon our return to London I insist you contact her about creating a new wardrobe for you." He dabbed at the bits of creamed haddock sticking to his lower lip, beaming munificently.

She blinked at him uneasily. She considered the gowns she now owned far and away sufficient for what her life would be from here on in. "Thank you, sir, but I have no need of more gowns. I've a surfeit of gowns, as you will see, for Gunna should soon be arriving with them."

"Who's Gunna?" Cora asked.

Fia turned to stare at MacFarlane's youngest child.

"Your nurse is coming to live here?" Kay's voice chimed in, drawing Fia's bemused glance. Kay was Gregory's nine-year-old son—and heir.

Children. At the dining table. Speaking without first being addressed. None of the few books she'd read made much mention of children, and certainly none of them described a child taking its meal with its parent. Why, even as Carr's doted-upon daughter, she'd never actually sat down at table with him and his guests.

"Why would you need a nurse?" Kay continued.

"I don't."

"Well," Kay said, "I hope, then, that she's coming for Cora, because *I* am too old to have a nurse."

Fia frowned. "No. She won't be nurse to either of you."

"Then why is she coming?" Kay demanded.

"To help me," Fia said, befuddled at finding herself answering the demanding inquiries of a nine-year-old boy. "Gunna arranges things and sees to things—"

"Ah!" Gregory exhaled. "She's here to replace Mrs. Osborne as housekeeper! Good. There now, Kay. You have your answer. Please don't speak anymore. At all."

"Would you play a game with me after breakfast, Mama?" Cora suddenly asked with suspicious ingenuousness.

Fia set down her fork and looked desperately at Gregory. "The girl called me 'mama' again!" she whispered urgently. "Why does she *do* that? I have asked her at least half a dozen times not to call me that, yet she continues to do so!"

Gregory shrugged. "She's teasing you."

Fia went utterly still. Her mouth parted, closed, and parted again. *"Teasing me?"*

No one had ever teased Fia. No one had come closer than offering a rude double entendre. This was different. The feelings flooding her were indescribable. She sat back in her seat.

No, things had not gone according to plan, but perhaps she could adapt.

Chapter 1

BRAMBLE HOUSE
THE SCOTTISH LOWLANDS
AUTUMN, 1765

Your father is here," Gunna whispered. She stood in the doorway, looking over her shoulder as if she expected Satan to be behind her. Nothing scared Gunna. At least, Kay MacFarlane thought interestedly, nothing until now.

And Fia, who usually seemed as composed as one of his tutor's mathematical theorems, flinched. "My father?"

"Aye." Gunna bit on the tattered scrap of her lower lip. "I could say yer gone."

Fia's black skirts rustled as she stood up. "No. I'm only surprised he's waited this long. The lawyers were here four months ago. Kay and Cora, please stay here with Gunna."

She disappeared into the interior of the house.

Gunna hesitated, fixing both children with a stern glare. Cora hastily closed her open mouth and went back to her needlework.

"You two'd best wait here if ye want to go to bed with blameless bums tonight," Gunna warned, and hastened after Fia.

"The kitchen," Cora said, popping to her feet.

"Don't be such a child, Cora," Kay chided her. "You can't mean to eavesdrop. It's so juvenile. Besides, 'tis nearly dinner. There'll be so many pots and pans banging around we won't be able to hear anything anyway."

Cora gave him a sour look and disappeared. Kay waited a few minutes and then rose. It wouldn't be right to set Cora a bad example, but he would be a poor excuse for a stepson if he didn't bother to find out what had upset Fia enough to make her flinch.

He headed down the hall for the servants' staircase, on his way nabbing a glass goblet from the sideboard in the dining room. The chance reminder of their father caused him a moment of melancholy.

Father had died five months ago. Dead of one too many treacle puddings, or so they said, and was it a wonder? Last time Father had been to Bramble House he'd looked like a prize bull but without any of the bullish parts and naught left but fat and bluster.

The thought saddened Kay, for he remembered Father as stout and solid a man as Bramble House was a manor. He pushed his sadness away. Something important was happening. Though in all the years she'd lived here Fia had never spoken about Lord Carr, Father had more than made up for that oversight.

On his rare visits home he'd been full of tales of his bosom companion, Ronald Merrick, Lord Carr. Fia hadn't liked that much. Her skin would tauten up and her eyes would grow flat with every mention of Lord Carr's name. Not that Father had noticed—but then, he hadn't been a very "noticing" sort.

Upstairs, Kay dropped to his knees and upended the goblet on the bare floorboards. It took him a few tries, but finally he found the best vantage for listening. Fia's voice, low and throaty as a spring warbler's, vibrated through the glass.

"—surprised you didn't have him done away with at once."

"And play right into your hand, m'dear? I should hope I have more restraint than that. Why, if I had, you'd have inherited a rich estate. You'd have been completely independent. Oh yes, Fia. I knew your plan from the moment I heard you'd 'eloped.' "

"You're forgetting his children." Fia's voice was a bit breathless. "His heirs."

The man laughed. "You know as well as I that had MacFarlane died when you'd first wed you would have had the management of his estate until the boy came of age. Still, from what I hear you didn't know about them, did you?

"How that *must* have pricked! I truly do wish I'd been a fly on the wall at that particular meeting."

There was a pause and Kay heard footsteps, measured and heavy. Lord Carr. When next he spoke it was directly beneath him but in a voice so low Kay only caught phrases.

"—enough faith in your imagination—"

"—sure you'd married with a plan already—"

"—dispose of the little—"

Then Fia's voice, cold and flavorless as ice. "Why did you come? You'd already sent your lawyers."

"I know the lawyers already told you," Carr purred, "but I could not deny myself the pleasure of repeating it to your face."

Fia's response was mostly lost but ended in the words "—how much?"

"Why, everything, my dear. *Everything.*"

There was a long pause, then Fia murmured something indistinguishable.

"I should think you would be happy I did," Carr responded. "MacFarlane was certainly delighted to have me vouch for him. And carry him. And accept his notes. And his collateral. I believe," a pause, "I believe he saw it as evidence of our friendship."

"You befriended him for one reason." Fia's voice was clear this time. "To avenge yourself on me."

"You are wrong. Well, *mostly* wrong. Oh, Fia, we are so alike, you and I. I wouldn't expend my energy on simple vengeance for anyone but you, dear daughter. Is that not proof of my paternal regard?"

Fia did not reply. The silence beneath Kay swelled, bloated on the black stew of emotions he sensed in the room below. He did not fully understand what was being said, but instinctively recognized it as vile. He'd begun to rise to his feet when he heard Fia again.

"What exactly do you want?"

"Nothing much. Simply for you to fulfill that role I assigned you on your birth, that role that you should have fulfilled five years ago but which you circumvented by running off with your Scottish groom. The role you were bred to perform."

Something fell on the floor below.

"What's this? Emotions, Fia? Oh, my dear, you *have* grown soft here in your little country estate. It's quite quaint, isn't it? All greeny and flattish. Not to my taste, but I see you've grown fond of it. And you can keep it, too. *If* you follow my wishes."

She said something. Her words were muffled.

"Well," Carr replied, "first off, you must come with me to London."

Chapter 2

The aria came to an end. The stout Italian bowed in acknowledgment of the applause and the impresario joined him to announce an intermission. Immediately a din of conversation filled the air as gentlemen and ladies jostled their way toward the lobby.

Captain Thomas Donne remained where he sat. Beside him his companions, Edward "Robbie" Robinson and Francis Johnston, lounged indolently while young Pip Leighton stood up and looked around eagerly.

Thomas had met Pip and his sister, Sarah, at an assembly to which his friend and shipping partner, James Barton, had brought him. Normally Thomas would have eschewed such affairs, but as his ship would take weeks to repair, he owned free time to spare. For a few days thereafter he had enjoyed Miss

Leighton's company, until it became apparent that she sought more than a casual friendship.

He could never offer his name to any English lady. Not because he did not want to—indeed, he wanted very much to have the sort of relationship James had enjoyed with his sweet Amelia before the influenza had taken her last year. No, he could not give his name because he no longer had one to give.

He was a convicted felon, deported as a Jacobite traitor and returned here under a false name. No one knew his true identity was Thomas Fitzgerald McClairen. Not even James Barton.

It had grieved Thomas to hurt Sarah, but at least he still held the good opinion of her brother, Pip. He was glad. He liked the young man.

"Her Christian name means 'dark promise,' " Pip suddenly crooned.

He smiled at the boy's impassioned tone. Apparently Pip had a new infatuation, some woman named Mac Farlane. The smile softened the hard lines of Thomas's dark, lean countenance and burnished the adamantine gray of his eyes to a warmer hue. If his stillborn brother had lived, he might have been much like Pip, not only in age but in coloring, having a shade of hair similar to Thomas's own mahogany.

If things had been different. If war and strife and Ronald Merrick, Earl of Carr, had not happened.

The thought of Carr frosted Thomas's smile.

"I'll be damned. There's the Black Diamond now," Francis Johnston breathed. "And as severe a beauty I never hope to see again."

"Is she here? Where?" Pip's head swung around.

"Up there, lad," Robbie remarked. "Watching from Compton's box. Or rather, being watched."

"Oh!" Johnston chuckled. "Imagine the consternation amongst the other fair ladies. They don't stand a chance by way of comparison."

"The Black Diamond?" Thomas asked, without looking about. Society was filled with high-class courtesans with interesting sobriquets. Unfortunately that was usually the most interesting thing about them.

" 'Tis a name one of the club lads conferred upon her. 'Tis said she's as rare and hard and black-hearted a beauty as that fabled gem," Johnston said.

"She's absolutely riveting. But *why* is she so riveting?" Robinson mused. "She doesn't utilize any of the usual tricks. No fans, no sidelong glances or teasing pouts . . . I'll be damned if I can see how she does it."

"And never will, Robinson," a wit behind them drawled. "See how she does it, that is. Not even if your older brothers were all to up and die. No mere viscount for that lady. You'd need a coronet at least to discover just how she *does* it."

The double entendre gave rise to rough, if embarrassed, laughter and cool disdain. Except from Pip. The lad's downy cheeks burned brilliant red.

"Lord Tunbridge!" he exclaimed, glaring behind them. "I demand an apology on behalf of the lady."

Dear God, Thomas closed his eyes in exasperation, *spare me indignant youth*. Of all the men the boy could have chosen to take issue with over some light-skirt, Pip had to pick a renowned swordsman. True, Tunbridge's skill might have been hampered as a result of having his hand—and the card he'd been trying to palm—impaled against a tavern table some years back. Had not Tunbridge fenced with either hand.

Tunbridge laughed. "Tell me, gentlemen, am I mistaken or has this pup just challenged me?"

Calmly, Thomas turned around. The years had not been good to Tunbridge. Once thin, he was now near skeletal, the cheekbones jutting painfully in his face, his eyes sunken into sulfur-colored flesh.

"Ah," Thomas said, smiling lazily. "If it isn't Tunbridge, by Jove. Tunbridge, do beg pardon of the lad so we might enjoy more songs. 'Tis too early in the eve to contemplate a duel." Neither his drawl nor his insouciance was as smooth as they'd once been but Tunbridge did not seem to notice.

"I'd take it as a personal favor," Thomas added.

A flicker of startled recognition awoke in Tunbridge's sunken eyes. When Thomas had first returned to England seven years ago, he'd fashioned himself the persona of a dissolute, expatriate Scot. Tunbridge had been a central figure amongst the gaming hells, pleasure houses, and taverns he'd frequented.

Thomas's goals then had been to first befriend and then destroy Carr's son Ash, on his way to doing the same to Carr. He'd nearly achieved his goal—and found that the role of Judas had damaged him more than Ash. Soon after Thomas had left England.

"Who's this? Donne, isn't it?" Tunbridge's eyes narrowed. "Chased out of the Highlands when you refused to fight for your Bonny Prince, wasn't it?"

Thomas continued to smile. He'd put the story out himself, as part of his masquerade.

"I will have my apology, Lord Tunbridge!" Pip declared in mounting indignation.

Drat the boy. Tunbridge would have forgotten him if he'd remained mum.

"Eh?" Tunbridge half turned his head, his eyes flickering uncomfortably over Thomas's gently smiling face and hard, toned body. "What? An apology? But of course. Sorry. No offense meant . . ."

Pip scowled. "Well, I most assuredly took—"

"None was taken," Thomas interjected. He gripped Pip's arm in an iron clasp that belied the casual gesture. "I daresay we all mumble things we regret. *Don't we, Robbie?*"

Robbie's compressed mouth relaxed. "Quite right. Men are always making asses of themselves over women who won't spare them a glance."

The barb missed its mark, however, for Tunbridge had backed away from the group, eager to be off. Probably scuttling off to inform Carr of something or other. Tunbridge had ever been Carr's creature.

Pip tried to pull away and follow but Thomas refused to release him and the other gentlemen, unwilling to allow the boy to throw his life away so effortlessly, immediately interposed themselves between Pip and the departing Tunbridge.

" 'Sblood," Robbie said, clapping Pip on the back, "if I were to account for every thoughtless remark I'd made, I'd be filling ledger books for months!"

Johnston had an even better notion of how to distract the ruffled youngster. "Will you look at that? More lads have entered Compton's box. Begad! They'd best watch out lest the damned thing break free of the wall and crash down on the cits!"

Thomas followed Johnston's amazed gaze. His eyes narrowed on the gilt box. "Hand me your binoculars, Robbie," he murmured, scowling.

He took the ivory set and raised them to his eyes. As though guided by fate, he found himself looking directly into her eyes.

Fia Merrick's eyes.

He could not be mistaken. She'd flitted like a beauteous wraith at the edges of his imagination for years, a phenomenon he'd never allowed himself to examine too closely. But now . . . His breath caught in his throat.

She was, had always been, the most ravishing creature he'd ever seen. She was even more ravishing now.

The passage of six years had only refined her luminous, otherworldly beauty. High, exotic cheekbones, pure expanse of smooth forehead, the jut and delicate angularity of her jaw, time had only sculpted them more resolutely.

The creamy white skin clung with more conviction to the bones beneath. Her eyes, always crystalline, looked bluer and harder than gemstones. Her mouth was both fuller and softer. Against all of fashion's dictates she wore her unpowdered hair down and loose, black cascading ringlets of it, its darkness devoured by the black, daringly low-cut bodice.

"Fia," Thomas murmured.

"You know her?"

"Fia Merrick?" Thomas lowered the binoculars. Pip didn't stand a chance if the likes of her had beguiled him. "Aye."

"Not Merrick any longer, old son," Johnston said. " 'Tis MacFarlane."

So she'd wed. Not surprising. Carr had been grooming her since infancy to adorn some power broker's arm. Though the name MacFarlane was not familiar.

"Which one is her husband?" Thomas could not think why he asked the question—except he wanted to know what the man looked like who could afford Fia Merrick.

"None of them," Robbie answered. "Ah! I forget you've been gone a year. You see, Lady Fia ain't got a husband. That is to say she had one, but she's hasn't anymore. He died. . . . Seems to me 'twas over a year ago. But then, if it had been that long, she'd have abandoned mourning, wouldn't she?"

"Why should she?" Johnston asked softly, eyes on Fia. "When she wears black better than night itself?"

Robbie chuckled. "Did you hear that, Donne? Lord spare us if Johnston ain't come all over poetical!"

But Thomas was not attending. Carr had had a nasty habit of losing spouses. Did Fia too? "Her husband is dead, you say?"

"Yes," Robbie answered, his smile fading. "Didn't know him meself. Older fellow. Stolid Scottish merchant. Caused quite a stir when Lady Fia ran off with him."

"She *eloped* with him?" It made little sense. Why would Fia have eloped with a Scottish nobody?

"A short month after her arrival," Johnston said, "and I know for a fact that she'd received three offers before MacFarlane took off with her."

"He was a wealthy man?" Thomas asked sardonically.

"Exceptionally wealthy."

Pip swung about. He'd apparently been listening after all. "There is only one reason a lady of Lady Fia's quality would elope. *Obviously* she was in love."

"Obviously." Johnston's head bobbed in innocent agreement.

"Without a doubt," Robbie concurred.

Pip nodded gruffly and went back to studying Fia.

"How did Carr take the news of his daughter's elopement?" Thomas asked.

"Carr?" Robbie's nostrils flared delicately, as though scenting tainted meat. "Can't recall. Though later MacFarlane and he became boon companions. The two were inseparable."

"Lady Fia must have been relieved there was such accord between her father and her husband," Thomas said.

"One couldn't say," Johnston said. "Lady Fia never came to town. Quite withdrew from society once she'd wed. Spent five years marooned at MacFarlane's country house. Lord, she must have hated it for—"

Johnston leaned forward, glanced circumspectly at Pip's back, and whispered, "—to be perfectly blunt, she came back into society months before her mourning period was officially over."

"Who can blame her?" Pip cast about angrily.

Johnston sighed, looking upward as though to ask heaven how the lad's hearing could be so keen.

"A beautiful young woman like that?" Pip continued. "Kept in some heathenish backwoods when she should be celebrated, admired, and revered? Why, 'twas abominable of MacFarlane to keep her there!"

"Precisely!" Robbie agreed.

"My thoughts exactly," Johnston nodded vigorously.

Thomas did not want to ask but the suspicion forming in his mind would not let him remain silent. "Was she able to comfort MacFarlane in his final hours?"

"That's the tragedy of it!" Pip flung out his hand. "He was in town and she was in the lowlands."

She hadn't killed him.

"That's right," Johnston agreed. "MacFarlane was here, with that . . . with Carr. The man ought to be brought up on charges of murder."

Murder. A knot abruptly tightened in Thomas's stomach. "Why is that, Johnston?"

Johnston's eyes flashed. "Carr led him on such a dance through society's hellholes that MacFarlane's old carcass finally just gave out. Drinking, gorging, gaming, wenching, up for days on end, week upon week. You could actually see MacFarlane deteriorate. It was vile."

"Whatever Lady Fia's father's infamy, it should not be allowed to reflect on her," Pip exclaimed. "She is innocent."

"Quite right," Robbie said.

But was she? Thomas asked himself. Or was she simply more circumspect than her father? No, his hatred of Carr biased him. 'Twas probably no more than it seemed, an elderly man chasing recklessly after his youth until his heart gave out.

Pip inclined his head with bitter exactitude. "If you gentlemen will forgive me, I must pay my respects to Lady Fia."

"I'll go with you," Johnston said. He swung his arm around the younger man's shoulders, shepherding him through the crowd and keeping up a bright line of chatter as he went. As they were about to exit to the outer lobby he glanced back and waggled his eyebrows.

Robbie burst out laughing. "Quite a young hothead you've taken under your wing there, Donne. He'd best learn to control his temper, though, especially if he's going to become infatuated with the likes of Lady Fia."

"Why is that?"

"The woman is a notorious heartbreaker. Half of society won't let her through their door whilst the other half besieges her with invitations. Gads, Donne, will you please drag yourself off the docks on occasion and pay heed to what's going on around you?"

"Forgive me," Thomas said. "Here I thought I had been attending—*your* cargo, if I remember correctly."

Robbie grinned. "Well, in that case, I shall make an exception for you and apprise you of the pertinents. The fact of the matter is that in the last month the Black Diamond has been at the center of no less than four duels. Four!" Robbie said.

"Well, now that you tell me that, Robbie, I see your point. I shall tell young Pip to be more discriminating as soon as he returns," Thomas vowed ironically.

Robbie sighed. "You're right, of course. When does a young man heed advice when it comes to his . . . to matters of the heart?" He shook his head. "Do you remember your first infatuation, Donne? I'll never forget mine. Lyssie Carter."

Thomas didn't respond. He couldn't. He'd been imprisoned when he was thirteen for having taken up arms against Lord Cumberland's troops when they'd come north to teach the Scots the meaning of the word "reprisal." His older brother John had been hung, drawn, and quartered for the same crime of treason.

Because of Thomas's youth he'd been spared, sent first to prison, then to a transport ship, and finally to a cruel bondmaster in the West Indies. There had been no fetes, card parties, no masques or dinner table flirtations for him. The only females he'd known had been those as desperate as he for a few hours of physical release from their wretched lives. But even then Thomas had never confused desperation with love.

The simple fact was, he'd never had a "first" love. He'd never had a "love" at all.

"Your reluctance to name names shames me," Robbie said, dismissing the topic and looking around. "Ha! Your young friend has managed to shoulder his way to his goddess's side." Robbie chortled. "Though it looks more like he's trying to throw himself prostrate at her feet."

Thomas raised his opera glasses to his eyes. Fia had engaged Pip's hand, either taking pity on the lad or, Thomas thought cynically, realizing that the boy's imminent fall from the box might cast a pall over her party's spirits.

Her unique smile deepened and her eyes lit up in welcome. Johnston was right. There was nothing overtly seductive in either her attitude or her expression. Indeed, one would swear that she greeted Pip in the same manner as she would a friend.

Thomas's eyes narrowed. What could she think to get out of her association with Pip?

As Thomas watched, a man's tanned hand appeared in his binoculars' view and touched Fia's shoulder. Thomas raised the glasses.

It was his partner, James Barton.

On the opposite side of the opera house, another pair of opera glasses had long been raised as Ronald Merrick, Earl of Carr, languidly scanned the crowd. Stilted conversation hummed behind him, though it was a travesty to call it conversation; that art had apparently been lost to London society during the long years Carr had been relegated to the Scottish Highlands.

Carr's gaze continued idly roving the crowd. It was a testament to his superior nature that he'd found worth in his early misfortunes. If he hadn't gone to Scotland, he wouldn't have married Janet McClairen, whose fortune had become the basis for his own. He glanced over his shoulder, wondering if Janet's ghost was here—one never could tell when she would appear; once he'd seen her at Covent Garden picking through cabbages.

"Looking for someone, Lord Carr?" his host, Sir Gerald Swan, asked. Swan was a member of Parliament who'd been elected on the basis of a reputation for personal integrity. Carr, however, had in his possession a document that quite put the lie to that integrity nonsense.

Carr regarded Swan placidly. Carr was no fool. He knew better than to tell anyone about Janet. It might begin a rumor that he'd become a spiritualist. As if he would align himself with such idiocy! Accepting that ghosts existed and believing that they mattered were two separate things entirely.

"No," Carr drawled. "I was simply hoping to find something to distract me from an encroaching ennui."

Society, Carr had long since decided, was simply no longer what it had once been. In fact, over the last few years he'd decided that ruling society was much like leading apes in hell—a rather fruitless and low occupation for one of his stamp.

Of late he'd set his eyes on a new prize. Since he no

longer wished to rule society he would rule England. To do so, he would achieve power as men since time immemorial had, through the accumulation of other men's power. Little men. Like Swan.

Swan cleared his throat. "I see Lady Fia is in rare good looks tonight."

Carr's brows rose. "Is she?" Fia hadn't told him she would be attending the opera tonight. "Where is she?"

"In Compton's box. The third tier on the far side."

Carr brought the glasses up to his eyes. It took him a few seconds to find the correct box, but when he did he immediately recognized Fia's exotic features and her long, unpowdered . . .

Carr frowned. Good Lord, he hoped society did not take to brushing the powder from their wigs because of Fia. He touched his elaborate powdered periwig. Beneath it his hair, once golden, had begun to fade. He didn't think a black wig would suit him. What with the scar on his face . . . No, he would simply look too unapproachable.

He readjusted his opera glasses. Fia was chatting amiably with some puppy. As Carr watched, a broad-shouldered, thickset man entered the box and pushed his way to Fia's side. He looked familiar. Ah, yes. 'Twas James Barton, captain of some merchant ship, if he recalled correctly.

A long time ago, Carr had been on the cusp of adding Barton's name to the list of people who could be counted upon to do him favors. Somehow things had gone awry. It didn't matter. Barton had only been a struggling seaman. But now, studying the ruby winking from the man's neckcloth and the intricate gold embroidery decorating his cuffs, Carr regretted he'd not pursued the association. A huge diamond sparkled on Barton's rough hand—Carr checked and stared— the same rough hand that descended on Fia's bare shoulder.

Carr's mouth flattened. She couldn't be so stupid. She must know he would never agree to her whoring for some . . . nobody! Not now. Not when he was so close to deciding who would be her next husband!

He dropped the binoculars, vexed beyond repair. Was it not enough that society considered her just this side of the pale? *Just*. And she knew it. She purposely fed the gossips, promoting the ribald stories about her, the result being that her more illustrious suitors had yet to come up to scratch. Which was just exactly what she counted on, Carr thought grimly.

Carr glared, willing her to feel his wrath. She didn't. Even if she did, he knew her too well to believe she'd acknowledge it. Fia never gave anything away. Not since that day he'd met with her at . . . what was the name of that damned house he now owned? Babble House? Brummel?

"Lord Carr," a hoarse voice spoke. He turned around. Tunbridge stood in the doorway. Behind him, Janet ducked behind a potted palm.

"What is it, Tunbridge?" Carr asked, wondering if he should find a priest to perform some sort of exorcism. Ever since Janet had fled Favor McClairen's body—or had she never actually been *in* Favor's body? He was still a little vague on that—she'd been pestering him. It wasn't frightening; it was annoying.

Tunbridge sidled closer. "There's a man here you ought to know about. Thomas Donne."

Donne? Carr lifted his binoculars again and trained them where Tunbridge pointed. Begad, Tunbridge was right. There stood the tall, broad-shouldered Scot, his face as dark as a savage's, his pale gray eyes raised to—Carr moved his glasses upward—Fia. And with *such* an expression of cold condemnation. Now that *was* interesting.

Poor Fia. Donne was the one man whom, to Carr's knowledge, Fia had ever wanted, and here Donne stood studying her with as much approval as he would give a fanged serpent. Carr smiled.

Thomas Donne, né McClairen: the last laird of the McClairen, the dispossessed son, and the exiled chieftain. Carr had known Donne's real identity for years. As far as he knew, he was the only one who did. He'd assumed that Donne remained safely off English soil. It was interesting that he'd returned.

Carr dismissed Tunbridge with a wave of his hand, and the thin man dissolved back into the shadows.

Casually, Carr put away his binoculars and rose to his feet. He secured the silver-tipped walking cane he'd needed ever since the night Wanton's Blush had burned to the ground, and prepared to quit the box. Thomas Donne—formerly McClairen—interested him. More so than the opera and certainly more than Swan.

"Lord Carr?" Swan stumbled to his feet. "Can I get you a refreshment? Is something wrong?"

"No, Swan, nothing is wrong," Carr said with honest surprise. "I would never allow it."

Chapter 3

She's not worthy of you, Jim." Thomas raked his hair back in exasperation. They'd been at it ever since Thomas had come upon James tying his neckcloth in front of the hall mirror. He'd sarcastically asked just how tightly Lady Fia liked her men trussed.

He shouldn't have said it. But once started the silence he'd imposed on himself for the past week broke lose. Jim's subjugation to Fia Merrick worried and disappointed him. All week he had heard tales of her sexual exploits, her wildness, and her profligacy. Added to which, being a devotee of Lady Fia's was bad for one's health. Her reputation stood constantly in jeopardy and therefore stood constantly in need of defense.

James must have heard the same stories, yet it

seemed not to matter to him. Every night he hurried to Fia's side with exotic baubles and expensive gifts. Thomas's hands clenched.

"You do not understand, Tom," James said. His voice, a moment ago raised in anger, was now placating.

"Oh, I rather think I do," Thomas muttered. He understood that Fia's bosom was snowy and full, her mouth inviting, and her gaze beneath the thicket of curling black lashes as impertinent and wise as Lilith's. "After what you had with Amelia, how can you be besotted of a—"

"Don't." James's eyes, usually so placid, blazed. "You're perilously close to being called out, Tom."

"I won't duel with you, Jim."

"I've used my fists before."

Thomas gave a short, bitter laugh. He owed this man so very much, not the least being his own miserable life. It had been James Barton who'd purchased Thomas's bond from the sadistic animal who'd originally owned it. Within a week, James had released Thomas of the year left in his indenture and hired him to work on his ship.

James had never asked Thomas anything about his past and Thomas had never spoken of it, though he had told James his intention of someday quitting the sea and rebuilding his ancestral home in Scotland. He considered telling James about his association with the Merricks, but discarded the idea. James would only point out that Fia had been a babe when Carr had betrayed the McClairens and stolen their home.

"What spell has she cast over you?" Thomas asked in exasperation.

"You're so damn set against her. She told me you would be. But you don't *know* her, Tom." James's face grew earnest.

Thomas ignored his entreaty. *"She told you?"* The ramifications flooded Thomas's imagination.

Fia knew he was in London. She knew he and Barton were partners and she'd warned Barton that he would oppose any relationship between James and her. The bitch had preempted him! Fury uncoiled within him and coiled back in on itself, vibrating with intensity.

"What did she tell you?" Thomas asked.

"That you were once her brother's only friend and that you came to their home and ate their food and slept under their roof and then betrayed her brother, nearly costing him the one thing in life he required, the woman he loved."

The sharp spear of guilt was unexpected and thus all the sharper, for it was true. What Fia had told him was true. And yet there was so much more to it than that.

"I told her she must be mistaken. Just as you are mistaken in her, Thomas."

"I'm not mistaken in this," Thomas said stubbornly. "She's made you her lapdog."

"Damn it, Tom!" James burst out. "There's more to this than you understand. Much more."

"Tell me."

"I can't. I gave Fia my word. God! It's all such a muddle."

Thomas nodded sardonically. Fia had always "muddled" men's minds. Thomas only hoped the poor fool didn't live to regret his infatuation. The thought burned like acid. He snatched his cape from the back of the settee where he'd tossed it.

"You're going out?" James asked.

"Yes." Thomas's voice was curt. "And I won't be back this night." He did not think he would handle returning and finding her here, with James.

Tomorrow, he would visit Fia—just to make sure she knew that James had a friend as well as a partner. Until then, he would go toward the river, where he could find a way to work off his anger in the haunts of hard men and harder women.

Though he doubted they could hold another woman as hard as Fia Merrick.

The clang of steel on steel echoed through the dark predawn air. Thomas peered past the links boy who'd lit his path across the cobbled street.

"Ye don't be wantin' to get involved wid them what's down there." The boy jerked his head toward the black maw of an alley. The glare from the torch made cruel work of his young, pinched face. "Best go this way."

"And why is that?" Thomas's voice was a soft rumble, slipping easily into dockyard cant. "You wouldn't be havin' a chum waitin' in a yard down there to nab me purse, would you, lad?"

"Nah," the boy answered, the glance that traveled over Thomas's tall frame as impersonal as it was assessing. "Yer too big. Yer knuckles is too large and yer eyes is too canny. 'Twas a friendly word of advice, is all.

"That down there goes to the York Stairs what leads to the river. Dark place. Out of the way, like. The watch don't even like going there. So's it's a grand place fer the bloods to stick each other."

"Dueling? Is that what we're hearing?" Thomas asked.

The lad shrugged and Thomas tossed him a penny. Up the narrow street a door opened. A pair of staggering nabobs emerged from the bright rectangle of a tavern's door. The links boy trotted off to offer them his services in navigating the dark, muck-filled alley.

Thomas turned toward the embankment. Long rows of smudge pots lined the top, their ghostly haze unfurling spectral tendrils into the dank night air. The salty bite of brine and the thick stench of sewage clotted in his nostrils.

He walked on. If all went right and his little discussion with Fia had its desired effect, perhaps in a few days he could escape this city and go north to McClairen's Isle.

The affinity he felt toward the isle and its castle mystified him. He'd never lived there, and had seen it only a few times as a youngster. Yet like a lodestone it exerted a powerful pull not only on him, but on other McClairens, too. Perhaps it was simply that they were an exiled people tired of wandering.

"Next time you conceive a desire to spill blood, I suggest you find a better reason!"

Tunbridge's voice echoed up from the riverbanks. The hairs at the nape of Thomas's neck rose. He strained his ears to discover the exact direction of Tunbridge's voice.

Damn. London's perpetual fog and the twining stone corridors conspired to confuse the senses and throw back sound as though it came from every direction at once. Boot heels beat a sharp tattoo against cobblestones. A man shouted once for aid, other voices answered, fading in a hollow echo.

"Where are you?" Thomas shouted.

"Here!" a young man's voice returned frantically. "Dear God, please hurry! He's unconscious and the blood— Help!"

Thomas followed the voice down a long, dark alley that ended in a small yard surrounded on three sides by tall buildings, their rude stone walls wet with brackish slime. At the opposite end of the yard a vaulted area stood at the top of one of the river's many flights of steps.

"Where are you?"

"Here! Oh, thank God you're here, sir! Help me!" A figure moved beneath the vault. Thomas went at once and found a young man crouched beside another youngster, a pool of glistening black spreading beneath his prone body. Pip Leighton.

One hand clutched a kerchief to his breast; the other lay twisted beneath his body. Beside Pip lay an obscenely pristine blade. Another lay a few feet away, its broken tip dark with blood. All this Thomas saw in a matter of seconds.

Wretched, stupid boy! Savagely he kicked Pip's sword away, sending it clattering down the steps. He turned to the other youngster. "Who are you?"

"Albert Hennington, sir," the boy answered in a quavering voice.

Thomas barely heard him. He knelt and carefully removed Pip's useless rag. Quickly, he studied the wound. It was high on Pip's breast and deep . . . very deep, no slashing of the meat. Driven in and jerked out. Pip's blood flowed freely but did not gush from the wound, nor did it bubble as would indicate his lung having been pierced, nor well up rhythmically, as an arterial wound would have done.

Thomas felt little rewarded by the discovery. Pray God it had not severed whatever pathways served to make the arm functional. He let the blood flow a minute longer, having noted in a life all too conversant with injuries that those puncture wounds that bled most freely less often grew gangrenous.

He ripped the fine Brussels lace from the cuffs on Pip's shirt and, pressing his own folded kerchief over the wound, bound it tightly to Pip's chest with the torn lace.

"What the bloody hell was he doing here?"

"It was Tunbridge, sir," Albert said. "Pip saw him at a drum we attended earlier. He accused Tunbridge of offending Lady Fia and demanded satisfaction! Tunbridge only laughed. Pip waited until Tunbridge left the ball and then confronted him."

"The fool!" Thomas whispered. "Well, boy, you'd best pray your friend here lives to regret his folly."

Gingerly, he slid an arm beneath Pip's knees and another under his back. With a grunt, he heaved himself and his burden to his feet. "Come on, then, Albert."

"But, sir! Perhaps I should wait? Tunbridge sent for a surgeon!"

"Bloody unlikely," Thomas said, "but satisfy yourself." He strode out of the vaulted cavern.

The boy waited a full five minutes before the sound of a wharf rat scuttling toward the scent of fresh blood sent him scuttling, just as ratlike, to retrieve Tunbridge's bloodied sword. He waved it threateningly at the rodent. The rat sat on its haunches and commenced to clean itself.

Ten minutes later Albert caught up with Thomas.

Thomas brushed past the stammering footman guarding Fia's front door to find a stately-looking butler blocking his way. "Where is your mistress?" he demanded.

"If you'll inform me of your name, sir," the butler said coldly, "I will see whether Lady Fia is—"

Thomas gripped the man's front coat and jerked him forward. He was dimly aware that he was bullying someone who could not respond in kind, but anger crowded such considerations from his mind. "*Where . . . is . . . your . . . mistress?*"

Amazingly, the butler refused to speak, as if inspired by loyalty. Only the flicker of his gaze in the direction of the stairs gave away any information.

With an oath, Thomas flung the man from him and took the stairs two at a time. Of course she would still be abed. It was not yet noon.

At the top of the stairs a frightened maid bearing a stack of linens pointed a shaking finger in response to his demand. He stalked to the door she indicated and pushed it open without knocking.

Though it was only midmorning, a full half-dozen men crowded Fia's boudoir, offering their opinions on her toilette. They ringed her rosewood dressing table, their primped and carefully painted faces reflected in the huge velvet-draped mirror sitting atop its lacquered surface. One man sat on a tufted stool by her feet. Another knelt beside her, peering into a silver dish containing beauty marks. The others stood close. James was among their number.

Thomas dismissed his friend's presence, turning his attention to Fia.

Like a rose in a field of bracken, she reclined against the tufted back of a small gilt chair, glorious and feminine in her fashionable dishabille. Her black, spiraling tresses trailed over her spare, smooth, white shoulders, naked above the filigreed lace edge of her negligee. Sheer, shell-pink silk flowed along the curves of her body and pooled about her feet.

As a child her beauty had been disconcerting; as a woman it was devastating. An untried boy would have no chance of resisting such as she.

She'd not remarked his entrance, Thomas noted bitterly. Why would she? What could one man more in her chambers mean to her? Or the absence of one boy? *Nothing*.

He cut through the ranks of her admirers until he stood within a few feet of her. The men's heads turned, irritated at the appearance of yet another contender for Fia's attention. When they saw what he carried, their irritation gave way to alarm.

Thomas lifted Tunbridge's broken, bloodstained épée like a talisman. He pitched it into the air and seized the middle of the bare blade in his fist, feeling the edge cut into his palm. The men's mutters faded, the room grew still with expectancy, and Fia, who'd been leaning back and sideways as she listened to the poor sot kneeling beside her, froze.

She turned her head slightly, her eyes still downcast, as if assessing his presence with senses other than sight. Her lashes swept across the creamy curve of her high cheekbones. Her nostrils flared delicately. She was unearthly beautiful.

He waited for her to look up. She would acknowledge him, damn her, *before* he spoke. Her brow knotted, smoothed, and slowly her gaze rose. By God, her eyes were just as startling a blue as he'd remembered. Mayhap more so.

"Lord Donne." Her voice was slight, breathless.

"Lady Fia."

"I say, Lady Fia, who is this fellow?" the swarthy man at her feet asked.

"Lord Donne is a very old friend of the family." Her eyes remained locked with his.

"Thomas?" James spoke.

Thomas ignored him. He didn't want to be here. The thought drummed, angry and desolate, in his mind. He'd thought himself finished with the Merricks. Above all things, he desired to be done with them.

But she, damn her, had drawn him back into their poisonous web and he resented it, almost as much as the regret with which he registered the fine lines at the corners of her magnificent eyes and the shadows beneath her cheekbones. He steeled himself against the unexpected compassion these signs of her weariness awoke.

She'd played havoc with a boy's heart, a boy's life. Common knowledge said it was not the first time she'd done so in her brief but lethal career. She played, now she must pay the price of her sport.

"I've brought you a memento," he said.

A line of consternation appeared between the dark wings of her brows. "A memento?"

"Of a particularly successful seduction."

"Thomas . . ." James laid a cautioning hand on his forearm. Thomas shook it off. James was in her thrall. 'Twas a fitting term, for couldn't he himself feel the draw of her, the potent attraction she wielded with such blithe disregard?

"Here." He dropped the bloodied blade on her lap, staining the fragile silk of her dressing gown. "You can add this to your collection."

She looked down, instantly recoiling. He waited, the pulse beating thick and urgent in his veins. He could not see her expression. Her face remained bowed over the blade, her hands arrested in the air above it, her tumbled locks masking her face.

"What is this?" she asked in a low, hoarse voice.

"By God, Thomas, you go too far!" James ground out.

"Do I?" His gaze slew to James, white-faced and trembling. "And here I'd thought *she'd* gone too far, for 'twas for her sake that the boy offered himself up in a demonstration of Tunbridge's art. For her—"

"What boy?" Her head snapped up.

"Are there so many?" He smiled mirthlessly.

"What boy?"

"I'd best describe him lest you have forgotten his name," he said. "A boy of eighteen years but looked less. Red-haired and fair-skinned—"

"Not Pip." Her eyes looked stricken and for a moment his resolve wavered. But then, he remembered, she had an audience to woo.

"I see you do recall him. He'll be gratified. Phillip Leighton. Pip. Not rich Pip, not powerful Pip, but as capable of love as any grown man. Indeed"—his gaze swept through the group of poseurs like the blade he'd so lately discarded—"more so. But then, the young love so ardently, so wholeheartedly, don't they? So very, very foolishly."

"Yes. They do," she said quietly. "Or so I've been told. Where is he now? What happened?"

"Your name was being besmirched," he said. "Pip would have none of it. The young fool challenged Tunbridge to a duel. Tunbridge accepted. They fought.

Young Pip, as you can see"—he looked tellingly at the bloodstained épée—"lost."

"Is he dead?"

"Not yet. The blade pierced his breast but no vital organs." The tension in her eased. She wasn't going to get off so comfortably. "If he's very lucky no nerves will have been severed and no infection will set in and he'll live to learn a lesson from his ill-advised gallantry."

"Perhaps we all will," she said softly before raising accusing eyes. "And what of you? Apparently you have some feelings for . . . this lad. Were you his second? A man of your years playing second for a boy? Could you have not stopped it?"

"I knew nothing of the duel." How dare she place the onus for Pip's fate on him? "I heard the sound of the duel and followed it. It was done by the time I got there. Pip is not much of a swordsman."

And having been stung by her inference that he had let the boy challenge and fight an opponent that Thomas knew to be superior, he repaid her in kind, by attacking. "When did *you* first come upon him? Pip, that is. You could have circumvented this then, by simply *letting the lad be*. He couldn't have presented much of a challenge. Not for you."

"No," she said tautly. "No challenge at all."

" 'Sblood, man," James burst out. "Continue and I'll be forced to call you out myself!"

Fia put her hand down on the chair's arm and pushed herself upright. The sword clattered to the floor, leaving a dark smear on her pale skirts.

The sharp sound shattered the shocked paralysis holding the other men in the room. The swarthy young man on the stool surged up and struck Thomas's cheek.

"Name the place, sir!" he ground out.

"No."

"Coward!" another gentleman spat.

The swarthy man's jaw bulged in frustration. He raised his hand to deliver a backhanded blow to Thomas's other cheek but Thomas caught his forearm, stopping him.

"Don't do it," Thomas advised coldly. "She's not worth a broken wrist, let alone your life." To emphasize his point he tightened his grip until he felt the man's bones grind together.

The dark man's brows snapped together in startled pain. Helplessly he tried to yank free, but Thomas's grip had been honed holding his own weight one-handed from a yardarm fifty feet abovedeck while he secured a sail with the other.

"I will not tolerate your insult of this lady!" the man panted, fear causing his voice to break.

"Thomas, desist!" James commanded as harsh exclamations erupted around them. Faces grew livid. Feet shifted.

"Stop it!" Fia's voice rose above the rising clamor. "Let him go!"

Thomas turned on her with a snarl. "Don't fret, madam. Your conscience will not be marred on my account." He looked at the man twisting angrily in his grip. "You can call me out as many times as you like, *sir.*" His gaze swept over the rest of them. "Any one of you can, but you won't find any satisfaction. Not now, not ever. Enough blood has been spilled because of her and her own. And from the look of you pitiful fools"—he included James in his scathing scrutiny—"more will be. But not mine. *Never* mine."

With a muttered oath, Thomas released the man's wrist. He snatched it to his chest, backing away.

Thomas waited, sure the fool would retaliate. Thus he did not hear or see Fia move. But he felt her suddenly, close behind. He swung around. She stood less than an arm's span away, her blue eyes brilliant and fierce and gorgeous.

"If *anyone* calls you out, Lord Donne, 'twill be me," she promised in her low, vibrant voice.

"And that," Thomas retorted as he turned his back on her and her coterie of sycophants and panderers, "is one challenge I might accept."

He strode from her chamber and down the hallway. And so did not hear her whisper in a voice so low even those nearby did not make out her words, *"En garde!"*

Chapter 4

*H*ave the coach wait. I shan't be long," Fia said upon alighting from the carriage. "Gunna, if you would wait here, please."

"But, lass," Gunna protested sharply, her Highland accent further distorting the inflection her deformed jaw gave all her words. She disliked the thought of Fia opening herself to yet more rudeness. "If his family has been listening to all the gossipmongers, they might—"

"Please wait, Gunna."

The tiger—a black lad of eight years with more snobbery than half the bucks in London—jumped from his post atop the back of the high-sprung carriage and scooted up the stairs to a modest front door. He sniffed, clearly disgruntled at knocking at so hopelessly middling a sort of door. His rapping soon produced an answer.

"What? Who? Oh, my!"

A flustered-looking serving girl stood in the doorway, her jaw loosened in surprise at the ducal carriage at the curb—the carriage being on indefinite loan from Lord Stanley, one of Fia's more distinguished admirers. The girl's gaze slowly traveled to Lady Fia. "Oh, dear."

"Tell your master Lady Fia is here to convey her concern and her sympathy for Master Leighton," the tiger pronounced.

The girl bobbed her head, gulped, and backed hastily into the hallway. "Right away! If you'd be pleased to enter, I shall inform the family at once."

"So certain I shall be admitted, then?" Gunna heard Fia murmur. The sad, ironic tone never revealed itself on Fia's face, which remained composed as she mounted the few steps. But Gunna saw the rapid rise and fall of the black lace covering her bodice. The evidence of her fear and her refusal to show it caught at Gunna's gruff heart. She offered up a hasty prayer that the Leightons would be kind.

A short time later Fia emerged from the house. Gunna glanced at the watch fob pinned to her bodice. Less than ten minutes. The fools had expelled her! The door to the carriage swung open and Fia entered. She did not meet Gunna's eye.

"Did they disrespect ye, then? Ye didn't care what the lot of them thought, now, did ye?" Gunna asked.

"They were surprised."

"And the boy?"

Fia's brilliant blue eyes rose. Gunna had once seen an iceberg. Deep within the heart of it, it had been so intense a blue it had seemed hot. Fia's eyes were like that.

"He can move his hand and arm freely. But he's very weak." She offered no more.

"He was happy to see you, though."

"Oh, yes. Most glad."

"Then I'd say that's all that matters," Gunna said, pulling back the velvet drape covering the window as the driver called out to the horses and they lurched into motion.

She hated Fia's life. Hated that each day Fia seemed to grow ever more inured to her role as a Jezebel. Only Gunna knew how much that role cost the lass and fretted over how much of her soul Fia had left to spend before she . . . Gunna scowled, refusing to let such thoughts take root.

"Ye'll see the boy agin a few more times," she muttered to herself. "Bring him a book, a lock of yer hair, and pet his hand. Soon enough he'll be back at yer feet—"

"No."

Gunna looked up, startled by Fia's vehemence. Fia was shaking. Fia, her little statue, her sphinx. The old woman darted across the carriage and slid next to Fia, wrapping her arms around the girl's taut form.

"No, I will not," Fia said roughly. "I should never have befriended the boy. I should never have let him in when he came calling. But . . ."

"But what, Fia?" Gunna asked softly.

Fia turned. Raw vulnerability had whittled away much of the mask she habitually wore. Such pain. Such hurt. Gunna rocked her gently.

"It's just that he reminded me so of Kay," Fia whispered. "He treated me so naturally and I . . . missed that and so I . . . God help me . . . I encouraged him to visit." She gave a little laugh, which was half a sob. " 'Struth, I fear my selfishness might be his death!"

"Oh, my dear."

"They didn't want me in their house," Fia said in a stark voice. "But they didn't know how to ask me to leave. I shouldn't have been there. I only brought embarrassment to them and false comfort to him."

"There now," Gunna said, stroking Fia's midnight-hued hair. "He's a boy and boys are always doing what they can to inspire their own deaths. Weren't it you, it would be some other . . ." She faltered, looking for a word.

"Some other jade," Fia finished.

"Some other woman," Gunna corrected her.

"*He* told me I should have left Pip alone." Fia's forehead had smoothed. Her face stilled. The last signs of her vulnerability disappeared and Gunna lamented their absence. It had been months since Gunna had witnessed some honest emotion in the girl. Each incident grew more rare. "He all but said that I couldn't resist ensnaring every man I saw."

"Who said this?" Gunna asked.

"Thomas Donne."

Gunna's breath caught. Years ago, Thomas Donne

had been Carr's guest at Wanton's Blush. He'd shown Fia an absentminded sort of courtesy and halting interest. Fia, young and achingly alone, had become smitten with the tall Scot. Small wonder. He'd been one of the few men she'd known who was neither a leering rake nor a scraping sycophant.

Her infatuation had ended abruptly. Gunna had never known what Thomas had done or said, but overnight Fia's puppy love had turned into cold enmity. Fia had grown up after that. Before, her shell of cynical sophistication had been a thin one hiding a confused and passionate girl. After Thomas Donne, both the cynicism and worldliness had become real.

"Where did you see him?"

"He came to my rooms this morning. He confronted me."

"Curse him for a righteous ass. He's wrong."

Fia lifted her head. Her eyes shimmered brightly, but her mouth was hard. "No. He is correct, Gunna. But being correct does not give Donne the right to judge me. His soul is easily as black as mine."

Gunna scowled, confused.

"Remember when Ash was at Wanton's Blush and Rhiannon Russell disappeared?" Fia asked tonelessly. " 'Twas Thomas Donne who brought Ash the news that Rhiannon had left him and nearly broke Ash in that telling. He had something to do with it, I vow. I was there. I saw them, Carr and Ash and Thomas Donne. No bearer of hurt looked better pleased to be speaking than Thomas Donne."

Gunna drew back. Thomas Donne had never seemed the sort to her to take pleasure in another's anguish.

Fia straightened. Only her words betrayed the depth of the emotion driving her. "I swear, I'll bring him to his knees before I'm done."

Fia mounted the curving staircase to the second floor, passing a housemaid polishing the railing and a footman replacing the candles in the crystal chandelier. The shining silver bowl on the table at the top of the stairs held fresh red roses that filled the corridor with their exotic aroma. The landing window above sparkled. She barely noticed any of it.

She opened the door to her boudoir, where the new French style of decor found expression. A bombé-shaped chest stood against one wall, a new Meissen snuffbox had been added to the collection crowding its surface. Opposite this sat an inlaid dressing table, the mirror above draped in crimson damask. More deep crimson damask covered twin settees.

She walked across the room without feeling any pleasure in its beauty. None of it was hers. All of it, the town house, the furnishings, the decor, her clothing, the servants, and even the food, Carr had rented, bought, employed, provided for, and maintained. All for one purpose, to lure wealthy and well-connected suitors.

Fia pushed open the door that led from the boudoir to a small antechamber, where she went directly to a delicately fashioned writing desk. She stopped before it and pulled out the gilt chair tucked beneath it. Despite her outward calm, her heart raced. She needed to be careful.

Carr employed all the people in the house, with the exception of Gunna and the butler, Porter. All of them were his spies and agents and sneak thieves.

With a few deft movements of her hands, Fia removed the padded seat from the chair. In a small hollow area beneath lay a slender packet of letters. She smiled, a smile that in no way resembled any of those she wore outside this room. It bespoke an honest, easy, and uncomplicated pleasure.

They were letters from her brothers and their wives, collected over the past five years, eight each from Ash and Raine, five from Favor, and six from Rhiannon.

With the air of a connoisseur she selected one of the thin envelopes from her stash and gingerly unfolded it. It had been read so often that the folds had grown thin with wear and the edges frayed.

It was two years old and from Raine, sent all the way from his sunny estate in northern Italy. For months after it had first arrived she'd imagined she could smell the nectarines her brother had once described.

> *My dearest sister,*
>
> *Glad news! This morning Favor was delivered of a daughter, as beautiful as her mother and, I quite proudly own, just as vocal. We have named her Gillian Charlotte, after no one because, as Favor so*

succinctly says, she must be our future and we shall not look to the past.

My lovely wife, as you can see, is not much of a sentimentalist. But she did ask specifically to be re-membered to you in this letter, so perhaps there is hope for the frightful wench yet.

I wish you and Gregory well. Perhaps the day will come when you, too, will begin a family. I own I, with all of nine hours' experience, am utterly besotted of the experience.

With my deep regard, your brother,
Raine Merrick

Fia carefully refolded the letter and returned it to its envelope. She hesitated a second before replacing the seat without reading another, wanting to dole them out judiciously so that the pleasure of reading them might stay fresh and alive for years to come.

Gillian. Gilly. And a year later a son had been born, Robert. Ash, too, had fathered a son, a redheaded boy to inherit his Cornish horse-breeding enterprise.

Fia shook her head in wonderment. Her brothers were either far more fearless than she was or far less fearful of the suspicion that had ruled her. Or perhaps they had simply forgotten whose blood ran in their veins— God! If only she could!

But then, what did she know of her brothers? They had been virtual strangers to her when she'd been growing up, and she'd always assumed they'd had no feelings for her. Too late she'd come to realize that

Carr had manufactured the distance between her and her brothers.

Heat stung her eyes. The control she donned each waking moment slipped. Reflexively she shored it up, forcing herself to confront those thoughts that threatened to undermine her self-discipline. It was an exercise she always insisted of herself.

There was much she'd discovered late and she recalled too clearly the day her naivete had ended. She'd been a pitiful, lovelorn little girl who'd sneaked out of the castle to follow her hero, the handsome Scot, Thomas Donne, and the lovely Rhiannon Russell.

It had begun storming, hard. She remembered how he'd held himself to take the brunt of winds, protecting Rhiannon, while Fia had hunkered down, drenched by the downpour, contemptible and pathetic, straining her ears to hear his words. She'd heard, all right.

"Carr killed his first wife then killed the next two."

"He left his sons to rot."

"Fia is nothing but Carr's whore."

There, Fia thought with satisfaction, her gaze fixed impassively on her fingers. No trembling. Not even a hesitation. The memory no longer had the power to set her heart racing and her body shaking. She had healed even harder than she'd originally been. But crooked, like an ill-set bone, flawed and twisted. Sometimes she wondered if, like that ill-set bone, another break could set her right. Not that it mattered.

Yes, she was tainted with Merrick blood. But even that could be put to use. Who else besides she, raised from birth to be his accomplice, could anticipate Carr? And if she could use the poisonous gift of her upbringing to checkmate him, then she would get down on her knees and thank God for the stigma of being Carr's favored child.

A knock sounded.

"What is it?" she called.

"A gentleman to see you, madam. A Mister Do . . ." Porter's voice lowered discreetly.

Her pulse began to race. "Mister Donne, did you say?"

"No, madam," the answer came back. "A Mister Dolan."

Her shoulders slumped—nay, relaxed. "Tell Mister Dolan I am not at home."

"As you wish, milady."

Her thoughts turned to earlier this day. She'd been immersed in her role of seductress, painstakingly feeding her own legend with lurid, salacious, and ultimately false stories. It kept the choicer suitors from seriously considering offering for her hand. And if no one asked for her hand, how then could Carr give it?

She'd known who stood over her before she'd ever raised her eyes. And when she did, she'd wished she hadn't. Thomas had worn the face of a guardian-warrior, devoid of compassion or uncertainty. He'd never been overcome by the enemy within or any enemy without. Thomas Donne did not know defeat.

Tall, lean, and broad-shouldered, he bore little resemblance to the indolent roué who'd gamed at her father's tables.

He was even more arresting now.

His dark rumpled hair was salted with gray. His body looked harder and more powerful. His skin was so dark and weathered that no amount of powder or cream would ever conceal the evidence of years spent on a ship deck or erase the lines that fanned from the outer corners of his clear gray eyes. His lips were carved wide and hard, his jaw square and lean.

For a moment she'd been a girl again, helplessly in the throes of a deep infatuation, hopeful for his notice, desperate for his good opinion, and deep down within, wishing that his power and ferocity were on her behalf and that he'd come to vanquish her foes.

But *she'd* been the foe he'd come to vanquish. Amazing that it should have hurt so much when he'd accused her of practicing her wiles on Pip—that poor, decent boy. The phantom of the girl she'd once been had shuddered and died all over again. Abruptly she'd remembered who she was and what.

She *wasn't* a good woman. She'd married Gregory MacFarlane because he was rich and malleable, but most of all because he'd been Scottish and when he died she'd inherit his estate. But things had not worked out the way she'd planned. Once more she was her father's puppet. But it *hadn't* been a role of her choosing.

She lifted her chin and walked through to the boudoir. She had little left to recommend herself except a perverse and deep-rooted pride. It had served her well after she'd discovered what her father was; it had driven her to elope with MacFarlane. Pride had seen her through her marriage and her husband's ever increasing dependency on her father, and pride had allowed her to meet unbowed the news of MacFarlane's death and her renewed subjugation to Carr. Pride had kept her from giving up and yielding to her father's machinations.

And pride was at the root of the vow she'd made—and meant to keep—to Gunna in that closed carriage a few hours ago.

If Thomas Donne thought her *bad*—well, she would show him just how *bad* she could be.

Chapter 5

"Come with us, Tom. You can't spend every hour playing nursemaid to that ship of yours," Robbie urged.

"Heed him, Thomas. Robbie's an expert on reckoning the exact amount of gaiety a man must have to maintain his vigor." Francis Johnston approached the table at which Robbie and Thomas sat and pulled out an empty chair. He motioned for the proprietress to bring him a cup of coffee, and groaned. "Three o'clock in the afternoon and I'm still not awake. However shall I conspire to revel this evening?"

"You might try forgoing the revelry for once," Thomas suggested dryly. He tilted back, lacing his fingers across his flat belly.

"And miss attending the Portmann's masque?" Francis's blond brows climbed. "Never! 'Twill be the event of the Season. They expect a horrible crush and to accommodate it they're said to have erected special venues in the fields behind the house."

"It sounds to be a pleasant time but I'll likely spend the evening with Pip," Thomas said.

"Oh, for God's sake," groaned Johnston. "Grant that poor family a temporary reprieve. They must be nigh well sick of seeing you."

"Come, Johnston," Thomas replied. "I've visited five times in the past two weeks. I'm hardly living in their pockets."

"Loath as I am to point it out to you," Johnston said, his tone growing mild, "as Miss Sarah's former—if undeclared—suitor, your presence in her home can only cause her embarrassment."

Thomas frowned. He wouldn't knowingly cause Sarah Leighton distress. In his concern for Pip had he been lax in his sensitivity to her situation?

"Blast!" he muttered. "How blind an oaf can one be?"

"Exactly," Robbie said approvingly. "So now that you won't be going there this evening, you might as well come with us."

Thomas did not reply at once. The repairs on the *Alba Star* were taking longer than expected. At this rate it seemed unlikely he'd be able to deliver the cargo by New Year's Day as he'd promised.

Perhaps he could persuade James to take the route round the Cape of Good Hope on his new ship, the *Sea Witch*. Then, once the *Alba Star* was seaworthy again, he would take James's shorter route along the northern coast of Africa. It was an idea worth pursuing—and one he would pose when next he saw James. His expression grew grave.

He'd seen little of James since they'd parted company the morning of his assault on Fia's house—no, he corrected himself with brutal honesty, his assault on Fia. His actions had been inexcusable. Once more his passionate distrust of the Merricks had cost him some of his hard-earned self-esteem.

Yet he'd only to see Pip's drawn face to feel again the wrath that had led him to Fia's door. 'Twould be best if he never saw her again, and he'd sought these past two weeks to ensure that he didn't.

"Come on," Robbie urged. " 'Twill give you something to tell Pip about during your next visit."

Thomas looked up. "Why would Pip be interested? Will Lady Fia be there?"

Robbie blinked. "Lady Fia? I don't think so. She ain't been seen in public for over a week now." He chewed on his lower lip. "Layin' low, most like, what with those nasty rumors circulatin' about her and—"

"And whether she was responsible for Pip's misadventure," Johnston hastily cut in.

Thomas turned his gaze on Johnston. Johnston smiled blandly, not fooling Thomas for a moment. Johnston had heard about his visit. Well, Thomas needn't give a damn about Fia—as long as she didn't embroil James in any of her schemes.

In the meantime, if he had an opportunity for a night of good-natured revelry and one where he could be relatively certain of not seeing that black-hearted siren, he might well take it. He was accomplishing nothing by hanging about the dockyard.

"Will I need a costume?" he asked.

"Good Lord, no!" Robbie exclaimed, laughing. "You can go just as you are and people will think you a splendid specimen."

"Specimen of what?"

Robbie and Johnston looked at each other and grinned. "A pirate," they answered in unison.

The Portmanns had devoted eight years to the construction of their enormous Palladian home. Unfortunately, by the time Tiburn House had been completed the popularity of its architectural style was already waning. At least the Portmanns could congratulate themselves on its site, that being less than a half mile north of Grosvenor Square.

It would only be a matter of time before the city overtook Tiburn House and the flat, unadorned sheep fields surrounding it were filled with a swarm of fashionable squares and streets. But for now Tiburn House marked the exact point at which countryside met city, its front facade greeting its urban neighbors while its back overlooked a great, dark, rural expanse.

Johnston's reports proved accurate. Beneath an indigo sky, striped pavilions had been erected. Farther out, winding paths had been mown in the grass. Tall wands, top-heavy with glass globe lanterns, illuminated various vignettes, a company of actors posed in *tableau vivant*, and a troupe of minstrels.

A short distance from the back gardens a large circle had been cut for country dancing. Around its perimeter, bull's-eye lanterns directed rays of light across the center, to be caught by mirrored lanterns and returned. Thus the whole circle was crisscrossed with brilliant beams, and the dancers in their shimmering silks and glistening brocades flickered in and out between the slender threads of light like silver minnows in some giant fisherman's seine.

Thomas stood back, nursing the cup of negus a harried servant had pressed into his hand, and watched the crowds disperse and regroup. There were easily five hundred people in the field and probably half again as many in the house. All of them were in costume, including amongst their numbers a half-dozen Cleopatras, twice that many Spaniards, several Chinamen and Indian princesses, a disconcertingly large number of men in women's garb, and a full complement of pirates.

Thomas had bowed to convention by clubbing his hair, clipping on a gold earring, and donning a nobleman's ragged coat, stripped of its ornamentation, that he'd found in a Cheapside market. Most of the revelers had much more elaborate disguises. Though Thomas knew that Portmann's guests would have hotly denied the word "disguise" as being misrepresentative, he could not put the term from his mind, for all about him the anonymity afforded by masks and dominoes and face paint had purchased licentiousness.

Already the wine flowing from fountains and the potent punch passing amongst the revelers had affected the mood of the crowds. Gaming tables had been hauled out of the house onto the back-facing balcony. Laughter erupted, flushed like grouse from little queues of guests, and the dancers reeled in each other's arms even though the current dance called for no "reels" at all.

"Damn poor excuse for a costume," a slurred voice hailed him. Thomas turned to find a portly figure draped in a red toga weaving his way.

"Do you think so? And here I'd thought I made a right nasty-looking pirate."

"No," the man sniffed. "Just look disreputable. I came afoul a pirate once meself, so I know, y'see."

"Don't say," Thomas murmured, trying to place the man. He'd the look of a banker, complacent and shrewd.

"Mmm." The fellow nodded. "Off the north coast of Madagascar. A pirate vessel overtook the ship I was on. I, of course, wanted to fight but the captain would have none of it, and so we were boarded." He paused to belch.

"Heathenish creatures they were," he continued, "a menagerie of nations and types. Foul, hard, and"—he peered woozily at Thomas—"as brown as you. Very well, I grant you're the proper shade, but a real pirate would never dress so shabbily."

"Really?"

"Ought to be wearing your booty, or whatever you call it. Ought to be showin' off."

"Perhaps I'm not a very successful pirate," Thomas demurred.

The man leaned forward and pressed a stubby finger to the side of his nose. "That's not what I hear."

"Oh?"

"I hear"—the man cast a furtive glance to his left and right—"I hear that you do right well by yourself— and some"—his smile grew unctuous—"lucky investors. Perhaps I ought to hire your vessel for my next shipment, eh? Double me profits like our most ravishing toast has done."

Thomas smiled mildly as every one of his senses sharpened. Over the last few days he'd overheard dozens of such mysterious allusions. But each time he'd confronted the speakers they'd backtracked and feigned ignorance. This was the first time he'd come close to any real information.

"I'm afraid I don't take your meaning."

The fellow scowled and peered more closely at Thomas's face. "Blast me. You ain't Barton, are you? Oops." The man hid his smile behind his hand, like a naughty child. "Well, damn me for a loose-lipped limpet. No offense meant. Thought I was talking to your partner. Both of you bein' the same color and all . . ."

He scurried off, leaving Thomas to consider whether to follow and press him for more information. But a party was hardly the place. He would have to wait.

Preoccupied with his thoughts, he continued along one of the dark, winding paths.

"Such a terrible scowl, Monsieur Buccaneer," a French-accented female voice whispered behind him. Before he could turn around, the end of a pistol barrel prodded him in the back. He'd felt that distinctive impression too many times to be mistaken. He stood very, very still.

"*Tch, tch*. Nothing to say?" she asked.

He forced his shoulder muscles to relax. "Indeed not. Not yet."

"Oh? Then you foresee a return to eloquence in the near future?" The end of the pistol jabbed him again.

"I don't know that I can promise eloquence, milady, but certainly some few words."

She laughed, and he smiled involuntarily.

This was madness. Not only that she'd provoked a smile in the midst of threatening him but that she threatened him at all. They were only a few yards from other people. She couldn't possibly seek to rob him here and get away with it. But what better place for a thief to ply her trade then at night at a masque held in an open field?

He lifted his hands from his sides. "May I turn?"

"Certainly," she whispered. He turned slowly around and found himself looking at the ivory-knobbed handle of a closed fan—the "pistol" barrel. He raised his gaze to an extraordinarily gorgeous pair of blue eyes.

Their brilliance was only slightly dimmed by the shadow cast by her artfully wrought silver mask. It covered her upper face and left exposed a luscious and naughtily curving mouth, a delicately angled chin, and a long graceful neck—a neck he'd dearly love to set his hands about.

"I hope you enjoyed yourself, Fia." He would have known her anywhere.

"Not Fia," she said. "But yes, I did." She snapped open her fan and flirtatiously covered her mouth.

A soft, slender egret's feather dangling from her ear caressed her bosom, drawing attention to the creamy skin embraced by a low-cut black bodice. Black and silver composed the entire gown, the ebony material some matte, light-eating fabric, the silver so reflective that it gleamed like a mirror. Shadow and starlight, darkness warring with light.

His gaze traveled up and for the first time he noted that she'd completely covered her blue-black curls with an elaborate silver-lacquered wig bedecked with black roses.

"Do you want to know my name?" she teased in a sultry voice. "Do you want to know who I *really* am?"

She moved closer on a whisper of taffeta and velvet. Slowly, purposefully, she raised an elegant hand as though to touch him. He waited, suddenly restive to discover what so many other men before him already knew. Her hand hovered. Neared . . .

The blue gaze lifted to his. Her lips formed a slow, all-too-knowing smile. Her hand dropped to her side.

"I have many names." She stepped back and he followed, drawn in spite of himself. "The Queen of the Night. The Black Damsel . . ." Her eyes glittered with merciless amusement. "Lady Longing."

She moved past him, leaving him behind as she drifted out of the torchlight's range and into the shadows beyond. He waited. Watched. Her heavy skirts bruised the midsummer grasses, bringing forth their rich, sweet scent. She paused and curtsyed deeply, the silver in her dark robes gleaming and disappearing. "Good night, fainthearted pirate."

She was mocking him. In a few broad strides he caught up with her, took hold her arm, and spun her to face him. He expected her to resist. Instead, she tumbled easily into his embrace, as though she'd expected it.

He should release her. Walk away. Damn her provocation and her triumphant smile. But she'd nestled close—or had he pulled her there? Either way, he held her hand tight against his heart.

He looked down into her masked and upturned face. She did not look frightened. The blue eyes gleaming up at him held a rich, complicated brew of humor and anger and triumph. But no fear.

Impression after impression crowded his senses. The scent of her seductive, night-blooming perfume, the silken texture of her skin, the flavor of her warm breath, and the overriding realization of how very small she was, how light and petite.

It would be so easy to hurt her.

To stop her.

To kiss her.

He dropped her hand. She laughed again, as though she'd foreseen this, too. And why not? She was an expert in such matters. She played him as easily as she did Barton.

"I've no taste for this game, Fia."

"Why do you persist in calling me Fia when I've told you that I am not the lady you assume me to be?" she asked with sly merriment.

"Well, there's one way to find out, isn't there?" He raised his hand to her mask. Her smile froze. Her breath grew shallow.

"You won't unmask me," she whispered.

"Why not?"

"Because you came willingly to a masque and thus have tacitly agreed to abide by the rules, the most important of those being never to expose one unwilling to be exposed."

His finger stroked a ruffled black feather edging her face mask.

"And," she said quietly, "because I've asked you not to."

"You're very certain of me."

"I know your kind."

"And that is . . . ?"

"Why, you are a gentleman."

He laughed at that. Perhaps this woman wasn't Fia after all, for once upon a time, at Wanton's Blush, Fia Merrick had witnessed him at his most ungentlemanly when he'd betrayed her brother's friendship. Surely Fia, of all women, would never have mistaken him for the role his ancient proud lineage ordained but which raw experience had forbade him.

And she did not *act* like Fia who, however outrageous in her behavior, moved and spoke and gestured with exquisite and ladylike grace. This woman moved like a gypsy . . . and laughed easily and brightly. And her eyes, though they might have been the same color—hard to say, shaded by her mask as they were—sparkled and shimmered with blatant amusement. Fia's eyes were bright but deep, like glass over dark water—impossible to plumb.

She reached up and caressed his cheek with the back of her fingers. Desire, red-hot and rapacious, instantly awoke and he resented it and she read that, too.

"Faint heart ne'er won a lady, Lord Pirate. Why stop now when we are so close to an understanding?" The whispered voice taunted, yet beneath it lay some other emotion. His anger thinned as he considered the implications. He looked down at the masked countenance, searching for clues as to the identity of its owner.

Was she Fia? And if she wasn't, what did she seek from him?

"What understanding would that be?" he asked.

"Why"—she tilted her head to a saucy angle—"the understanding that all men strive for and to which all women are eventually privy: You understand how to fulfill your desires and then share your knowledge with me." Bitterness now, and no attempt to mask it.

"And what of *your* desires?"

"What manner of man ever troubled himself with such concerns?"

"If you think that which might exist between a man and woman ends at the man's procurement of his pleasure, why would you seek to further the 'understanding' between us?"

Her soft, pliant mouth grew taut. She'd not foreseen him questioning her, Thomas realized, and it displeased her. "Fie, sir," she said irritably, turning away. "You would make labor out of simple pleasure."

"Something informs me, madam, that no pleasure would be simple with you."

She turned back smiling, her moods as mercurial as the shifting darks and lights of her gown. "Mayhap, sir, you are right. But pleasure hard won is more oft savored than pleasure chanced upon."

"You speak obliquely, madam. I pray, be forward."

"Now of *that*," she purred, setting her hands on her hips, "I *have* oft been accused." A sudden gust of wind whipped her dark raiment about her legs and teased a nimbus of silvery gilt from her head.

"But if forthright speaking you would have, then here's what I have in mind. A game of chance. A card game." She gestured toward a lonely, unattended bench a short walk away. "Loo."

He glanced sideways, instinct urging caution. Be damned, the woman *had* to be Fia. No other female could have set his skin prickling in equal parts awareness and wariness. "And the stakes?"

She touched her lip, posing at rumination. Thomas was not fooled. He was certain that she'd long since decided on the stakes, as he was that every line she'd spoken and every line he'd returned had been if not preordained at the very least anticipated, and that all that had gone before had led him to this place, to making this wager. He disliked the idea of being manipulated so adroitly.

"I know," she said with no convincing attempt to convey sudden inspiration. "Since you are so certain I am a lady of your prior acquaintance, if you win you have my leave to remove my mask."

"And should you win?"

"Then"—the torch guttered in brisk wind—"then I win the right to kiss you."

He smiled wolfishly. "The stakes are patently lopsided. How can I lose?"

Her answering smile was just as smooth as his voice. "Such facile gallantry, sir. I had hoped for more. Though not expected it."

Her words pricked . . . as he was sure she'd meant them to. "You don't warrant kissing you a prize? You value yourself too little."

"Ah!" She wagged her finger playfully. "How like a man to hear what he wants to hear and not what is said. I said *I* would kiss *you*. Not the other way around. *You* must remain absolutely still."

His gaze grew hard.

"What say you?" she asked.

At least she'd chosen a game without bias toward

the dealer. He'd never have played her at a game of
faro. Carr's daughter had been raised at the gaming tables, and Fia, if this lady was indeed Fia, already had
too many advantages.

"Lead on, lady."

Chapter 6

The first trick is yours, Lord Pirate," the silver-and-black-clad woman said, drawing a murmur from the small crowd gathered about them.

She'd done that, made known the nature of their bet, thus assuring them an audience. Even Johnston was amongst the spectators, having hastened over after spying the gorgeous creature who'd wagered a kiss against her unmasking.

Thomas gathered the trick he'd taken: her king of hearts trumped with his king of clubs. His gaze remained fixed on his hand. He led with the ace of spades, knowing she must, if she was void in spades, trump it or lose yet another trick. She trumped in with the eight of clubs.

"That would be mine," she said, sweeping up the

cards and immediately playing the knave of clubs, another trump.

Thomas pondered. He took the knave with his queen trump and played the eight of spades. She had no spades, which meant she must trump in or lose the trick. If she did not have any more trumps, he did: the nine of clubs. The odds against Fia holding the ten *and* another trump were monumental.

She trumped it with the three of clubs, taking the trick and bringing them even. "The moment of truth," she whispered.

"Nay, lady, that will be the moment of your unmasking. Enough theater."

She laid down the ten of clubs. His gaze shot up to meet hers, sparkling in the shadows of her mask.

"I win."

"This round, lady," he conceded. He stood up. "I look forward to you collecting your winnings."

She rose, too. "You have not long to wait, for I would take my prize now."

He regarded her coldly. "A public spectacle out of what began as a private wager? I think not."

"But do you have a say in the matter? I don't recall a discussion about when and where the loser would reward the winner," she said challengingly. She spread her arms in a beseeching gesture and turned to their audience. "What say you, gentlemen?"

"She has you, old son," said a dandy dressed in Turkish robes. Others, including Johnston—damn him for a disloyal dog—voiced their agreement.

Thomas forced a smile. "And I don't recall agreeing that the public might be called upon to moderate."

"You didn't," she answered, her arms slowly falling to her sides. "So I must appeal to your sense of sportsmanship and your honesty. You *are* honest?"

"Do you doubt it?" he asked tightly.

"I?" she asked. "I don't *know* you, sir. No better than *you* know *me*." Her voice had grown cold. "At least I have the advantage of realizing my ignorance. But that," she said, her voice abruptly returning to its former teasing lightness, "is beside the point. I will assume you are a fair man and ask this: If you had won the game, would you have been content to unmask me at some future date?"

She had him.

"No." He sketched her a mockingly short bow. "I am, milady, of course, entirely at your service."

Not well done, he thought as the men about them broke into snickers and her exposed flesh grew rosy.

"I suppose it would be asking too much for you to come to me?" she asked in the tone one used on a spoiled child.

"Not at all," he responded, and in two broad steps covered the distance separating them. He looked down at her, very conscious of how he loomed over her. "What would you have me do next?"

Her head tipped back. "Nothing."

He did not look away as one of her hands stole up his chest. Their gazes were locked in some contest neither was willing to lose. It was ridiculous, nonsense,

Thomas told himself, and yet . . . and yet it seemed so damned important.

Her fingers crept about the back of his neck and winnowed through his hair. The shadowed blue of her eyes deepened with a lambent quality. Her lips parted, revealing a sliver of the dark mystery within. Her nostrils flared delicately, as though she'd scented his arousal, and her cheeks flushed in response.

"You are too tall." Her other hand joined the first behind his neck and she stretched against him, pressing her soft breasts to his chest as she raised herself slowly on her tiptoes and pulled his head down. She made a throaty sound, like a purr, and then her lips were skating just above the surface of his jaw, so close he could feel their warmth, an electrical tingling.

And he wanted more. He wanted the velvety plush mouth pressed to his flesh. . . . No, to his mouth.

"Turn your head, sir," she whispered so that he alone could hear. "For while I am sure *you* would never ask for more than a lady would willingly give, *I* am not made of so strong a moral fiber. I want what I want, Lord Pirate, and I want to kiss your mouth."

She smiled slowly, and slowly touched her lips to his mouth, teasing him, tormenting him with what she withheld.

He would not let her win. He would not turn to force a fuller, deeper union. He stood rigidly and felt the light trill of her laughter wash over his lips.

The very tip of her tongue touched the sensitive corner of his mouth.

Desire speared him and he jerked back. Behind her mask, her eyes gleamed with maleficent satisfaction. Then, quick as a cat, she pulled his head down and swept her little tongue fully across his lips. Before he could react, she danced back, smiling.

Suddenly Thomas became aware of the men all around them. Most were strangers to him but all stood silent and fixed, the air charged with ill-suppressed sexual excitement. She'd awoken something there, something primal and predacious. Something dangerous.

She ran her tongue lightly over her lips, tasting. "Brandy. And a good brandy, too. I believe the Pirate King takes his share of the profits in liquor."

She noted it then, the unnatural silence of the spectators. The smile died on her lips. Her eyes moved slowly over the still, intent crowd, a spark of dawning fear in their shaded blue depths.

They were still far from most of the crowd and the paths leading back to the dance circle were dim and poorly lit. She held up her hand, motioning him near.

Grim satisfaction flooded through him. She would need to appeal to him now, to the "gentlemanliness" she'd derided, and ask that he accompany her back to safer ground, away from the impulses she'd so heedlessly awakened with her little performance. He moved to her side.

"We are quits, milord pirate," she whispered. She smiled mockingly. She'd known that, too, that he would assume she'd appeal to him for help. "Goodbye." She moved away.

"Wait."

She paused.

"An honest gambler would allow his opponent a chance to recoup his losses."

"But I'm not an honest gambler—which should come as no surprise to you." She turned, looked back over her shoulder, and pitching her words so that only he could hear them, said, "And even if we were to play again and this time you were to win, are you so certain you would know me even without my mask?"

She did not wait for his answer. With Fia's unearthly grace she moved toward the phalanx of men. She did not pause as she approached them, and this—and her absolute and imperial refusal to acknowledge them—caused such disconcert that they stumbled apart and allowed her to pass.

A man near the edge of the circle swung around, his dark eyes marking her departing figure. The others milled uncertainly. He started after her.

"I wouldn't," Thomas called out calmly.

The man checked, glanced back at Thomas, his upper lip lifting in a sneer. "She made arrangements with you, then?"

The others looked at Thomas, their faces variously filled with jealousy and resignation. Only Johnston looked unhappy and confused.

"Aye. She's mine." It didn't matter that it was a lie, he thought, watching her disappear into the light.

As long as he remembered it himself.

*   *   *

The lighting in Tiburn House did not begin to do justice to him or his costume, Lord Carr thought critically.

He turned his face this way and that. Perhaps it was this damned mirror. Made one's skin look splotchy and tended to emphasize the middle of the face, which happened to be the nose, which was no longer perfect. He would have to see he repaid his son Raine for that someday.

He returned to contemplating his reflection. There was also the irksome matter of some other people here wearing the same costume as his. He'd been quite certain his costume was unique. In fact, he was *still* certain his was the original notion, and when he returned to his town house he would have a little discussion with his current valet about the importance of discretion. Hopefully the fellow would survive to benefit from the lecture. Breaking in new valets was such tiresome work.

"Lord Carr." Another face joined his in the mirror. A cadaverous-looking Spaniard with an imbecile fake goatee and a perfectly noxious black velvet doublet.

"What is it, Tunbridge?"

"She's here."

He already knew that. "Do you think my complexion looks uneven, Tunbridge, or is it simply these cheap tapers Portmann is using?"

Tunbridge flushed, and Carr smiled. How Tunbridge hated his position as lickspittle. Poor fool, even though he must realize that the more his hatred of

Carr grew the more delight Carr had in tormenting him, he still could not mask his loathing.

"Well? An honest answer, now. You know how I depend on your honesty," Carr purred.

"The tapers, sir. Without doubt."

"Hm. As I thought." Carr turned to face his toady, glancing about to assure himself they were alone. "What have you learned about Captain Barton and his relationship with my daughter?"

"Barton's last two voyages met with disaster. A Swiss company insured the first. I have been unable to ascertain whether he collected on his losses or not. The last was insured here in London, and that Barton definitely collected on. He's bought a new ship and he's been spending money hand over fist. Most of it on Lady Fia."

Carr's mouth grew tender. "How enterprising of her, but alas, how futile."

"Sir?"

"Why, it's apparent, isn't it?"

A stumper, apparently. Tunbridge wrinkled his brow. "They're lovers and she's taking him for all she can get?"

"No, no, no. Really, *think*, man. What do you know of Fia? Other than that you once had the audacity to think she—or more to the point, *I*—would ever consider allowing you to marry her."

Tunbridge did not reply. His face . . . well, now *that* was a splotchy complexion. Carr glanced at his own reflected visage, but seeing Tunbridge's slack expression of bewilderment mirrored behind his own regal countenance, he sighed, resigning himself to once more having to illustrate to a lesser intelligence what was abundantly clear.

"They're not lovers. They're *partners*."

"Partners?"

"Yes, you dimwit. Oh, he's courting her, all right, but Fia is, after all, my daughter. Would she be content with sitting at the table waiting to receive whatever bones this . . . this *colonist* is willing to throw her, when she could have the entire feast?" He snorted at the very notion. "Hardly."

"But," Tunbridge stammered, "but if she's his partner, why is he showering her with all these gifts?"

Carr stared at Tunbridge. He couldn't believe he had to explain this. When Tunbridge's brows lowered in fierce, if unfruitful, concentration, Carr gave up. "She's accepting his gifts *at the same time* that she's bundling away her portion of the insurance. That way she reaps more than a half share." His gaze grew fond. "Savvy little beast, ain't she?"

"How do you know this? How can you be sure?" Tunbridge asked, eyes wide in his cadaverous face.

"You don't imagine for an instant that I rely solely on *your* reports for my information, do you?" He didn't wait for an answer. "I've looked into the matter. Fia has invested nearly a thousand pounds in various instruments since Captain Barton's arrival.

"Besides, if they were lovers Fia wouldn't be going about flaunting her availability to every man in town, would she?"

Tunbridge's expression hardened. The fool still had

feelings for Fia, though from his expression it was clear they were no longer of a romantic nature. "*She* might."

"She might if her lover were *you*, Tunbridge," Carr conceded dryly. "I doubt, however, that she'd play so fast and lose with a man like Captain Barton. No, she hasn't committed any acts of insanity, such as taking a colonist water rat for a lover." And insane it would be if Fia were to put herself beyond the pale once and for all.

Carr considered further. He'd encountered Fia earlier in the evening, on the terrace. It had quite startled him to see her mouth was tremulous beneath her silver mask and the mantle of angry color covering her shoulders and throat. His daughter, usually about as easy to read as Chinese characters, looked near to sobbing with fury.

A few minutes later Thomas Donne had stalked across the back lawn, his face set in taciturn lines. Had the tall Scot given his little Fia a set-down? Oh, if only he had been there to witness that!

He glanced up and noticed Tunbridge still hovering miserably. "Well?" he snapped irritably. Toadies were all very well and good, but even baiting one such as Tunbridge palled after a while. "You've said what you came to say. Unless you have further information of a pertinent nature, be gone."

Tunbridge dipped at the waist and began to scurry off. Carr, his attention once more focused on the mirror, frowned. "Tunbridge!" he called.

The thin figure came to a quivering standstill by the doorway. "Yes, milord?"

"You don't think the pink was a mistake, do you?"

Tunbridge's hand curled at his side, the side hidden from Carr's view. "No, milord. A most flattering shade."

Carr nodded complacently, accepting the compliment as his due. "That's what I thought. Go on, now. I don't want people getting the lowering notion that you and I are associates."

Without responding, Tunbridge disappeared, leaving Carr still examining his reflection. Perhaps it was time to rejoin the party, he thought. There were still people to meet, secrets to hear, intelligence to be gathered. He composed his lips into a smile, adjusted his pink, lace-covered bodice, snapped open his ostrich-plume fan, and sallied forth.

Chapter 7

Thomas stepped out into the early afternoon sun and snapped the papers he held against his thigh. His mouth still held the grim lines it had taken on during his interview with Sir Ffolkes, one of Lloyd's Insurance Company's senior partners. He'd run into him on leaving Portmann's masque two nights ago. Ffolkes had invited Thomas to his offices for an "informal conversation." His curiosity piqued by Ffolkes's somber manner—he knew the man only superficially but had always gauged him a decent, even-tempered sort—he'd agreed.

The information he'd gathered in the last half hour had been worth the effort. It had also infuriated him that the rumors surrounding James Barton had reached so far and been taken so seriously. Thomas had assured

Ffolkes that Barton was not guilty of insurance fraud and offered to supply proof. He looked down at the copy of the manifest for the *Iona* still clenched in his fist. He'd promised Ffolkes he would have a letter from the Swiss company that had insured Barton's shipment confirming that it had, indeed, been delivered. He would dearly like to find who was at the root of these foul accusations.

In such a mood he descended the steps and crossed the street, maneuvering through the swelling throngs of carriages and lorries to the park opposite. For once, the perpetual haze shrouding London had lifted, leaving the sky above clear except for an occasional puff. Soon the sun warmed on his shoulders and Thomas slowed his pace, his temper dissolving.

The park was crowded with Londoners taking advantage of the fine weather. The air was filled with sound: the dull strike of hooves on the bridal paths, the merry squealing of playing children, the creak of light carriages moving sedately along gravel avenues, birds trilling from the shrubbery.

He had no appointments to keep so he decided to walk back to the town house, following the footpath through the heart of the park. He'd reached the Serpentine Road and stopped to purchase a hot meat pie from a boy when he noticed a nearby couple, a woman standing over a young man sitting on one of the park benches.

Even from a distance it was clear the man was in distress, and from the manner in which the woman hovered it was equally clear she did not know what to do about it. Pricked by a feeling of familiarity, Thomas bade the lad keep the extra pennies and started toward them. As he drew near he recognized Sarah Leighton and Pip. Alarmed, he hurried forward.

Sarah looked up at his approach. For a second her expression betrayed her unhappiness at seeing him but then concern for her brother overruled her distress.

"Captain Donne, I . . . we . . . Pip has come over ill."

"So I see." Thomas sat down next to the boy. Pip's chin rested on his chest and his breathing was labored. His pale skin glistened with a thin coating of sweat. Quickly Thomas secured the boy's wrist. His pulse was steady, if rapid, and his skin, though warm, was not unduly hot. The young fool had simply over-reached himself.

"He seemed so much better and he'd been moving about the house so easily that when he . . . when he re-marked how he'd like to walk in the park, I thought a short turn could do him no harm and so brought him here."

At this Pip smiled weakly. "Chased after me, she did, Tom. Thought I would go out of my head if I sat in that damned house one more day. Didn't give her any choice. Not her fault."

"I'm sure not," Thomas said, smiling at Sarah. She ducked her head, refusing to meet his eye.

"Would you be so kind—"

"Of course." Thomas rose, looking about. Though the avenues were filled with carriages, none was for hire. It was a good quarter mile to the boundaries of the park and while Thomas had no doubt he could carry the lad, the possibility that in doing so Pip's wound would tear open made him hesitate to suggest it.

A light carriage drawn by a single horse rounded the avenue. With relief Thomas saw that the driver was James Barton. He strode to the center of the lane and hailed him, and James reined in. Too late Thomas identified the passenger beside him. It was Fia. The black tricorn she wore at a rakish angle shaded her face but the taunting smile beneath gave evidence that she had recognized him.

"Thomas?" James called.

"Pip Leighton is over there. He is in need of assistance."

"Of course." At once James maneuvered the carriage off the drive and onto the grass verge, tied the reins, and leapt to the ground. "How can I help?"

Sarah, too, had seen, and apparently recognized, the notorious "Black Diamond." The color bled from her face but she lifted her chin. "If we might impose upon you—" She broke off, coloring at having addressed a stranger so boldly.

"James Barton, ma'am," James supplied, bowing. His worried gaze moved from Sarah Leighton's distressed face to Pip's.

"Lady Fia!" Mortification marked the boy's face as he attempted to rise.

Thomas put a hand on Pip's shoulder, pushing him

down. "I am sure Lady Fia will forgive you for not rising."

"Good heavens, Pip, sit still!" Fia said sharply.

Thomas looked at her, surprised by the real dismay in her voice. She continued watching Pip, her expression troubled.

"I have missed you," Pip whispered, seeing in her countenance all the concern and care a smitten youth could hope for.

"Oh, Pip." The tone was tender but then, as suddenly as a door slamming shut, her expression smoothed. " 'Tis no wonder." Her voice was breezy and offhand. " 'Struth, I've been so damnably pressed for even a moment to call my own, I swear I miss myself! When last did you come calling? Was it this week or the week before?" She laughed. "I really should keep better track of my visitors."

The intimation that she had forgotten that Pip had been injured fighting a duel over her honor was beyond cruel. Beneath Thomas's hand he felt Pip tense. Sarah's cheeks colored with surprised anger. James gnawed his lip miserably. "Fia . . ."

"Can you drive Pip to his house, James?" Thomas asked.

"But of course."

Thomas glanced at Sarah. She stood rigidly, her gaze fixed beyond the carriage as she strove to pretend that the ruthless, ravishing creature who'd besotted her brother did not exist. Useless endeavor. 'Twould be like staring at the sun and denying it burned the eye.

Thomas pitied Sarah, knowing she would loathe his pity as much as she would hate accepting his escort home. But James's carriage had been built for two occupants and while it might accommodate three there was no possible way it could hold four persons. James hesitated, obviously reluctant to leave Sarah but unable to think of an alternative.

Thomas bent his head in her direction. "If Miss Leighton would do me the honor of allowing me see her home . . ."

"But why should she have to do that?" Fia asked. "She must ride with her brother, of course."

"But . . ." James said, looking back and forth between the two women, one so clearly overset, the other just as clearly amused. "But what of you, Fia?"

"Why, I shall impose upon Captain Donne to escort me home. He already knows where I live." Her smile was wicked, her gaze dancing with a message for him alone. In this situation, under these circumstances, such flirtatiousness was outrageous and she knew it. But at least her willful naughtiness had the boon of saving Sarah Leighton from further distress and her outré behavior might at last waken Pip to her true nature.

"I would be delighted," Thomas said formally.

"Then it's settled." She rose, and lifting her coal-black skirts, held out her hand in a commanding attitude. He had no choice but to take it. She alit as softly as black swan's down beside him.

Pip's face was naked with hurt astonishment. Fia

did not look at him. Her winsome, wicked smile was
for Thomas alone.

It took only a few minutes to see Pip into the carriage and Sarah beside him, and then James, with one
last troubled glance at Fia, whipped up the bay, taking the Leightons home and leaving Thomas alone.
With Fia.

Fia waited until the carriage disappeared from sight
before turning. The saucy smile she'd fixed on her
face vanished, leaving her face as smooth and enigmatic as ever. Without a word, she started walking,
and Thomas fell into step beside her.

Her heart pounded uncontrollably. She hadn't expected to see him again so soon. She glanced sideways,
noting as she did so how strong his dark throat looked
above the snowy collar and remembering too clearly
the feel of his skin beneath her lips and the desire in
his gray eyes.

"I know you were the lady in the silver mask at
Portmann's ball." His words caught her off guard.

"I don't know what you mean," she said.

Her actions at the Portmanns had been a mistake.
But James had been otherwise occupied that evening
and she'd come unannounced to the fete, and when
she'd seen Thomas there, she'd decided to teach him a
lesson regarding his own susceptibility to what he so
openly disdained. Instead she'd only learned about her
own weakness. It had been impetuous and she was
never impetuous. She couldn't afford to be.

Besides, she was above this. She was no green girl

come begging for kindness, like the kindness Thomas had given Sarah Leighton and like the kindness she had so ruthlessly withheld from Pip.

She'd been selfish. So certain that because Pip was only a boy it would be safe to befriend him. And because he'd reminded her of Kay and in this tempest of plots and counterplots she'd so wanted a friend with whom she could just stop acting.

Well, no more. She would never again let her "want" threaten an innocent life. She was wiser now.

"Do you ever wear anything besides black?" Thomas's voice startled her after so long a silence.

"I should think you a man partial to black and white. It saves you the bother of trying to identify any subtleties."

He laughed, and her heart trip-hammered in response. He wasn't supposed to have laughed. He was to have taken offense.

"I own it's flattering on you, lady," he said. "As was the gown you wore to the Portmanns' masquerade the other night."

She smiled, neither denying nor admitting his renewed charge. "Why, Captain Donne, you'd best be on your guard lest you fall under my sinister influence." She said the words ruefully and was surprised when he scowled.

"It was good of you to offer Miss Leighton your place," he said shortly.

But she knew her role now. She arched one brow, donning the bow-shaped smile men found appealing. "Oh, Captain. I think we both know that 'good' is hardly an appellation that springs to mind upon hearing my name. It suited me to walk. With you." Her gaze slew provocatively toward him. "And so I am walking. With you."

"I don't believe that."

She shrugged. "As you will."

The day had grown warmer, making even her cloak uncomfortable. She loosened the silk frog at her throat.

"You knew that Sarah Leighton does not approve of you and yet you still let her have your seat."

"Is that what this is about? Well, lest you seek my sainthood prematurely, let me explain. Sarah Leighton is a pitiable drab." Beside her Thomas grew rigid with distaste. Good. "She is simply not worth considering a rival. Actually, she's not worth considering at all."

The lie tripped easily from her lips. In truth, she rather admired Sarah Leighton. The woman was decent and kind and her concern for her brother was honest. But that wasn't an insight she was willing to give Thomas. Because insight meant advantage and she trusted Thomas Donne with an advantage less than any other man she knew—including her father— because where her father's power over her was limited to threats, Thomas's . . . She would not pursue that thought.

She went on, the quality of her voice hard and gaudily bright, like cheap-cut glass. "No. However worthy Miss Leighton is, she offers no competition for James's attention. He is quite certainly mine. And

Pip is already under my sway. Which leaves only you standing so valiantly as proof against my charms."

"You're lying," he said flatly.

"Ha!" She managed a good laugh. Light and amused. "You, better then most anyone here, know my background. I am a gambler, from a long line of gamblers. Is it any wonder I'm unable to resist a new challenge instead of contenting myself with prizes already won?"

She looked at him from beneath the thicket of her lashes. "Besides, 'twas you yourself who issued the challenge."

He shot her a startled glance.

She stopped, beckoning him near so that he had no choice but to lean near to hear her words. "In my boudoir," she whispered, letting the warm exhalation brush his ear. "When you came to chastise me. You said I was the one challenger you might not refuse."

He did not draw back as she'd expected but turned his head to speak. Their lips were inches apart. His pale eyes glinted like polished pewter in his dark face. "That's not what I meant and well you know it."

She would not be the one to draw back. It had become a contest now, a game of dare and daren't that she could not afford to lose, never ask why. She lifted her face, bringing her cheek close to his. He smelled of sandalwood and coffee. His skin was smooth. He'd shaved mere hours ago. "But it's what *I* meant."

He moved slightly so that the bright sun dazzled her eyes. She averted her face, blinking. Her lashes fluttered against his cheek. She heard him catch his breath, and suddenly his hands were on her waist, spanning her, holding her still.

For a second she could not say whether he intended to pull her close or push her away and she had the distinct notion that he didn't either. She felt the imprint of each long finger, the breadth of his palm, his thumbs above her hipbone. She should move, slap him, berate him, but all she could think was that Thomas Donne was touching her with something less than eagerness but something more than indifference.

Every fiber of her body awakened. Her pulse hammered wildly. She couldn't breathe and so held her breath and thus heard the ragged, ill-timed measure of his exhalations, passion's obligato. His gaze searched hers, troubled and angry and confused. She swayed, and the movement caused her unhooked cloak to slip from her shoulders and pool at her feet.

One of his hands left her waist and traveled slowly up her spine to the nape of her neck. Her eyelids slid shut. His fingertips were rough, callused, and warm. She angled her head back, turning his touch into a caress, all of her concentration focused on the sensation.

His hand dropped.

The hand at her waist withdrew.

"You're wearing Amelia Barton's necklace." His voice was hollow, devoid of inflection.

Well, yes. He would hate that. Amelia Barton had been, quite simply, the loveliest woman Fia had ever known. No doubt she'd been the loveliest woman

Thomas had known, too. Perhaps he'd been in love with her.

She opened her eyes. He still stood very close. His eyes made up for the lack of emotion in his voice. They burned. "Is it?"

"You know damn well it is. James gave that necklace to Amelia on their wedding day."

"Really?" She wanted to tell him that it was all window dressing. Part of the game. Part of the act. But she couldn't trust him. She *didn't* trust him. Thomas hated the Merricks. He'd done everything he could to hurt her brother Ash. There was no reason to think he'd treat her any more kindly. He hadn't yet.

"He should never have given it to you," Thomas went on coldly. "It's been in his family for generations."

She bent and retrieved her cloak. She stood up; he'd moved back. Casually she settled the light wool over her shoulders. She was cold. Chilled through to the bone. "How very flattering of James."

"Leave him alone, Fia."

"I'm afraid it's a little too late for that, wouldn't you say?"

"He deserves better."

"Than what?" she demanded, stung. His words prodded the temper lurking beneath her chill composure. He'd touched her, caressed her. Now he looked at her with loathing, implying that she sullied a dead woman's necklace simply by wearing it. "Better than *me*? James is quite capable of determining what he does or does not deserve."

"Listen to me, Fia. I know you're trying to involve

James in some sordid intrigue or other. I won't have it. Do you hear me? James Barton is a decent, honorable man and I *won't* let you drag him down."

Exaltation briefly flared to life, for a moment banishing her anger and hurt. If Thomas had heard rumors then others had, too.

Thomas read the triumph in Fia's expression and mistook it for gloating. He buried the . . . the thing that had momentarily distracted him. Call it lust, for want of a better term.

For a short time he'd believed in a chimera: a Merrick with a heart. He'd imagined he'd seen wistfulness in Fia's fading smile as she watched Barton's carriage drive off. He'd thought then that she'd purposefully hurt Pip in order to keep him from a deeper hurt. And when he had touched her . . . how to explain the quickening, the surge of desire and tenderness? God help him, yes, tenderness. For her.

He could not believe his idiocy. A Merrick with a heart? He doubted this one had a soul. When had he become a vapid romantic instead of the realist life had made him? His hands ached to punish her for being beautiful and false and pitiless and for so effortlessly imitating something else.

"I'm warning you, Fia."

"That sounds like a threat . . . Thomas."

"No," he said. "It's a promise."

She laughed, quicksilver and bright. But still, God help him, it sounded as though it hurt her to make that quicksilver sound, like razors stropped her heart to make it. Against all reason and all his hard-earned knowledge, he almost reached out to her.

But then she turned and walked away, heedless of being alone and unchaperoned. He followed her at a discreet distance until they reached the street, where she hailed and entered a carriage.

Chapter 8

"Ye look done for," Gunna said flatly.

" 'Tis your imagination," Fia said, her needle flashing in and out of the small hooped frame she held. Needlework, she'd discovered from one of Cora's nurses, was a soothing occupation.

Across the room Kay studied one of his schoolbooks. His unexpected arrival yesterday had been not altogether welcome. Fia had canceled her plans for the evening, unwilling to let Kay roam the town house unsupervised. Thank heavens Mrs. Littleton's Academy for Young Ladies, which Cora presently attended, did not allow their charges to hie off as Oxford apparently did.

"And is it my imagination or my failing eyesight that has yer eyes lookin' red-rimmed and yer voice hoarse as a bittern's call?" Gunna said, interrupting Fia's thoughts.

"Honestly, Gunna. I am fine."

In truth, she felt worn thin. The interminably long nights of posing and posturing were taking their toll. Too often she felt light-headed and started each day trembling with exhaustion.

Her confrontation yesterday with Thomas hadn't helped. Ever since, she'd felt irritable and tearful—she, Fia Merrick, queen of self-possession—and her much-vaunted composure was strained to near breaking. She did not know how much longer she could keep this up. But it wouldn't do any good to admit that to Gunna. The old woman would only fret, and when all was said and done, her fretting wouldn't change a thing.

"It's not natural to live like this, changing day to night and night to day," Gunna grumbled.

Fia shot a sharp warning glance in Kay's direction. Kay did not know about her reputation and Fia wanted him to remain in ignorance as long as possible.

"Drinking and riding and carrying on . . ."

Fia looked at the old woman with a mixture of exasperation and affection. Apparently Gunna had decided not to heed her unspoken warning.

"Well, it's day now and here I am," Fia said with false brightness, "awake and alert, ensconced in my own home, blamelessly embroidering, and yet still I manage to invoke disapproval."

"Don't use that tone on me, Lady Fia MacFarlane," Gunna said. "It's yer own good I'm lookin' after and—"

"And I appreciate that, however inappropriate," she cut in, once more looking in Kay's direction.

"Cannot we quit this place and go back to Bramble House and take up where we left off?" the bent woman asked for the hundredth time. Fia had never told Gunna everything about the arrangement she'd made with Carr.

As long as her father wanted Fia in London, in London she would stay. When he'd told her she would marry whom he said she would marry, she'd agreed. If she didn't she would lose Bramble House, and she would not even contemplate that. Of course, Carr did not know that. He thought she acquiesced to his demands through fear—of himself and being poor.

"No. We cannot," she replied. She put her fingers to her temple, rubbing little circles. "You know, Gunna, I do feel a bit fatigued. Perhaps a restorative might help. Would you be so kind as to make me one of your tisanes?"

She felt a soupçon of guilt when she saw the concern flood the exposed half of Gunna's face and witnessed the alacrity with which the old woman shot to her feet and scurried from the room. But it was surely kinder to give Gunna a problem she could fix rather than have her worrying uselessly about something over which she had no control.

Kay glanced up as soon as the old woman had left. "Gunna's right. You look pasty."

"Such flattery. You shall give me a conceit of myself."

Kay, used to Fia's calm irony, went back to his reading. At fifteen, Kay still looked very like the boy she'd met six years ago. His expression was still as open, his hair still had a tendency to cowlick, and he still took people at face value. She wondered when that would change and if she would be the instrument of his eventual awakening.

She steeled herself against the possibility. The world's wisdom, she'd long maintained, eventually seeks those who do not seek it. Indeed, 'twas possible she did Kay a disservice in shielding him. She picked up her hoop.

A few minutes had passed when a shadow filled the sitting room door. Only one person would have the temerity to arrive in her home unannounced.

"Hello, Father," Fia said, finishing a stitch. Every muscle in her body tensed with anticipation. She'd been waiting for this visit for a long, long time. She forced herself to relax, taking whatever time was necessary to search the cool, tough persona she'd worn so long for any egress. Finding none, she lifted her head.

"Can I help you?"

Her father, resplendent as always in an embroidered copper-colored waistcoat and a blue jacket, idly perused the room. He lifted his silver-topped walking stick and pointed at Kay. Her heart skipped a beat.

"What is that boy doing here?"

She glanced in Kay's direction, allowed a hint of surprise to touch her features, as though she'd forgotten him. "Oh. That's Kay. MacFarlane's boy."

Kay rose hurriedly to his feet, his expression openly interested.

No, Kay, she silently begged him. *Don't make him take note of you.*

"Oh?" Carr murmured. "MacFarlane's heir, eh?"

"One of two, actually," Fia said in bored tones. "The other's a girl. She's at school."

"You can afford to keep her at school?"

"Well, the alternative is to have her here," Fia explained smoothly. "And while society is lenient and my suitors hardly sticklers, I do think they might take exception to me tossing MacFarlane's children out on the streets. Don't you?"

Carr considered the matter. "Perhaps. But why is he here, then?"

"He's leaving," Fia answered. "In fact, right now. Go away, Kay."

Kay's cheeks grew ruddy. His youth and embarrassment made him graceless. He executed a short, awkward bow, and hurried from the room.

Fia watched him go impassively. He'd survive the assault to his dignity. He might even thrive if Carr could find no use for him—say, as a bit of leverage to induce his daughter to do his bidding. But then, for Carr to suspect she held the boy in any sort of regard would presuppose Carr to have imagination as well as heart. No, Kay was safe. Unless something betrayed her feelings.

"Won't you be seated?" she said after Kay had gone. "Tell me, to what do I owe this visit? You pine for my company, perhaps?"

"If that's the sort of banal sarcasm you try to pass off as wit, 'tis no wonder you are surrounded by such common men."

"And here I'd thought there was another reason entirely," Fia said smoothly. "And one having nothing to do with . . . *wit*."

Carr's lips twisted. "You haven't learned a bit of humility, Fia."

He moved across the room, the slight limp he'd acquired on escaping Wanton's Blush barely noticeable as he made his way to a nearby chair. Once seated, he placed his cane across his lap. "I have come to tell you that I know what you are doing and I shan't allow it."

"What I am doing," she repeated.

"Let me save us some time. I know that you have inveigled Captain James Barton into a partnership wherein you purchase cargo, insure it at twice its value, and have it loaded on one of his ships."

He held up one well-manicured hand, forestalling her denial.

"Captain Barton then scuttles his ship, collecting on whatever value it has, while you collect the insured value of the cargo." He turned his hand over, inviting comment. She obliged.

"But what a delightfully artful plan," she said. "I only wish I had thought of it myself."

"You did," Carr said. "I have looked into the matter extensively. You have been, I will allow, clever. And careful. I could find little concrete information. But plenty that is suggestive.

"So much, in fact, that when tallied, the sum of the various particulars I have uncovered leave but one explanation, the one I have already told you and which you already know."

She raised her brows. "You have suspicions but, by your own word, nothing else. Certainly nothing you can use as—what is that fanciful term you have for extortion? Oh yes—impetus. And that being so, tell me, Father, exactly *why* are we having this conversation?"

Carr pursed his lips. "Just because I am unable to blackmail your . . . friend does not mean you are free to do as you wish.

"You still have no home, Fia. And no money. You have nothing of your own except the very nice gifts with which Captain Barton has been attempting to buy his way into your bed. Ah, yes. I know all about that necklace and the ring and the paintings. Sell them all and you'll be able to live for less than half a year in the style you currently enjoy."

She allowed him to see her tense, just a little. His smile spread thinly across his face.

"Ah, you wouldn't like that, would you? No. I didn't think so. Really, Fia," he drawled, "while your enterprising partnership with Barton might eventually have brought you within eyeshot of being independent, did you think I'd allow it?

"You, Fia my dear, will marry who and when and where I say. You are not independent. Not now. Not soon." He feigned a pout and shook his head. "Not ever, I'm afraid."

She voided her expression of anything resembling emotion. "What do you want?"

He smiled. "Ah! Finally. I feel so much better when there's real understanding between us, don't you?" Abruptly his smile, too, vanished. He simply removed it. "I want in. I want your portion. Your share in the partnership."

She waited half a heartbeat, then invested the smallest hint of anger into her voice. "I can't do that."

"I truly hope for your sake you are wrong. Did you know the Marquis of Mannett has been asking after you? An unprepossessing-looking man, what with the gout and those open ulcers, but I am sure— well, relatively hopeful at any event—that they are not caused by the French pox, as is rumored. Ugly things, rumors."

"You can't make me marry him," she said, breathing heavily.

"No. But I can make sure you don't marry anyone else. By any means necessary." His eyes were as flat and unfeeling as a dead man's. She shivered, this time for real.

"I can't, I tell you—" She broke off abruptly. Took a deep breath. It was imperative she not overplay her hand. "As you yourself noted, Captain Barton has been most careful. There is no evidence. Nothing to use to pressure him into letting you in on the arrangements."

His gaze met and held hers. "You underestimate yourself, Fia. So unlike you."

She met his reptilian stare with one equal to his in

blankness. "Are you suggesting I trade my favors for your share?"

If the idea repelled him, he did not show it. Instead, he merely tipped his head back and stroked his chin thoughtfully. "No. I know Barton's sort. Romantical. As clean-cut a business transaction as that would only give him a disgust of you. No, he'll have to be wooed. He'll have to be made to think that in taking me on he's winning you."

"Impossible," Fia said. So close now. She must be smart. Take her time. *Lead* him to it. "Everyone knows I hold you in contempt."

Again, what naturally would have hurt a father caused not a ripple of disconcert in her sire. "True," Carr said. "So, you'll have to find another way."

She tapped her fingers lightly against the arm of her chair. Narrowed her eyes as though concentrating. "He'll need to be offered something he thinks I want. Something he'll feel will win my capitulation."

"What would that be?"

"I don't know. Something he'll think I'll find irresistible. Something grand enough to make the risk of taking you on as a partner seem worth the obvious drawbacks." Her smile was humorless. "Though I doubt he'd know enough to ask for the Crown Jewels."

"Most amusing. Think."

"I don't know— Wait. Bramble House."

"What?" Carr leaned forward. "MacFarlane's farmhouse? It's in the middle of nowhere."

"Yes. I know." Not too much now. A subtle mixture of truth and deception. Hadn't he taught her that?

"Barton is always carrying on about 'the pleasures of rural living.' I have fostered his belief that we share the same feelings about the countryside. He might think to buy it as our love nest. He might think it just the thing to win my favor. And he would like to own it anyway. He's spoken of wanting to acquire land."

Carr was watching her carefully. "Perhaps," he finally muttered. "After all, I have nothing else on this man, do I?"

"Not as far as I know," she said coolly. "But then, you have never let me see your assemblage of 'leverage materials.' "

It was the power base from which Carr worked, an accumulation of deeds, mortgages, promissory notes, indiscreet letters, and stolen church records. She'd seen them once, neatly bundled and hidden in Carr's library at Wanton's Blush. She'd long suspected that Carr had been scarred retrieving them. Too bad they hadn't burned. Along with him.

"And never will, my dear." He dropped the silver tip of his cane to the floor and pushed himself erect. "Perhaps you ought to stay away from Barton for a while."

She blinked at this unexpected suggestion. "But why?"

"Oh, 'Absence makes the heart grow fonder,' that sort of nonsense. 'Twill make Barton more avid to make you his. An anxious man is a willing dupe."

"I'll think about it."

Carr sighed heavily. "Must we always end our

conversations with one of your tiresome assertions of autonomy? Just do as I say, Fia."

She did not reply, neither did she rise, nor bid him good-bye when he left. It would be out of character. She set down her needlework. It had gone well. Now all that was needed was for James to play his part.

Lord Carr exited the town house and waved his carriage off. He wanted to walk tonight. He felt wonderful, so wonderful, in fact, that when he saw Janet peeking out of an upper-story window, he bowed chivalrously and kissed his fingertips to her. She disappeared, and he laughed, a full-blown booming sound.

Dear Fia! Who would have guessed she would be so entertaining? And she'd done it so well, damned if she hadn't. His chest swelled with paternal pride. If she'd been pitting herself against anyone but him she might well have ended up with Bramble House.

But she *had* pitted herself against him. He shook his head, chuckling fondly. Unfortunately for Fia, he hadn't forgotten the reason she'd eloped with that disastrous toad-eating Scotsman or that she'd willingly stayed in that horrible little hamlet for all the years of her marriage, proof that she would do anything—yes, *anything*—to be out from under his power.

This is how she'd planned to regain her freedom, by having him sign over that rude little manor to a man who would then hand it to her.

Oh, Fia! He dabbed at his eyes. Doubtless she thought he would have no choice but to sign over her little farm if he wanted in on the Barton and Donne

Shipping Line's insurance ploy. But he wouldn't. He didn't need to.

For while 'twas true he didn't have anything on James Barton, he most certainly had something on Barton's partner, Thomas Donne. Or rather, Thomas McClairen.

Chapter 9

"Trading our routes is the most sensible solution." Thomas stretched out his legs. He cupped the balloon-shaped brandy snifter in his hand, heating the amber fluid with his palm.

On the other side of the fire, James Barton sat in repose. It was one of the few nights James hadn't left the house to trail after Fia like a faithful—if not particularly bright—hound, and Thomas was determined that tonight they would mend the rift Fia had caused between them. He would avoid all mention of her and stick to matters of mutual interest, specifically the shipping business.

"The *Alba Star* won't be seaworthy in time for me to be able to make our delivery date," he went on. "It will be at least another month before the new sails are ready, and the final coats of varnish need to be applied. If I don't make the deadline we'll have to bid adieu to a very nice bonus."

James's lower lip thrust out unhappily. "I hadn't planned on leaving London so soon. It might prove inconvenient."

"Inconvenient? How? Don't tell me it might interfere with your social obligations. Since when have such become so important to you?" Thomas asked mildly.

"They haven't." Tenacity gelled in James's blunt features. "There's simply some unfinished business I'd like to conclude before I sail. I'm not certain I can bring it to a conclusion so swiftly."

Conclusion or climax? Thomas thought bitterly, but held his tongue. Would James heed his intellect if it denied his heart? No. It would take more than that to sway his friend. Certainly Thomas had yet to find the way.

Once more he considered telling James about the sort of family he was becoming embroiled with. That his own family had been decimated by Carr, that Carr had stolen the McClairen birthright and the McClairen lands, had been responsible for the death of a half-dozen McClairen men, including his brother and uncle. He swirled his brandy in his glass, gazing deep into the burnished liquid.

But that would mean revealing that every time Thomas stepped foot on English soil he risked being exposed as a returned deportee and executed. He'd purposefully kept the knowledge from James, not because he didn't trust him, but because James, who was open and candid in nature, had never been able to keep a secret. And it was imperative that Thomas keep his past a secret because there were others who depended on his not being found out.

Besides, if Thomas told him, James would only ask what that had to do with Fia MacFarlane. James was besotted.

"I have an idea," James said suddenly. "Couldn't you captain the *Sea Witch* round the Cape, and when work on the *Alba Star* is finished I'll take her on the North African route?"

Thomas shook his head. "A ship is like a woman, James. You'd best know her better than your own mistress, in the waters we sail. Unfortunately, you're not privy to this wench's secrets, James."

James's mouth tightened. "I was speaking of a ship, Thomas."

"As was I," Thomas said. "But now that you have broached the subject, I would be a poor friend if I didn't warn you once more against Fia MacFarlane."

James set his own glass of brandy on the floor and pushed himself to his feet. "I don't understand your animosity. It is unlike you to hate without cause and your hatred of Fia is nearly palpable."

Hatred? Thomas thought, stunned. He didn't hate Fia, and the notion that James thought so vexed him. "I don't hate her. I fear her. For your sake."

"Why?"

"Her father—"

"She's not her father, Thomas."

"She's her father's daughter."

"What proof of that do you have?"

"I would think her reputation is proof enough."

James made an impatient gesture. "Gossip and rumor. By God, man, can't you see—" He broke off abruptly and swung around to stare out the window.

Thomas drained the remaining liqueur in his glass in one swallow, his temper frayed. "If only that she-devil disappeared from this earth and vanished back to whatever dark and hellish fairy realm she left," he muttered.

"Don't say that, Thomas," James said, spinning to face him. "You don't know what you're talking about."

"For God's sake, man! Look at what she's done to you!"

"And what exactly is that, Thomas?"

"I had a meeting with Sir Ffolkes yesterday, James. He wanted to know what had become of your last two shipments. He implied that you purposely lost them to collect the insurance."

The fury and amazement Thomas had expected did not appear. Instead, James's expression grew pensive. "Oh? And what did you say, Tom?"

"I said it was a lie."

James nodded. Nothing more. Thomas stared at him, apprehension trailing up his spine, chilling him with possibility. James should be deeply, grievously offended. He should be penning a note to Ffolkes this moment, demanding an interview. At the very least he should be swearing his determination to discover who had spread these vicious lies. But he wasn't.

"By God!" James was watching him, abrupt realization manifest in his expression. "You don't put any credence in Ffolkes's suspicions, do you, Thomas?"

"No. Of course not."

"I swear to you I have done nothing illegal," James said stiffly.

He heard the sincerity in James's avowal and he believed him, yet at the back of his mind he could not shake the image of Fia laughing as she told him that James was hers. Or of Amelia's necklace encircling Fia's throat. "Of course."

"Of course," James repeated bitterly, sensing his doubt. "Well, what would you have me do, then, Thomas?"

He should ask for nothing. By doing so he admitted questioning James's integrity. It would be a blow, perhaps even a fatal blow, to their friendship. But if he could remove James from Fia MacFarlane's influence, it was worth the risk.

"All right, James," he said coolly. "I want you to trade routes with me, as I suggested. I'll remain here while the repairs to the *Alba Star* are finished and deal with Ffolkes and any other questions that arise."

A vein bulged in James's throat. His lips disappeared into a tight, fine line. "All right, Thomas," he said. "If this is what you think is necessary. When must I ship out?"

"Three weeks."

Both men understood that there was nothing more to say, and so nothing more was said.

My Dear Fia,

I know you prefer I not commit to paper any communication between us. But I cannot see you this evening or the next and feel the information I am about to impart is of a pressing enough nature to take this risk.

Your concerns about Thomas Donne may have some merit. Indeed, I fear he means you some form of injury, and while I will never believe he means to do you any bodily harm, his words this evening caused me concern, for he spoke quite heatedly of wishing you vanished.

If only you would release me from my promise not to speak of our relationship. Until then I will, of course, abide by your wishes. Other than hope this warning proves needless, I can do nothing more.

There is more to relate but being ever mindful of your cautions, I will wait until we meet in person to tell you this very important news.

Until that time I remain, as always, your servant,

James Harold Barton

Carr waited within the carriage while his liveried lackey dashed up the stairs and rapped sharply on the town house door. The young night was already dark. A thin rain had begun and beneath the lamps bracketing the front door, the whitewashed steps glistened like bones.

A servant answered and, after an amazed look at the carriage waiting on the street, slammed the door shut.

Carr gazed out incuriously. 'Twasn't the first time his appearance caused such a reaction. Awe, he supposed. A woman suddenly appeared perched atop the lamppost at the corner of the street. It was Janet.

"Now, what are you doing here?" Carr murmured. He would have called out but the experience of the past five years had taught him the uselessness of doing so. She'd only fade. She always did.

Janet was apparently enjoying a prolonged ghostly snit. She was miffed at him for something or other. It couldn't be because he'd killed her. She'd forgiven him for that or she wouldn't have bothered warning him to leave on the night Wanton's Blush had burned down. So there must be some other reason for her stubborn silence.

He couldn't begin to guess what. Not that he particularly cared. Better a silent ghost than a nattering one. It's just that he felt a bit injured by the unfairness of it— Sure enough, she'd begun to shimmer and then fade and finally she snuffed out. He turned his hand over, studying his nails.

The door at the top of the steps swung open again and the footman bowed low. Carr's servant leapt down the steps and flung open the carriage door.

Carr alit and mounted the steps slowly, ignoring the flustered footman as he moved without hesitation into the hall and down the narrow corridor to the open door on the left. These little town houses were all patterned the same. This could only be the sitting room. And of course it was. He entered. Thomas Donne stood in the center of the room, awaiting him.

Carr looked about. A pleasant, pedestrian sort of room. The requisite bookshelves holding gold-embossed leather works, the blue velvet draperies, the Aubusson carpet. Everything quite standard.

"Lord Carr," Donne rumbled, his gray eyes canny in his sun-darkened countenance. "It's been a long time. Won't you be seated and tell me to what I owe this visit?"

Carr shrugged off his light cloak. The footman flitting nervously behind him caught it before it hit the floor. "You may go now," Carr dismissed him. The man looked at Donne and, after receiving his nod, backed from the room.

"I have a salve that might be able to help that," Carr said, taking the seat Donne indicated.

"Sir?"

"Your skin, man, your skin. I have a salve that can bleach out some of the tan."

"Thank you, but no." Despite the smile and mild tone, Thomas did not relax but prowled along the edges of the room. Carr remembered the attitude well; Thomas Donne had lounged and moved and stalked through society like one great Bengal tiger. He'd been quite an attraction for the women on the few occasions he'd visited Wanton's Blush. "I doubt you've come here to advise me on cosmetics."

Carr planted the tip of his cane between his feet and folded his hands over the heavy knob. "Of course not. I have come to blackmail you."

He'd hoped to disconcert the bruising Scotsman; he'd failed. Which, now that he thought of it, seemed to be becoming something of a pattern lately. Indeed, the last few times he'd made that particular announcement, he'd been met with only impassive resignation. No histrionics, no shock, no horror—as though his victims resigned themselves to their fate before he even had the fun of stating his intentions. Rather mean-spirited of them.

"Oh?" Donne finally sank down into a chair opposite Carr, resting his right boot on his left knee. "How?"

"I know who you are. I know you are Thomas McClairen."

Donne's gaze remained impassive. He waited for Carr to continue. Wise man. At this point in the conversation so many of Carr's victims began a tedious string of denials, epitaphs, and explanations. This was rather a nice change of pace.

"I have only to—"

"Yes, yes," Donne interrupted impatiently, "you have only to say the word and I'll be hanged. Threat duly noted. Can we get on with it? What do you want?"

Carr pursed his lips, disgruntled. The man was a killjoy after all. It wasn't as if Donne were pressed for time. He obviously hadn't been about to leave for some engagement or other. Yet here he was . . . rush, rush, rush.

"Well?"

Carr released a long-suffering sigh. "I want in on the insurance fraud you and your partner are involved in."

Not a flicker of anxiety. "We're not involved in any insurance fraud."

Ah, this was more like it.

"Really? And here I am, come straight from my daughter, who, by the way, is so covered with the profits from your scheme that she's a walking advertisement for it."

"She *told* you James was involved?"

"No, my dear. *I* told *her*. *She* did not deny it."

"Doesn't sound very convincing to me."

"Oh, it was. Believe me. Indeed, my little black-headed lambikins had obviously been anticipating my arrival. She had a plan all drawn up for me to convince Barton to let me become his partner."

Donne watched him silently. Had the man no conversation? Gads! "It seems my darling wants the ownership of Bramble House."

"Bramble House?"

"Yes." Carr frowned at the fold of his cuff and gave his hand a little shake, resetting the gossamer lace more elegantly about his wrist. "Oh, don't fret if you've never heard of it. No one has. 'Tis a country house once owned by Fia's dead husband, now owned by me. MacFarlane deeded the place over to me some months before his demise—as well as a good many other things. Too bad for Fia . . . and his son, of course."

"MacFarlane had a son?" Donne asked curiously.

"Has a son. Weedy, unprepossessing creature."

Donne's mouth flattened with distaste, why Carr

could not yet say. "Why does F—your daughter want it?"

"She wants it because it's a wealthy property, and the estate vast enough, and the lands fertile enough, that were she to own it she would be able to live quite comfortably on the income it produces."

Donne's expression tightened. Carr rested his chin atop his hands folded over the cane handle, watching. He wasn't about to inform Donne of Fia's rather desperate desire to be free of him. It might awaken some kindred spirit in the tall sea captain, though Carr rather doubted it. Even when Donne had been a guest at Wanton's Blush and Fia had pursued him with all the guileless ardency of fresh womanhood, he'd withstood her charms, her allure, and her less than subtle offers.

Poor Fia. For Thomas Donne nothing would ever alter or mask the fact that Fia was his enemy's daughter, would always be his enemy's daughter; nothing Fia did would ever make him forget that.

"But enough about Fia," Carr said. "And Barton. It's you I am interested in. Shall we come to some sort of agreement, Donne—or should I say McClairen?"

Donne shrugged. "Mind you, I am not convinced James has done any wrong, but clearly your daughter has been pressuring him to some such ends. If I agreed, you would have to stop Fia from coercing James."

"I wouldn't have to do anything," Carr said. "If we enter partnership, Barton will terminate his operations soon enough. I mean, even a besotted fool must see that for every ship in a fleet to catch fire or be way-laid by pirates would be a bit much.

"And Fia? Once Fia realizes she's been outmaneuvered she'll quickly release her hold on Barton and turn her not inconsiderable faculties toward trying to find yet another means to secure her"—he paused; he'd been about to say "release"—"house."

Thomas regarded him narrowly. "And if I refuse you'll tell the authorities who I am."

"Exactly! Of course, if you're lucky you might be able to escape England, but you'd never be able to dock safely in an English harbor again, and since England owns the seas . . ."

"I understand."

"I was sure you would." Carr stomped the end of his cane against the carpet, signaling a close to this end of the proceedings. "So. How do we go about the next phase in our partnership?"

Donne scowled into space, thinking. Carr allowed him the time. He despised hasty, emotional decisions.

"It will take a month or so," Donne finally said. "We'll need to buy cargo. It has to look right, though. I'll need to go to France and procure the sorts of things that might reasonably be insured at great value and shipped to foreign ports for profit. Brandy. Linens. That sort of thing."

His dark brow furrowed. "We won't need to find a receiver since there won't ever be any receiving. We'll load on and the night before we're to put out to sea, there'll be a fire."

"Excellent," Carr exclaimed, his eyes shining with inspiration. "But I have an even better idea."

"Do you?" Donne said dryly.

"Why not collect twice on the cargo? Load it, have it inspected by Lloyd's, and then, just before the fire, offload it. We can store it someplace and sell it later, too."

"Fine."

Carr pouted. "I thought it was a damned good idea and you don't seem at all enthusiastic."

"Forgive me. I take an unaccountable exception to being blackmailed. Besides, I fear for the lives of the men on the docks. Fire can spread far easily."

He feared for the dockworkers' lives? Carr thought incredulously, and could think of no reply other than a small "Oh."

Donne's lifted his gaze to Carr's face. "I want something out of this, though."

Carr waggled his finger chidingly. "Uh, uh, uh. Mustn't threaten the threatener."

"I'm not making threats. I'm telling you the only way you'll get what you want from me. I have no great love of England. Exile from this island wouldn't be relegating me to hell on earth, as you seem to imagine."

His words sounded real, all the more real for being sneered. Carr considered. He did not like making accommodations for those he victimized. But here, he intuited, he had no choice. Donne would flee without a backward glance. "What?"

"This . . ." Thomas leaned forward and began talking.

Ten minutes later, when Carr left the house, the footman who held the door heard the earl laughing.

It was not a pleasant sound.

Thomas hurled his brandy snifter into the fireplace. Flames exploded above the glowing embers, spitting raucously. With a growl, Thomas swung away.

He'd thought having James gone in three short weeks would be soon enough to pry him from her clutches. And he was not nearly as sanguine as Carr about the odds of Fia obeying his command to stay away from James. She might just do something desperate if she found her back to the wall.

Unfortunately for her, his was already there.

Chapter 10

*F*ia took the chair by the window. Earlier she'd angled it so that the light streaming through would fall full on the face of anyone sitting in it. After the strain of yesterday's meeting with her father, the morning sunlight would be unkind to her. Every line, every shadow, would be pronounced. Idly, she began sorting through the stack of letters in her hand.

"I don't understand!" Pip exclaimed. He had not sat down since his arrival ten minutes earlier.

Fia sighed heavily, clearly relating annoyance, and regarded the boy coolly. Though his flesh still had a waxy aspect and he'd lost weight, he moved without difficulty and his breathing seemed easy.

"What is it you do not understand?" she asked heavily. "I have made plans to travel out of the country with a dear friend of mine. I shall be gone a fortnight or longer. What is so difficult to understand in that?" The lie came easily. The thought of hiding here while everyone believed her to be abroad was heavenly.

"Who is this friend?" the boy demanded.

She picked up a silver letter-opener. She must not allow Pip to involve her in some emotional scene. Were she to answer in any way other than coolly, it would only convince him that there was, indeed, sentiment between them. "I don't think that is any of your concern, is it?"

"But . . ." The anger drained from his young face, leaving only pain and transparent confusion. "What have I done? You seem different."

"Do I?" Her voice rose in surprise. "In what way?"

For a moment she thought he would refuse to answer, but then, he was young and had been wounded and it was only natural that he should seek to wound in return. His lip thrust out belligerently. "You have become callous," he said. "And unfeeling. I want to know why."

She paused for a moment's aloof consideration, as though his harsh words had not affected her in the least. As though the dull ache in her heart did not exist. "Perhaps, m'dear, it is you who have changed," she finally suggested. "Perhaps coming so near a tragic end has changed your perceptions of things. And people."

"Are you saying that you were always cold and . . . and uncaring?"

She laughed. "Not at all. I *am* saying that perhaps I

never was quite the soppy little sentimentalist you apparently thought I was and that now you have realized this. I am sorry if the reality is a disappointment. But in my own defense, most men would not agree with you." She pouted slightly, fluttering her lashes. The boy flushed.

"Perhaps you are correct, Lady Fia," he said stiffly.

A knock sounded at the door.

"Come in," Fia said, glad of the interruption.

Porter opened the door. "Lady Fia, I was—" He saw Pip and stopped. "I am inopportune—"

"Not at all," Fia said. "We are done, are we not, Pip?"

The boy began to protest and then thought better of it. "Yes. But I would like to say, ma'am, that I already know 'the friend' with whom you will be traveling."

Fia's brows climbed. Since her proposed travel, as well as her travel companion, were completely imaginary, this was a most interesting turn of events. "Really?"

"Yes," the boy said gruffly. "And for the sake of that image of you I once held in my . . . in such esteem, I am duty bound to warn you against him."

"Do tell," she murmured. "And why is that?"

"Because Thomas Donne once claimed to be my friend and you can see for yourself how well he respected that relationship, since he used my injury to ingratiate himself with you and plans to go abroad with you!"

"Thomas Donne?" she repeated. "He told you he was leaving London with me?"

"No." Pip shifted uneasily on his feet but he did not recant his claim. "But he did say as how he would be leaving London for a few weeks. And when he came to see me whilst I was convalescing he spoke of you. I thought at the time his tone derisive and his manner disapproving but I see now that it only masked his real intent . . . to understand you better.

"I am not so stupid or callow, ma'am, that I cannot add two and two." He laughed bitterly, but he was not much good at it and his laughter broke. "And to think he had the temerity to warn me against you."

She recovered quickly. "Ah, yes, well. Men will commonly put their own interests above that of others. Even their friends'." For all Pip's jealous suspicions, Thomas's plan to leave London had nothing to do with her. She turned half away from Pip, aware of Porter standing with telltale silence on the threshold.

"Men?" Pip echoed sarcastically.

"And women, too, of course." She looked over her shoulder at him. "Ah . . . thank you for your concern."

He did not respond.

"I believe Porter had something of a private nature to impart to me." It was a dismissal and a not particularly kind one. Pip flushed and shoved his way past the butler.

Fia waited until she heard the sound of the front door slamming shut before saying wearily "What is it, Porter?

"I know it is not my place to try to discern the intentions of your friends and admirers, Lady Fia."

"Probably not," Fia agreed with a trace of irony.

"But I would be remiss in my duty if I were to suspect someone of perpetrating an unpleasantness on you and then neglected to warn you, would I not?"

"Oh, dear. Is this an ethical question, Porter? Because, if so, I gravely doubt I am qualified to answer it."

"Not at all, Lady Fia. I merely seek to ascertain your wishes."

"Ah, I see. Well, speaking for myself, yes, were you to suspect someone of a dastardly plan against me, I would certainly welcome being forewarned."

Porter nodded. "Then I must concur with Master Leighton's suspicion concerning Captain Donne."

Fia's ennui vanished. "Why?"

"Captain Donne came to call on you earlier today."

"What?" Fia said. "Why was I not informed of this?"

"Because Captain Donne specifically told the footman—a young fellow named Bob—not to bother you. The captain came early, far earlier than any society lady is likely to have arisen; indeed, earlier than many a woman in a simpler household rises. He asked to see you. When Bob said you were not yet receiving company, Captain Donne laughed with some embarrassment, alleging how chagrined he was at his eagerness to see you.

"At that point Bob marked Captain Donne down as another besotted swain. The captain then proceeded to ask him a number of questions about your habits: when you could most often be found at home, your daily routine, when you were most likely to be alone . . . that sort of thing."

Fia frowned. "And Bob told him?"

Porter winced slightly. "I am afraid so, Lady Fia. Captain Donne tipped him most handsomely and took his leave, asking Bob not to mention that he'd been here and explaining that it did nothing for a man's cause to have the lady suspect his eagerness. And Bob, a recently failed suitor himself, agreed.

"Bob only chanced to mention Captain Donne's appearance to me now because he saw Master Leighton come in and thought it odd that so many fellows were queuing up before luncheon. Bob's words, not, I assure you, mine."

"Of course," Fia murmured, her thoughts racing. She glanced down at the note James Barton had sent her the night before last. Then she had thought it merely James's natural wariness. But now . . .

"Milady?"

She looked up. Porter was waiting. Abruptly she came to a decision. "I thank you, Porter, for both your loyalty and your diligence. However much appreciated, your concern is unnecessary. I *am* planning on leaving London, you see. Possibly as soon as this very afternoon, but then again perhaps not. My plans are most liquid, you see, and contingent on another's whim. You may inform the staff."

Porter blinked once, but years of training stood him in good stead. "Of course, Lady Fia."

Fia was standing before her open wardrobe when Gunna came in bearing a tray laden with hot chocolate. The hunched woman looked around at petticoats, chemises, clocked silk stockings, and stomachers heaped on the bed, the chairs, the settee, and any other available surface in the room.

"You've gone daft, then," she said, nodding resignedly. "Well, no wonder. This city would drive a saint to sin and ye never were no saint, dearie."

"Hm?" Fia, her hand hovering above a silk faille underskirt, reached instead for the lisle print one beneath. "Oh, Gunna. Good."

Gunna set the tray on the dressing table. "What are ye doin', lass?"

Fia tossed four sets of stockings on the bed, frowned, and added another. "I'm preparing for my abduction."

"What?"

Hearing the amazement in Gunna's voice, Fia turned and smiled. It was seldom she managed to catch Gunna unaware. "My abduction," she repeated calmly, and glancing at the mantel clock, continued, "which ought to begin any time now."

Gunna did not return her smile. In fact, the exposed and crumpled side of her face looked decidedly grim. "Ye better explain, Fia. And it better be good."

"I don't have time."

"Ye better find time," Gunna pronounced tersely.

Fia didn't want to get into an argument with Gunna. The old Scotswoman would almost certainly win and, in winning, convince her to abandon the plan that had sprung full-blown in Fia's imagination when she realized that Thomas Donne planned to kidnap her in order to keep James Barton from her evil influence.

She did not want to abandon her plan. What better way to accomplish so many things? She would obey her father's directive and be absent during James's meeting with her father, which might help serve to explain James's—dear, honest James's—miserable mien at that conference. This way she could also keep Thomas from interfering with the plan and, last but not least, extract a bit of sweet revenge on that righteous Scot.

Fia opened her portmanteau and began stacking clothing. She must take care not to pack too much, lest Thomas's suspicions be awakened. She turned, her eye alighting on a particularly frivolous, feminine, and extremely provocative robe of violet tulle. There was definitely room for that.

"Fia . . ." Gunna's voice rose in warning.

She met Gunna's gaze levelly. "You are not to worry, Gunna. The purpose of this abduction is to keep me from seducing someone, *not* to be seduced."

"Ach!" the old woman exclaimed. "I'd never thought to see the day Lady Fia Merrick acted the gull."

"I'm not being gullible. Nor naive."

Gunna's one good eye peered at Fia. She was apparently satisfied with what she saw, for with a grunt she sank down onto the edge of the bed. "And who's this saint who's taken on the job of saving London's poor men from yer evil clutches?"

"Thomas Donne."

"Ach, no! Not that one! I'd soon as trust ye with a selkie. Ye've been smitten with him since ye were a lassie and I'll no have ye puttin' yerself in his hands."

"Gunna, dear."

"Don't 'dear' me. Ye never got nuthin' from 'dearin' ' me as a lass and ye'll find it works no better now that yer a woman grown."

"All right, Gunna," Fia said, giving up her wheedling tone. "Here it is, then. You are going to *have* to trust me. If I leave with Thomas Donne I can make sure he doesn't ruin my plans. Plans that will see us back to Bramble House. Plans that will once and for all sever my father's influence over me. Over us." She didn't bother to tell Gunna about the proposed revenge.

Gunna scowled and stroked her seamed cheek with her narrow fingers. "I don't know. . . ."

"It makes perfect sense. It is perfectly reasonable."

Gunna slapped her knee. "All right. I'll go with ye."

"No! I mean, no. He'll never agree to taking you with me and . . . and you need to stay here with Kay. And Cora. She might appear just as suddenly as her brother." It was unfair to use Gunna's affection for the children. But Fia had never learned the art of fighting for what she wanted by fair means.

"Ah!" The old woman shook her head. "I don't like it. Ye don't know *what* that man is capable of."

"Not rape," she said with absolute conviction.

Gunna glanced at her sourly. "I was thinkin' he's not the sort that needs to force his way."

"He'll not have his way with me," Fia vowed. It did not seem to comfort the old woman greatly but at least she protested no more. And after Fia closed the latch on the portmanteau and set it to wait by the bedchamber door and Gunna had kissed her cheek and promised to watch out for Kay and finally left, Fia breathed the words she'd held in check.

"But I surely intend to have my way with him," she whispered.

Chapter 11

The square containing the MacFarlane town house was quiet. Early morning languor hovered over the empty, cobbled streets as sunlight warmed the broad back of a dray horse standing in its traces. Later, housemaids would venture out to scrub stairs and run errands, but now, at seven o'clock, they kept to quieter pursuits so as not to rouse masters and mistresses who had taken to their beds only a few hours earlier.

Thomas vaulted over the stone wall encircling the town house's back garden and landed on the privy roof. From there he jumped lightly to the path leading through the garden and looked with satisfaction at the back of the house. True to the pattern three days of reconnaissance had made known to him, the library window stood open. He looked up. Overhead the draperies in Fia's boudoir fluttered in the window.

He needed to keep Fia out of town until James was safely aboard the *Sea Witch*. He'd planned carefully, from the man waiting at the end of the alley with the closed carriage, to the notes he'd left Carr and James claiming he'd gone to France to purchase merchandise.

Of course, when Thomas returned Carr would realize he had not bought any cargo and had no intention of scuttling his ship. Carr would then inform the authorities of Thomas's status as an illegally returned deportee and Thomas would flee—leaving behind the dream he'd worked so hard to realize, the dream of reclaiming Maiden's Blush from the ashes to which Carr had consigned her.

He did not regret his decision. He owed James Barton a few dreams and more. Besides, even if Thomas could not supervise the restoration himself, he could still find a way back now and then. And if he never felt the joy of one final homecoming, well, he'd still have the satisfaction of knowing that his clan had returned to McClairen's Isle.

No, he did not regret his decision. But that didn't make this, his proposed course, any more palatable. He'd never in his life mistreated a woman. And yet, in a few minutes he would abduct a woman from her home and keep her against her will.

He took a deep breath, placed his hands on the library windowsill, and pushed himself up and over, dropping noiselessly to the carpet inside.

"I say, most of Fia's friends use the front door."

He froze. The accent was undoubtedly Scottish, adolescent, and male. He turned.

A young man, even younger than Pip, sat in an armchair. In his lap was an open book. He regarded Thomas with dark, thoughtful eyes beneath a tousled fringe of brown hair.

Who the hell was this?

Thomas arranged a smile. "I admit, I didn't expect to find anyone here. Who are you?"

The boy closed the book on his finger. "I believe that is my line, sir."

Gads, but the boy had panache. His self-containment, the slight dryness of his tone reminded Thomas of someone. No nervous fiddling, an exceptionally calm, direct— The boy reminded him of Fia. Impossible for them to be related. Except for a likeness of expression, there was no other resemblance.

"You're not MacFarlane's boy, are you?" Thomas asked.

The boy's watchful air dissipated slightly. "You have the better of me, sir," he said.

Thomas broadened his grin, thinking. He needed to come up with a reasonable explanation for having entered through the library window, though surely a boy raised under Fia's care would be used to the sudden, unheralded arrival of strange men. "I am a friend of your stepmama."

"I never call her 'mama.' I call her Fia. She's only six years older than me, you know," the boy said, a defensive note creeping into his voice.

God spare him, yet another of Fia's conquests!

"It would be absurd for me to call her 'mother,' " the boy went on, before adding thoughtfully, "though Cora calls her 'mama' sometimes, but only to tease her."

"*Tease her?*" The notion of anyone "teasing" Fia was so outlandish that for a moment Thomas forgot himself. "Who is Cora that she teases Fia?"

"My younger sister. *Horrible* younger sister. Twits Fia something terrible. Not that I don't empathize. Fia is such an easy mark, don't you think?"

Thomas glanced about, nonplussed, half expecting to discover this Cora in some other chair. Fia an easy mark? An object of childish torment?

"Oh, don't worry." The boy had read his mind. "Cora is away at school. In Devon. The *far* side of Devon," he emphasized with unmistakable relish.

"I see." But he didn't. He should be upstairs, tying a scarf around Fia's lovely mouth in preparation for tossing her over his shoulder and making off with her. Instead, he was chatting up a boy.

The lad stood up and nodded in courtly fashion. "I am Kay Antoine MacFarlane."

"Uh, Donne. Thomas Donne." Thomas glanced at the door leading into the hall. A maid was bound to show up soon.

"Honored, sir."

"Likewise, Lord MacFarlane."

The adult veneer fell away and the boy grinned, his expression open and spontaneous in a manner Fia's could never be. "Just 'Kay,' sir. 'Twas an honorary title my father held and one I don't pine after. Being MacFarlane of Bramble House is enough for me."

Thomas found himself liking the boy and damning Carr for cheating such a decent lad out of his rightful home. The thought led back to his reason for being there.

"Well, Kay MacFarlane of Bramble House, I'd best be on my way before we attract one of the servants."

"And what way is that, Mr. Donne?" The guarded quality reentered his eyes.

Thomas held his hands out, palm up. "There's this little bet Fia and I have made. I claimed I could enter her house and take the bouquet from the upstairs vase"—*God, let there be a vase in the upstairs hall*—"and that no one would see me, including Fia." He shook his head ruefully. "Wouldn't she love to know that I'd no sooner entered the house than was discovered by you?"

The boy's lips quirked in amusement. "Aye. Fia crows somethin' awful when she wins, don't she?"

Crowing? Laughing? True, he'd heard Fia laugh many times—derisively, cruelly, scornfully—but never with the uncomplicated delight this boy was speaking about.

"We lads must stick together, don't you think?"

Kay studied him. "Perhaps."

"Come now, Kay. Fia's too used to winning. It's time we poor frail males had the upper hand, isn't it?"

The boy nodded, the hovering smile just waiting to be born.

"So what say you just go on doing what you were doing. Reading, was it? Something grand, I hope."

"*The Iliad.*"

"Ah! Nothing grander. You just read on—only do so in your own room, Kay. That way, you won't have to answer any hard questions later when Fia's discovered she's lost our bet." He winked at the boy.

"I suppose I *could* go to the kitchen. . . ."

"The kitchen it is!" Thomas said, clapping Kay companionably on the back and feeling utterly despicable. "Go on. There'd be no living with her if she never lost, would there?"

It tipped the scales in Thomas's favor. The boy nodded in commiseration. "You have the right of it there, sir."

Thomas laughed and swung his arm about the boy's bony shoulders, shepherding him to the door. Once there, he glanced both ways before giving him a little shove into the corridor.

Kay was halfway down the hall before he looked back. "How long do I have to stay in there?"

"Oh, a quarter hour," Thomas answered casually, "mayhap a bit longer, just to be sure. You know, in case I dodge into some room to wait for a maid or a footman to pass."

The boy nodded. A minute later the servants' door swung shut behind him. The smile vanished from Thomas's face as he took the stairs to the second level. He remembered which room was Fia's. He pushed it open and entered quickly, soundlessly shutting it behind him.

He looked around, spying the arched entrance that led from the boudoir to the bedchamber. He padded across the floor and peered in, fully expecting to see Fia asleep in her bed, unwillingly anticipating the picture she would make with her black hair flowing over white linen and her skin dewy with sleep.

She was not in the bed.

He peered around the corner. She was sitting with her feet tucked up beneath her in a wingback chair, a piece of needlework on her lap. *Needlework!* And she was wearing a simple yellow day-gown, the neckline modest, the sleeves trimmed with treble bands of white lace. The fresh color of it became her as much as her usual dramatic palette of black and white, though in a subtler manner, setting her skin to glow softly and the rippling black of her hair to shining.

She looked up. For a second her gorgeous eyes darkened, turning the brilliant blue dusky, like wood violet in shadow.

"Captain Donne." She showed only slight concern at his appearance, employing that unearthly trick she had of smoothing her features to impenetrable stillness. "To what do I owe this honor?"

He moved quickly across the room, seizing her upper arm and pulling her to her feet. The needlework fell to the floor. Her brow puckered in extreme distaste, echoing his own.

"I would dislike hurting you, Fia," he spoke softly, "but I swear if you raise your voice I will render you unconscious."

She pulled her arm free, stepping back and challenging him with a scornful look. "I have no intention of raising my voice. What are you doing here?"

He took a deep breath. "I may couch this in the form of a request, but make no mistake, Fia, it is not a request. It is a statement."

One dark, wing-shaped brow rose. "Pray continue."

"Will you come with me?"

The humor Kay had described flickered to life in her extraordinary eyes. "Where to? Oxford Street to visit that new French mercer? Or Covent Garden—though, I daresay, the fruits have been picked over by now. Perhaps you've in mind an excursion to—"

"I am taking you out of London."

Her humor faded. "I see. For how long?"

"An extended period of time."

Did her alabaster skin pale? He thought so, and he noticed for the first time that she wore no cosmetics this morning. The paints and perfumes and salves that created the Black Diamond no longer concealed her.

Why, in all the saints' names, had she ever covered such flesh with dross powder and paint? The tint of her skin was warm and translucent, as delicately shaded as the pink pearls he'd once purchased on an uncharted South Pacific island.

"Then this is an abduction."

"Yes."

She gave a businesslike little nod. "I see. And do I have any say in this? Of course not"—she shook her head at her own stupidity—"if I had a say, and I said yes, this would be an elopement, not an abduction. Semantics are so very important, don't you think?"

She was purposefully trying to overset him. He'd seen her do it to a dozen men over the past weeks, catch them with false candor that concealed more than it elucidated.

She moved closer, too close. She did nothing obvious as she had when disguised at Portmann's masque. She did not touch him, though his body stiffened in anticipation and his skin prickled with a phantom sensation of her hand on his chest.

"So little confidence, Captain. Has it not occurred to you that I might *not* be adverse to going with you?" she purred, a faint tantalizing smile playing about the corners of her lush lips. "Why don't you simply ask me?"

He caught himself just in time. She would say no and laugh. He saw it in the hard bright eyes that refuted the softness of her mouth.

When he didn't answer, a shadow of doubt dented her composure—slight but there. She'd expected him to ask her; she did not know how to take his refusal.

"Ah well, then," she said. "If you'll be seated, I shall gather a few things and we'll get started."

At his start of surprise she regained her mastery of the situation, bright and sharp and clean as a razor's wounding. "Why . . . you don't imagine this is my first abduction, do you?"

A trilling little laugh. "Oh, heavens no! I count it an utterly wasted Season if I am not abducted at least once. Though"—her voice turned reproachful—"most of my abductors at least do me the favor of telling me how long I can expect to be gone.

"I mean, a schedule would be so helpful. I could then decide whether to cancel that new dress I ordered—not much sense in having an especial gown made for the Bennetts' fete if I'm not going to be here, is there? And then the wine merchant should be notified to stop delivery for . . ." Her pause invited disclosure, but when he said nothing she went on in open exasperation. "*However* long.

"Added to which, I was to interview for a new housekeeper this week, meet with the hair stylist, Monsieur Gerard—you realize that if I simply do not show up for my appointment with him I may as well just kiss good-bye any future hopes he will arrange my hair—plus all the other mundane items of daily life that even an abduction cannot gainsay."

She sighed resignedly. "I suppose not telling me how long you plan to keep me makes it more romantic for you?"

Her words snapped the immobility holding him silent. "This is *not* a romantic tryst!"

She blinked at his angry tone. "Apparently not." Her eyes suddenly widened. "Rape, then?" she whispered.

"God's teeth, no!" he thundered.

"Oh. Good. What exactly is it, then? I do hope you haven't any wrongheaded notion that you might hold me for ransom? Because I assure you no one will pay a penny for my return."

He did not miss the small, unwilling note of bitterness beneath the amusement, but he was too furious, stung far more deeply than he would have imagined possible that she could think him capable of rape, to pay it heed.

"I very much doubt that, milady," he snarled. "But no, I do not seek ransom for your return. Now, do not ask anything else, for I will not answer. I will only say to you that no harm will come to you as a result of this . . . this . . ."

"Abduction?" she supplied.

"Abduction," he agreed tersely. "In time, you will be returned unharmed."

"Do you promise?" Until that moment he had not a clue that his proposed kidnapping had afforded her more than a ripple of concern. Now he saw that, for all her bravado, she felt vulnerable.

"I promise."

"Well"—she turned from him before he could gauge her reaction; her skirts belled gently as she moved away—"if you'll indulge me a few minutes?"

She crossed to a painted chest at the foot of her bed and tossed up the lid. A moment later she'd hauled out a large leather portmanteau and opened the clasp. "Hm." She bent over, rummaging within. "Chemise, corset, *echelles*, two underskirts . . ."

He stared. "You have a portmanteau *ready*?"

She nodded without bothering to look at him. "And a small trunk," she said, pointing vaguely in the direction of the closed armoire. A brass-bound traveling trunk rested beside it. "For a few gowns. Can you carry it or would you rather drive round to the back and I can have one of the footman take it down?"

He crossed the room in a few strides. She *must* be mocking him. But a glance revealed a neatly packed portmanteau filled with delicate, lacy . . . things.

She shut the bag and straightened. "Well?"

With a strangled sound he lifted the valise and stalked over to seize the brass handle of the trunk. He hefted it to his shoulder and turned. She was waiting by the door.

"Do not attempt to raise an alarm, madam."

"And miss discovering for what reason besides seduction or monetary gain a gentleman"—the emphasis on the word was slight but ironic—"performs an abduction? I daresay not! Come, the maids will be working in the front rooms yet. We can leave through the kitchen."

Thomas thought of Kay. "No. The library."

She shrugged and reached for the door handle.

"Wait."

She turned a questioning look on him.

"You will write a note, telling your family that you have decided to accept an offer to tour the continent."

Her brows climbed in surprise.

"I would not want them worried."

He expected her to mock his concern for her stepson but, after a short pause, she only said, "As you will," and brushed by him.

At her writing desk she pulled a thick piece of paper from a stack. She scrawled a few appropriate lines and folded the paper in half. On the outside she wrote "For Kay." She left it atop the table and returned to his side.

"Satisfied?"

"Yes." He reached past her and opened the door, making sure the outside corridor was empty before motioning her ahead of him.

Tensely he followed her down the stairs, the valise thumping soundlessly against his thigh and the edge of the trunk biting into his neck. He fully expected her to break into a run at any moment and, fool that he was, he'd ensured that he would be able to do nothing to stop her.

Part of him wished she would, wished she would suddenly lift her skirt and flee, freeing him from this mad plan. She did not.

Another part of him was glad.

At two o'clock the same afternoon, James Barton was heading for the MacFarlane town house. He'd made arrangements with Fia to go driving in St. James Park. He would then take the opportunity to tell her that he was leaving in a few weeks. At the same time he would make an ostentatious show of presenting her with a pair of spectacular diamond earbobs. They had belonged to Amelia. Amelia would approve, he thought with a sad smile. She and Fia had maintained a sporadic but affectionate correspondence until Amelia's death.

It had been to Amelia that Fia had given her invaluable aid seven years ago.

James and Amelia had arrived in London fresh from the colonies. He had been flush with pride, his pockets filled with the income of his shipping company's first successes, and avid to introduce his lovely wife to society. They had been taken up by people who brought them to Wanton's Blush.

There, he'd come to the attention of the Earl of Carr. Urbane, articulate, witty, and self-assured, the earl had cultivated their association, flattered James, but mostly encouraged his gambling.

In a week the profits James had earned during the past year disappeared. Frightened and uncertain of where to turn or how to tell Amelia, he'd taken to the gaming tables with increasing desperation. Soon he owed more than he owned.

That was when Carr had requested a private interview. He proposed that James "do him a favor" and in return Carr would see that his gambling debts were paid. The nature of this favor was never spelled out, but James knew with certainty that it would be questionable. He'd asked for a day to consider it, which Carr, with a knowing smile, had granted.

Finally, he'd confessed to his bemused and horrified wife. For some reason she in turn had confided in Carr's preternaturally self-possessed daughter. What transpired between them remained their secret forever. He knew only that Fia gave Amelia a cameo. A gorgeous diamond-studded piece of jewelry. Given. Freely. Without condition.

He never understood why. As far as he knew, Fia Merrick had never exhibited such magnanimity before nor was she to do so again. But then, he never pretended to understand that enigmatic woman. The idea of taking valuable property from a child offended every ideal James held dear. But eventually, Amelia had convinced him to accept it. The proceeds had been nearly enough to cover his debts. Paying off the rest of his notes had taken him a full year.

Eventually he had come to appreciate the extent of the debt he owed Fia Merrick. The rumors surrounding Carr exceeded James's original fears. The Earl of Carr was a pitiless puppeteer who extracted an ever growing price from victims.

Then, this spring, James had arrived in London and received a note from Fia. He'd gone to her immediately. When he heard her story he vowed to aid her in any manner he could, agreeing to her proposed plan without hesitation. If he had any regret, it was only that he could not explain his actions to Thomas Donne.

He halted the carriage before Fia's residence and climbed down. A footman opened the door and bade him enter. Kay, Fia's stepson, was in the hall. He greeted James with a look of surprise.

"Captain Barton, I'm afraid if you are looking for Lady Fia you are in for a disappointment. She's gone."

"Oh?"

"She's on a trip to the continent." The boy smiled. "Shopping."

James frowned.

"I am so sorry," Kay said politely. "I would have expected she would have told you, as one of her dearest friends, but from what her note says I gather her decision to leave was somewhat impromptu."

There was something wrong here. Why would Fia

leave the country now, especially without leaving him an explanation? "Left a note, did she?"

"Yes." Kay nodded. "Gunna delivered it to me."

"Gunna didn't go with her?"

"No." Kay smiled wryly. "And she isn't at all pleased about it. Been grumbling all day about Lady Fia's strong-willed ways. I believe"—he leaned in confidingly—"that they had something of a set-to about it."

"I see." He made his voice unconcerned, not wanting to alarm the boy.

"It isn't only you she's neglected to remember," the boy offered as a salve to what he assumed was James's wounded pride.

"Really?" James asked, slightly amused in spite of his concern. "Who else has our Lady Fia left wanting?"

The boy colored. "Oh! I daresay it's not the same thing at all. There was a gentleman here this morning; he'd made a wager with Fia and now it looks like it may be some time before he's able to collect his winnings."

"A wager?" James murmured distractedly, his thoughts racing to account for Fia's sudden absence. "Who was this gentleman?"

"A Mr. . . . Donne."

Apprehension touched James's spine.

"Do you think there's something amiss, sir?" A note of alarm had entered Kay's voice.

"Oh, no. Not at all. I know Captain Donne quite well. I was just wondering whether he'd won his bet."

The boy relaxed. "I couldn't say, sir. Gunna didn't mention him."

"I see," James said. "I'd best be getting on, then. I'm sure Lady Fia will have written me a note and I've only to return home to find it. Thank you."

He bade Kay good-bye and took his leave. At the curb, he mounted the carriage thoughtfully. He disliked Thomas and Fia disappearing on the same day. He disliked even more that Thomas had told Kay that he and Fia were engaged in a friendly contest, for though assuredly they were in contest, he doubted the term "friendly" in any way applied.

Most of all, he disliked that Thomas had taken the *Alba Star* out of dry dock before the work on her was complete, leaving James a note claiming he'd been contracted to pick up some cargo in France and paid a princely sum to do it if he left at once.

But then, Gunna, who had been Fia's dragonlike guardian for as long as James had known them, had spoken to Fia about her shopping trip. She and Fia had even had something of a quarrel about it.

The thought did not bring him much comfort. There was too much coincidental here. Though what he could do about it he was at a loss to think. He would soon have to ship out of London harbor. What with last year's disaster, their shipping company could ill afford any delays or setbacks. He was duty and honor bound to follow through on his promise to Thomas.

He would simply have to wait here in London until he shipped out, hoping Carr took the bait he and Fia had dangled before him. To leave now, following after Fia or Thomas, would destroy all their carefully laid groundwork.

No—he sighed, snapping the leads smartly and maneuvering the horse into the traffic—he could do nothing to either support or disprove his suspicions regarding Thomas and Fia.

But he might know people who could.

Chapter 12

The pungent scent of the sea swept in with the rising tide. Overhead a high wind shredded the clouds, leaving long white tatters stretched across a bleached blue sky. The midday dockyards were crowded with traders and buyers, peddlers and costermongers, sailors and stevedores loading and unloading the slighters that bobbed alongside the wharves. Farther out deep-hulled ships waited, a forest of masts in the harbor.

Thomas led Fia to the berth where the *Alba Star* was moored. She was not completely refurbished, half her sails were gone and the others ill-mended, some planking unvarnished. Still, she was seaworthy enough for this voyage.

He looked with affection at the sloop. Single-masted, sleek, and small, she'd been designed by her

Spanish builders for speed and maneuverability, to outrun the enemy's fleet. Since he'd captured her she'd served him well in outrunning privateers and pirates.

"We are going in this boat?" Fia asked as he crossed the narrow gangway and held out his hand.

"It's a ship, not a boat." She laid her hand in his and, even though her gloves encased her fingers, awareness tingled through him. This and the short hour he'd spent closeted with her in the hired carriage proved the wisdom of choosing to journey by sea rather than land.

Her fragrance had permeated the warm interior; the shadows clung with lascivious ardency to her cheeks and brow, the cut of her lip, the column of her throat. He'd forced his gaze outside, but imagination provided what he denied his senses and her image hovered in his mind's eye, taunting and enigmatic.

"I have never been aboard a ship." She said it without any discernible inflection yet Thomas sensed a tensing in her.

"It is a very safe vessel, Lady Fia—"

"You called me Fia not so many days ago and now that I am at your mercy you suddenly afford me the respect of my title? I commend you on your originality."

His mouth flattened. He'd only meant to reassure her and she'd seized the opportunity to upbraid him. But, some part of him insisted, wouldn't he have done the same thing in her position? Wait for his enemy to show weakness or inconsistency and then abuse him with it? Yes. In fact, he *had* done the same thing. To his bondmaster. He carried a few scars on his back to prove it.

She released his hand and stepped lightly down onto the deck. A deckhand, Portuguese as were most of the other members of the skeleton crew, came to take her meager luggage.

"I'll show you to your quarters," Thomas said. He led her across the deck, down a steep flight of stairs to a short corridor separating two main cabins. The crews' quarters were belowdeck. He pushed open the nearest door.

Inside the cabin was spartan, containing a single bunk attached to the bulkhead and a small table and chest of drawers secured to the flooring with bolts. A tiny window allowed in a single shaft of daylight. Her portmanteau and trunk filled the rest of the space.

"Charming," she murmured. She turned to him. "How long will I be here?"

"Three days, I should imagine. Perhaps four."

"Then I can assume we are not going to France?"

"No."

She did not react to his words but ducked her head and entered the cabin. She removed her hat and placed it carefully on the table. "Your compartment is across from this one?" Her tone invested a wealth of scorn and warning in the simple query and Thomas felt the blood rise in his face.

"Yes." Confound the girl!

"Then I suggest you go to it, unless you have some other captainly duties that require your attention. I bid you good day."

Her sangfroid was supreme. She dismissed him as easily as she would a servant. She also left him little choice but to leave her. To stay would be unconscionable.

"Do not attempt to leave the ship, Lady Fia. We will be under way within a quarter hour, and my crew is most diligent and most faithful."

"What a comfort to you," she replied without bothering to look around as she stripped off her gloves.

With a curt inclination of his head, he left.

As usual, the harbor was choked with traffic and threading the *Alba Star* through the city of tall ships, frigates, and pleasure craft took the rest of the day. By the time they'd left London behind and turned north toward the Suffolk coast, the sun hovered just above the horizon, its burning belly pricked by London's countless steeples.

Fia did not appear on deck and Thomas could only assume she was sulking. The explanation did not satisfy him. It was not what he would have expected of her, but then, what really did he know of Fia Merrick?

The notion consumed him as he worked. As a young girl Fia been untouchable in her isolation, and somehow pitiable, owning a sophistication that her tender years should never have supplied. She'd been Carr's shadow, Thomas remembered, watching the carnival at Wanton's Blush with brilliant eyes that gave away nothing of what she thought.

Yet on those occasions when he'd spoken to her

he'd been surprised by her reticence, the obvious effort it cost her to reply. It had intrigued him—in an entirely objective and dispassionate way, of course.

Then, for the next six years, though he'd heard plenty about Carr, there'd been no word of Fia. When finally he heard about her, it was through her reputation. He learned about her in seasoned roues' knowing smiles, in the betting books of "gentlemen's" clubs and, not least of all, in poor Pip Leighton's near-tragic introduction to the ways of a worldly woman. Now, for the first time, Thomas wondered why Fia had set herself on so infamous a course.

The mainsail luffed and Thomas pulled the wheel left, bringing the ship about and calling out for the crew to raise the jib. In minutes the smaller sail filled, rolling the ship to a gentle angle against the wind.

"Dinner in an hour, Captain," the thin, elderly man who acted as steward called up in Portuguese. Thomas raised his hand in acknowledgment and called his helmsman. He gave him the wheel and headed for Fia's cabin.

No sound answered his knock. He tried again. "Lady Fia?"

"Go away."

Her voice was muffled.

"Are you all right?"

"Perfectly. *Go away.*"

"I will. But if you want to eat, you'd best be in the galley in an hour."

"Go away!" Her voice rose in a thin protest. "I don't want to e—"

Begads! She was being sick. He'd heard that telltale sound too often to mistake it. He opened the door. She was sitting on the edge of the narrow bunk in her chemise and underskirt, her knees spread wide, her head hanging over the wash basin that sat on the floor between her feet.

Long, damp ropes of hair clung to her shoulders and throat. She looked up at his entrance, bringing her face directly into the shaft of the late-afternoon light. Her skin was a ghastly milky green, her dark-ringed eyes bleak with mortification.

"Go away!" she pleaded weakly.

He swung around, jerked open the door to his cabin, and ducked inside. He grabbed his water pitcher from the table, a tin cup, and a hand towel and returned to Fia's room. She hadn't moved, only hunkered down closer to the basin. He sloshed water into the cup and thrust it at her.

"Drink this."

"Oh, God."

"Drink it," he commanded. She glared up at him through the tangled ropes of hair.

"I—I can't—oh—oh—" She jerked forward and retched. A weak retch. Not much spirit to it. Not much of anything to it.

He sat down and wrapped an arm about her shoulders. Her skin was moist and clammy, the thin chemise damp with sweat. He lifted her chin up with his fingertips. Her eyes were squeezed tightly shut.

He brought the cup to her lips and tipped it slightly. Water dribbled over her lips and down her chin.

"Drink it, Fia. It will help. I promise."

She obeyed, too weak to argue, too ill to resist.

"Small sips, is all. There. Feel better?"

"No," she moaned softly. He pulled her closer, noting grimly that even though she was so ill she could barely hold her head up, she resisted. She was small in his embrace, so small it surprised him. He could trace the shallow rut between each rib, measure the deep dip at her waist and the gentle camber of her hip with a hand.

"Relax," he murmured, laying his palm against her cheek and pressing her face down against his shoulder. She didn't have the strength to fight, and grudgingly rested her head beneath his chin. The breath coming between her pale lips was shallow. Her small fist curled tightly against his breastbone.

How she hated this. He could not say how he knew but he was certain it was not humiliation at her physical state she felt, but a deeper distress. He sensed her vulnerability and her own deep contempt for it and remembered his own fury at the tears that had sprung to his eyes with the fall of the bondmaster's whip.

Hiding any sign of sympathy that would only increase her sense of defenselessness, he offered her more water. Eyes still squeezed shut as though unwilling to chance seeing his pity, she accepted.

After she'd taken a few sips he leaned sideways, carrying her with him. He dipped the towel into the pitcher and wrung it out as best he could with one hand. Gently, but with matter-of-fact sureness, he swabbed her forehead and eyes, her cheeks, lips, and throat.

"You won't die," he said after another dry wretch racked her body and subsided.

At this her eyes finally opened, sunken and clouded with misery. "That," she said, "is exactly what I am afraid of."

He grinned, surprised by her unexpected humor and surprised even more when an answering smile flickered briefly across her pale lips, a smile unlike any she'd ever given him. Their gazes met and held for a heartbeat and then she pulled back, a frown troubling her moist brow. She turned her head and shut her eyes again.

"You have the seasickness," he explained.

"Really?" she asked with devastating sarcasm, her icy composure wrenched back into place. "Thank you *so* much for informing me. And here I thought it but this morning's kipper—" Her eyes abruptly widened, her sarcasm ending in another dry retch.

He could have shaken her. He felt cheated and angered, and hated the flippancy she so readily assumed. Hated that the bit of—What to call it? Humanity? Honesty?—he had seen had been snatched away.

"Serves you right, you rancorous, viper-tongued wench," he muttered as he bent her forcibly over his forearm and rubbed her back between the delicate winglike thrust of her shoulder blades. Her head twisted and she shot him a startled glance.

"What?"

He grunted. "Has no one ever called you a rancorous, viper-tongued wench before?"

She blinked. Apparently not.

"Well, there's an oversight 'twould be hard to forgive! For had someone had the *balls* to call you out earlier on that caustic tongue, it might have been recast in a more genial mold. As it is, I fear whoever ends up wedding you, Milady Maleficence, will go to bed each night praying God he meets the next morning without having been bled dry, pricked a thousand times over by that savage tongue of yours."

The glance turned to wide-eyed wonder. "You! You! You—ohhh!" The tongue-lashing she obviously longed to deliver was subverted by another spasm, folding her in half over his forearm, shudders wracking her body. When she was done she reached for the tin cup standing on the floor and with a shaking hand raised it to her mouth. She took a short drink and straightened cautiously.

"*You* are no gentleman."

"Really?" he asked. "Thank you so much for informing—uff!" Her elbow caught him in midstomach. A look of open triumph lit her beautiful, disheveled face before another attack of nausea overset it, turning victory to misery and upending her once more over the basin. He held her forehead in his palm, bracing her.

"Thank you. Go 'way."

He hesitated a second before slipping his arm from around her and standing up. She did sound better. She'd drunk enough water to restore her body's fluids and it did neither of them any good for him to remain here when her opposition to his presence grew stronger with each second.

"You must eat. I'll have a plate sent down—"

"If you bring . . ." she paused, swallowed audibly, then went on, "*food* . . . into this room, I shall not content myself with merely pricking you with words. Do I make myself clear?"

"Abundantly. But I must insist, in all Christian conscience"—at this her mouth quirked—"that you'll feel better if you—"

"Don't say that word! *Get out!*" She picked up the wet rag from a puddle on the floor and hurled it at his head. He dodged it easily. She was indeed better. There had been real power in that throw.

He let himself out and only then discovered that he was smiling. What the hell was he grinning about? The girl had tried to do him bodily harm, shouted at him, and threatened him, and here he reacted as though he'd just received his first kiss. He was certainly mad.

But damned if later he could remember anything but the spontaneity of her smile.

And its beauty.

Chapter 13

She wasn't much of a sailor. In fact, she wasn't any kind of sailor.

This struck Fia—on the rare occasions during the next two days when she could give consideration to something other than how far away she was from the ubiquitous basin (which by the end of the voyage had supplanted castor oil in topping the hierarchy of her personal hatreds)—as being most unfair. After all, she'd spent her childhood looking out at the sea and dreaming about a tall ship that would carry her away. Tall ships and tall, strong captains . . .

That way led to disaster. Better to concentrate on making her way to the upper deck with what was left of the rest of her pride intact. She opened the doors at the top of the stairs and peered out before cautiously stepping onto the decking.

After three days of roiling seas the morning had dawned calmly. Above, the sky was thick and gray. The *Alba Star*'s sails filled with a weak wind that moved her sluggishly across the ocean's flat, mercury-colored back.

Fia tilted her face to meet the light spray flung back from the ship's cutting prow. It salted her lips and stung her eyes, but after three days huddled in her sour-smelling cabin she drank the clean air as a thirsty man drinks water. The sound of voices caused her to open her eyes. At once she spotted Thomas. One booted foot planted on the rail, his elbow on his thigh, he stood in earnest conversation with one of the crew. His eyes were narrowed, his dark brows dipped low over his bold nose.

The wind up top must have been stiffer than where Fia stood, for though Thomas had shed his coat, his shirt was plastered against his chest. It molded to the hard, flat contours of muscle and bone, billowing like the wind-filled sails above. As she watched, he nodded and straightened, stretching his great, long arms over his head and yawning hugely. He spoke and whatever he said caused the sailor to laugh. Thomas answered with a masculine, confident smile, reminding Fia powerfully that on this ship Thomas was king and the sea was his domain.

The sailor left and Thomas rubbed the back of his neck, his gaze eastward. The humor disappeared and his features donned a pensive expression. He looked tired and troubled.

Fia frowned. She did not want to see him vulnerable. She did not want to think of him as troubled or haunted. Not like herself in any way.

She glanced up again. He'd turned, facing squarely ahead, his fists planted on his hips, his legs straddling the decking in an open stance. The wind whipped his shirt across his lean flanks and teased open the laces at his throat, revealing the strong prow of his collarbone beneath tan flesh.

She shivered, pulling the light shawl she'd packed more tightly across her shoulders. She had always been attracted to Thomas Donne's strength, his strength of character as much as his physical one. When she'd met him at Wanton's Blush, she'd decided that Thomas Donne was the sort of man who would never allow himself to manipulated or blackmailed—not like the others at the castle.

It set him apart in her mind. No. It set him apart in her *heart*. His actions to her, courtly to a frustrating degree, had only cemented his place there.

How childish she'd been. Hindsight easily informed her that what she'd mistaken as his "courtly reticence" had been irony and that his chivalry had been nothing more than casual pity. Well, at least he was no longer casual about her.

She tipped her chin up to an angle that matched Thomas's. Her features smoothed to expressionless beauty, the exquisite camouflage that was so much a part of her.

She'd survived being Carr's child by facing bitter truths. She would not shy from them now. And the truth was this: In Thomas Donne's judgment she'd fulfilled the destiny he'd once foretold. She'd become nothing more or less than Carr's whore. That is why, or so he told himself, he'd taken her from London—to save James Barton from her.

Well, she wouldn't allow him the solace of being his comfortable victim. She'd allowed herself to be abducted in part because Thomas Donne needed a lesson.

She blinked fiercely, ridding her eyes of unwanted tears. She wanted Thomas to know a little of what it felt like to be stripped of one's illusions.

He'd betrayed the ideal she'd carried all these years. She'd held Thomas Donne up as an example of a man who was above animal pleasures and animal lusts, who desired only where the heart was engaged, who wanted only what he valued.

It didn't make a damn bit of difference to her that it wasn't fair to him, that he'd never asked to occupy the lofty position she'd assigned him. And it didn't matter to her that he looked tired and worn. This had nothing to do with fairness! She'd had little trade with that worthy notion and did not intend to start now. This had to do with retribution.

The Thomas she'd once created in her girlish imagination did not exist. Despite his low opinion of her, he *wanted* her. In spite of his contempt. In spite of his mistrust. In spite of all of what he presumed to know about her.

She felt it in the way his gaze fastened on her, in the hesitant compulsion that led him to touch her and, more important, made him refrain from touching her. She discerned it in the angle of his body when he drew near, in the scent of him, in the arousal he took such pains to disguise, in the space between them that nearly shimmered with awareness. Longing. And scorn.

She pulled the shawl tighter.

"Lady Fia!"

She came out of her bitter reverie with a start, distressed to find tears on her face. Quickly she dashed the backs of her hands across her cheeks and turned, startled to find herself trembling.

"Yes, Captain Donne?" Her voice rose above the snap of the sails, her vow to bring Thomas to his knees revived.

Thomas snatched his coat from the rail and descended the short flight of stairs to the deck. When he reached her side, he laid his jacket over her shoulders. Suddenly, she was drowning in the dense boiled wool, surrounded by him, her senses inundated with his scent.

"You are well? No more sickness?" he asked.

"Much improved." Blast the man for reminding her of the last few days. It put her at a distinct disadvantage—particularly for a woman bent on seduction. It is hard to be seductive when one's mind is filled with images of oneself bent over a slop bucket.

"You do not look well," he muttered.

She laughed. "La! Captain! I am at a loss as to how I shall respond to such gallantry. Tell me, just how bad do I look?"

Ah! That ought to fluster the great dark-skinned brute. His brows lowered forbiddingly. "Your illness has pared the flesh from you and bruised the skin beneath your eyes, but for all that you are as ravishing as ever and well you know it," he said grudgingly. "I can scarcely credit it, but were you on your deathbed from some wasting illness, I swear you would still be beautiful."

It was she who was flustered; she sought some tantalizing reply but could only find a shrewish one. "Do you intend to find more rough seas in order to make me sick again?"

He looked at her in surprise. "Why would I do that?"

"To satisfy your curiosity in regard to exactly at what point I might lose my looks."

His gaze grew sour. "I would not play so cruel a game."

"Wouldn't you? But here you've stolen me from what home I have, taken me from my friends and family, and are carrying me off to a location that you will not reveal." She smiled sweetly. "Can you blame me for mistaking you for a cruel man?"

"I have my reasons," he said.

"And what might those be?" She swept her arm out, gesturing over the sea. "We are, I should think, sufficiently well away from London for you to entrust me with the motive for your extraordinary action— extraordinary only inasmuch as you say it has nothing of a liaison to it."

"It hasn't."

"Well then?" She arched one brow in regal inquiry.

"I have brought you here not to seduce you, but to keep you from compromising my friend James Barton."

She tossed back her head and laughed.

"Oh!" She sniffed, dabbing at imaginary tears of delight. "Oh! How splendid. Let me see if I have this correct. Essentially, you've absconded with me so that your friend doesn't, is that right?"

His eyelids narrowed. "Essentially."

"You'll forgive me if I don't believe you?" she asked, still smiling merrily.

"It's the truth. You can do with it what you like. I don't care."

"But I care," she murmured, stepping nearer until his broad chest shielded her from the wind, while the warmth still contained in his coat cradled her. "Because I think you're a liar, Captain."

His head jerked back. If her gender had been different he would have struck her for saying that.

She went on, "I know you've told yourself that you're saving James from a terrible mistake. But in truth, a truth I'll have you admit ere I'm done, you took me because you want me. Not as a hostage. Not as a prisoner. But as your lover."

"You're wrong." He made the words a vow.

She laughed again. "You leave me no choice but to demonstrate."

His face reflected his distaste. "I'd have thought you too old for these childish games, Fia."

She flushed at the rebuke, put off by his attitude of frank disappointment. Men were rarely disappointed in her—sometimes they were disappointed in her decisions, especially those that did not acquiesce to their plans, but not her. She retreated behind her poise, pressing her hand over his left breast.

"I've warned you," she whispered. "I intend to break your heart."

"You'd have to own it first."

He did not look at her.

"I'll own your soul as well," she whispered.

At that he grinned suddenly, discomposing her once more. "Such dramatics, Fia," he said, finally looking down at her. "The London theater doesn't know what it's missing."

She blinked, struggled for some wordplay to return her the advantage. "I prefer," she purred, "an audience of one."

He snorted, encircled her wrist, and removed her hand from his person. "If you plan to seduce me, you'll have to offer less hackneyed fare than that, m'dear," he said. "I fear you've become accustomed to relying too much on your beauty to do your wooing. I am but a nearsighted fellow and rely on what I hear as much as what I see.

"If I might be so bold, may I suggest you author a few new lines to pique my interest—that is if you really feel inclined to make a go at securing my unworthy affections—lest I grow bored before the courtship e'er begins?"

"Oh!" Only years of practicing self-restraint spared her the ignominy of stomping her foot.

"Now, Fia," he said, though the smile did not fit quite as easily as it had before. "Don't let your good

mood grow foul over such a trifle. We're near to landing. Look."

Before she could react, he'd placed his hands on her
shoulders and spun her about. He pulled her against
him so that her back pressed against his chest, his big
palms cradling her shoulders and holding her still. His
heart beat steadily between her shoulder blades. His
hands were warm and strong, his body a ballast behind
her.

A sudden pitch of the sea knocked her off balance,
driving her buttocks against the lee of his hips. His
breath hissed on a sharp draw. His right arm swooped
down across her breasts, bracing her against him.
Sinew rippled beneath the sun-dark skin, pressed
deep against the soft, pale flesh swelling above her
décolletage.

For a long moment he held her thus. And though
she knew such intimacy would advance her objective,
she could not take advantage of their position. She
could not think of some witty, provocative comment;
she could not *think* at all. Every inch of her flesh urged
her to burrow closer. And then the ship regained its
even keel and Thomas shifted her away from him, re-
moving his arm and freeing her. He stepped back and
pointed.

"There." His voice sounded labored, breathless. Or
was it only the blood rushing in her ears that made it
seem so? She had to say something.

"What is it?" she asked stupidly.

"Land. Scotland."

Her gaze sharpened and she scoured the horizon. "Where?"

"There. That strip of darkness."

She swung around, staring up at him. His gaze did not waver from the horizon. "Where have you brought me?"

"Home," he said softly.

Chapter 14

Through the small window in her cabin Fia saw a light at the top of the headland pierce the fog. A short while later one of the sailors came to her cabin and made impatient gestures for her to follow him.

She wasn't sure why she should consider refusing but when Thomas had told her that the little slab on the horizon was Scotland, unnamed emotions had coursed through her like a riptide. Wherever she'd expected Thomas to take her, it hadn't been Scotland.

She watched as the sailor unceremoniously tumbled her belongings into the open mouth of her portmanteau. With a grunt he lifted the trunk, grabbed the portmanteau, and jerked his head in the direction of the door.

Forcing down her rising unease, she swept out of

the room and up to the open deck. Thomas was no-where in sight. Reluctantly her eyes moved toward the shore. They were close now. Through the dense fog, she could just make out the land's sheer walls and at its base a jumble of rocks that rose like jagged teeth from an animal's foaming maw.

It could only be McClairen's Isle. She waited for the expected anguish so that she could deal with it. None came. Instead she found herself studying the great island fortress with undeniable anticipation.

Home, Thomas had said. She'd not forgotten that Thomas owned a house fifteen miles inland from McClairen's Isle, and assumed when he'd said "home" that is what he'd meant. But he'd brought her to her home as well, and she recognized that with a warm sense of familiarity.

She knew each copse of trees on that island, each patch of bracken, where the harebells hid in the rocks come spring, and where on the side of the island it would turn crimson come fall. She knew the castle, too: where the priest's hole had been carved in the garden wall, which rooms' ceilings sparkled with light reflected from the ocean below, and how hard the wind needed to blow before the battlements sang as though manned by a hundred fife players.

Her eager gaze clouded. There were no battlements now, nor rooms with sparkling ceilings. Wanton's Blush had burned down six years ago. She'd left just before the blaze had started.

Carr had been there, though. He'd struggled from

the inferno with his precious papers intact; the price paid in broken bones and lacerations small compared to what the loss of his blackmail material would have meant.

"Go. Faster." The sailor snapped at her. Fia moved in the direction he indicated. At the side of the ship the sailor hoisted the trunk from his shoulder, called out loudly, and heaved it over the side. Fia rushed forward, certain he'd flung her belongings into the ocean. Angry cries erupted from below. The sailor laughed uproariously and slapped his thigh.

Fia looked over the gunnel. A small wooden boat bobbed a dozen feet below, its four crewman shaking their fists upward. One man, sitting beside her upturned trunk, rubbed his leg, grimacing in pain. Beside her, the Portuguese sailor hooted with malicious delight.

"What goes on here?" The laughter abruptly died, as did the shouts and curses from below. Thomas strode along the deck, a satchel tossed over one broad shoulder, his hair rippling in the breeze.

The Portuguese deckhand answered in rapid-fire fashion. The injured sailor below bellowed up what could only be a refutation. Without warning, Thomas dropped the satchel and snatched a handful of the Portuguese's grimy shirt.

Instinctively, Fia retreated. The sailor clawed uselessly at Thomas's wrist. Thomas shook him like a mastiff with a hare, speaking in a low, lethal voice. Whatever he said had a profound effect on the Portuguese. The man blanched and gulped, nodding frantically.

With a curse Thomas dropped him. The sailor fell on his bum and scuttled backward until he came up hard against the mast. He clambered upright, ducked under the boom, and hurried away.

Thomas bent over to retrieve his satchel, and in doing so spied her. He straightened slowly, his jaw taut, his eyes still dark and angry. She took another step back.

He frightened her.

In all the years of their association, in all the strained and unfortunate circumstances in which they'd met, not once had he ever truly frightened her. Not even when he'd stormed into her boudoir with Lord Tunbridge's bloodied épée, cursing her. But now he did.

With stunning force she realized how absolutely she was under his control, followed hard by another realization: She knew next to nothing about Thomas Donne.

He was some sort of Scots-French hybrid with a minor French title who'd come to Wanton's Blush as a gambler who didn't game much. His sister, Favor, had arrived at Wanton's Blush and captured the fancy of not only Fia's father, but Fia's younger brother, Raine, who'd escaped from a French prison and returned to the island unbeknownst to anybody but Gunna and Fia herself.

Raine and Favor had disappeared from Wanton's Blush the night it had burned down. They had married soon after. Favor had never mentioned Thomas in her letters, and neither had Raine or Ashton.

For the first time, she wondered at the wisdom of her game. She'd allowed herself to be kidnapped because she had assumed she knew what Thomas was capable of and had taken for granted that she would be capable of more. Judging from her lineage and her history, Fia had always supposed herself to be the most ruthless person in any given situation. Certainly the most dangerous.

It had been a source of, if not exactly comfort for her, at least liberation. If she was indeed the most ruthless type society had to offer, at least she knew the limits of what she was likely to encounter. But looking at Thomas's dark, hard face she found she could not gauge the depth of his anger, or say with any certainty what he would do. He'd looked near enough to killing that sailor—all because the poor sot had dropped her trunk overboard.

As if against his will, Thomas spoke. "I am the master of this ship. I am the absolute law here. And there." He jerked his chin in the direction of the land. "I make the rules and I enforce them. However I see fit."

Her mouth was dry.

"Goddamn it! Don't look at me like that. Just do as I say and you'll . . ."

"Not end up with my neck broken?" she suggested, the bravado she'd hoped for not quite reaching her voice.

His eyes went from burning hot to glacial cold in the space of a second. "Aye. I just might spare you. *Might.* Now, come here. I'll lower you into the boat."

She forced herself to move to his side. He dipped, snaring her behind the knees and shoulder, and lifted her easily into his arms.

Holding her high against his chest, he strode with her to the side of the ship and barked an order for a sailor to make a harness from a thick rope secured to one of the riggings.

She could not pull her gaze away from his profile while they waited. His eyes were not gray as she'd thought, but palest blue, flecked with green-gray shards as dark as the island's shale.

His arms tightened around her. "Hurry!" he shouted.

One of his men held out the rope sling he'd completed and Thomas set her in it. "Hold on to the rope," he told her. "I'll be below."

He released her and she swung out over the side of the ship. She gasped. The water looked far more than a dozen feet below, its dark, unreflective surface grim and expectant. Ever since she was a little girl and her mother had plummeted to her death, she had been unable to stand on a ledge and look down. Especially on water.

She clutched the rope in a white-knuckled grip. Her pulse raced, her head buzzed. "I cannot swim," she heard herself say.

"You will not have to," Thomas promised. He climbed over the gunnel, and hand over hand lowered himself by a rope into the boat below, barking out an order in Portuguese.

A second later the rope holding her jerked. She plummeted a few feet and snapped to a halt, bouncing. She slammed shut her eyes, spinning wildly in the harness. At once her seasickness returned, this time coupled with fear. She would have sobbed but her throat was too dry to make any sound.

She heard Thomas bark another order. She pressed her forehead against the rope, trying desperately to concentrate on breathing, on not letting go. She had an impression of more movement and then, suddenly, miraculously, she was in his arms again, her cheek pressed to his chest, his heartbeat as steady as her perch had been unstable.

He sat down, keeping his arms around her and settling her in his lap. She still could not open her eyes. Fear gibbered within, taunting her with her inability to control her unreasonable dread of heights.

She felt his hand move tentatively, brushing the hair back from her face. He spoke and the boat jumped forward as the men heaved at the oars while Thomas's fingers combed through her hair.

Long moments passed and he did not say a word and neither did she, the silence broken only by the slap of the oars against flat water. "You're afraid of the sea."

She considered allowing him to be mistaken, but what good would that do? Perhaps if she told him the source of her fear he might . . . What was she thinking? Fear had addled her brain. She told him anyway.

"Not the water. Being above the water," she said

faintly, reluctant to pull herself from his embrace. Why, she asked herself gruffly, should she not take comfort where she could? It was scarce enough she found it at all. So she stayed, feeling like a thief, waiting for him to eject her.

He did not. " 'Tis heights that frighten you?"

She nodded. He did not mock her. Or laugh. He said nothing. His arms continued sheltering her without any perceptible change. His heart continued beating in its steady, unbroken rhythm. His warmth seeped through the thin batiste of her gown and slowly, like a wax taper held close to a brazier, her muscles relaxed, her limbs loosened, and she felt her body grow soft and pliant against his.

So lost was she in the inexplicable pleasure of her rare quiescence that it took her long minutes to realize that the tempo of his heartbeat had quickened and that the broad planes of his chest rose and fell deeply in counterpoint. She knew the reason. If only unconsciously, his hard male body reacted to the softening of her own.

She should take advantage of it. But the anger that had made her vow to bring him to his knees was nowhere in evidence and the seagulls were calling a homecoming greeting and the silky whisper of the water across on the prow charmed the energy from her. And she felt safe. Truly safe.

For the first time in her adult life, Fia fell asleep in a man's arms.

*   *   *

He ached with wanting her.

She curled in his lap like an exhausted kitten. Her hair streamed over her shoulders and across her face. Her lips had parted and her breath stirred a few witchy tendrils with each exhalation. The long black lashes that made wicked her blue eyes now lay harmlessly on the upper curve of her pale cheek, a few tiny diadems of mist caught at their very tips.

One of her hands curled slightly beneath her chin, the other she'd tucked around his torso when a deep swell had wobbled the boat. Even through the linen fabric, he could feel each finger's imprint like a brand on his ribs, just as he could feel the svelte length of her thighs draped across his lap and the soft swell of her buttocks.

He lifted his gaze away from her, peering desperately through the thick blanket of fog for their mooring place. It had to be close. Pray God, it was close. He did not think he could take much more of Fia, so seemingly lost and exhausted and in need of protection, molded to him like this.

"Land ahead, Captain," Javiero called out.

Fia stirred and he silently cursed his crewman for waking her, fully cognizant that seconds before he'd been praying for deliverance from the sweet torment of holding her. But he did not want to relinquish her, either to wakefulness or to the land.

Her eyes opened, glittering with awareness. Of course, Fia Merrick would never wake slowly, yielding to conscious thought by degrees. She would come instantly alert from sleep's deepest abyss. Because—his brow furrowed with inspiration as he studied the brilliant blue eyes gazing with such penetrating solemnity into his own—to do less could be dangerous.

Chapter 15

$\mathcal{F}$ia awakened to find Thomas studying her. She struggled upright and he immediately shifted her onto the hard bench beside him. One of the sailors said something and Thomas replied by swinging his legs over the side of the boat and dropping down into chest-deep water.

"*¿Es mucho frío, sí?*" one of the Spanish sailors asked.

"Not nearly cold enough," Thomas replied in Spanish. The crewman laughed, casting her surreptitious glances.

"What did you say?" Fia demanded.

"I said the water was very cold."

He was lying. She could tell by the aggressive way he met her gaze. However, there was nothing she could do to force him to tell her the truth, and from the way the men were smiling at her, she did not know if she wanted to hear it. She was well used to the vulgar banter that followed her, and while she accepted that in London such banter was only what she could expect, given her provocative behavior, here she'd done nothing to deserve it.

Another sailor joined Thomas in the water. Together they grabbed hold of long ropes attached to either side of the boat and began swimming toward shore. When they were halfway to the beach they stood up, planted their feet, and hauled the boat toward the shore as those men remaining in the boat strained at the oars, rowing against the surf. Once past the breakline, the rest of the men jumped out and pulled the heavy boat up on the beach.

"Hail to ye!" a booming Scottish voice called out as a giant of a man strode from between a pair of boulders. He led a shaggy horse drawing an ancient cart. An outlawed tartan was belted about his thick waist and draped over a loose, rough-looking shirt of dubious color.

Fia looked about. They were on a thin crescent of sand at the base of sheer cliffs. The giant boulders strewn at the water's edge had kept the beach from being visible from the sea. A perfect smuggler's landing, and the man leading the horse fit the role perfectly. He also looked vaguely familiar.

"Jamie!" Thomas shouted, pleasure in his voice and the wide grin that carved deep dimples beneath his cheekbones.

The giant approached and dropped to one knee

before Thomas. A scraggly tail of reddish hair flecked with gray fell across his sunburned neck. He grabbed hold of one of Thomas's hands and brought it to his forehead. Even from a distance of some ten paces she could smell him. Her nose wrinkled.

"M'lord," he murmured, "ye've been gone too long. Welcome home to ye."

Thomas laughed, the sound rich and infectious. "Ach! If my absence teaches a heathen brute like you humility, I'll be chartin' a course round the Cape to finish yer domestication."

Fia watched Thomas in surprise. The burr was strong and musical and easy on his tongue. She'd known Thomas was part Scot but had never heard him speak with the Highland accent. It sounded natural, as natural as the smile still gracing his face.

"Yer the sorriest excuse fer a lord I've ever known, ye young rakehell," Jamie said, "but if ye've no regard fer yer proper station, I have. Ye'll not stop me from payin' me respects to me la—"

Whatever he'd been about to say was cut off as Thomas placed his boot on the huge man's shoulder and pushed him back. With an "uff" of surprise Jamie landed on his bum and then with a roar surged upright, overshadowing even Thomas's tall figure. "Tommy, yer not so big tha' I can't be teachin' ye to respect yer elders!"

A great grin cleaved Thomas's face. "Try me, ye great unwashed goat."

The sailors, alert to the promise of a fight, gathered in a loose circle. The anger in the giant's ruddy face abruptly vanished, leaving a delighted anticipation matched only by Thomas's own. Thoughtfully he rubbed his chin.

"Two falls out of three? Both shoulders to the ground?"

Fia stared at this Jamie's huge, beefy hands and thick, meaty calves. He'd kill Thomas.

"Sounds fine to me."

"Well, it doesn't sound fine to me." Dear Lord, had that been her speaking?

Both men turned to her wearing identical expressions of amazement, as though the boat had expressed an opinion.

"Who's the lassie?" Jamie's eyes grew round. "Mother of Mercy, dinna say ye've taken a bride! Lord love ye, son, we've waited fer this day—"

"No," Thomas snapped. "She's not my bride. She's—"

"His prisoner," Fia supplied matter-of-factly. She ran through her mind how she could use this situation to her advantage—and Thomas's disadvantage. Apparently this mountain of unclean manhood held Thomas in some regard.

The mountain narrowed his eyes on her for a long moment before turning to Thomas. "Just tell me this," he said stonily, "be she an Englishwoman?"

Thomas nodded, his face expressionless. "Aye."

Jamie let out a huge sigh of relief. "Ach. Snatched yerself a haughty bitch from the English dogs' own kennel, did ye? Good fer ye, Tommy. Have ye raped her yet?"

"No!"

Fia barely heard Thomas's roared denial, she was too busy staring at Jamie.

"Mayhap just as well," he said. "She looks the high-flown sort of fancy that carries the pox, if ye ask me."

"I never!" Fia exclaimed indignantly.

"Be quiet, Jamie!" Thomas thundered, coming to the side of the boat. "This is . . . Lady MacFarlane."

"MacFarlane? Tha's no English name. . . ."

Fia lifted her chin. "Before my marriage I was—"

"No one cares who you were before yer marriage," Thomas interrupted, his eyes dark with warning.

"I do," Jamie disagreed. "If she's a Scottish husband lookin' fer her, I'd best be warned."

"There'll be no one looking for her," Thomas said.

He hadn't meant to do it, but his words pierced like a little needle.

"Her husband's dead. A lowland Scot." He turned to Fia and plucked her from where she stood on the plank seating.

"We'll be staying at the house." The accent he put on the word "house" struck her as odd, so odd the protest she'd been about to make died on her lips. He bounced her once, redistributing her weight. She flung her arms about his neck, sure he would drop her.

"The house," Jamie repeated, his gaze traveling back and forth between Thomas and her.

"Aye. And see if Mrs. MacNab can help her doin' whatever it is she needs done."

"I don't need your aid or that of one of your servants."

Thomas snorted. "Oh, aye. You're a font of self-reliance, you are. And 'twas only to keep me near that you heaved up yer dinner each day."

"I didn't!" she clipped out as the blood boiled to her skin's surface and Jamie burst out laughing. She struggled to gain the upper hand in the only way she knew. "But"—her voice slid an octave lower, became a throaty purr—"mayhap I *did* want you near me." She walked her fingers up his chest before delivering the coup de grâce. "Fat lot of good it did me."

Jamie hooted with laughter and an unwilling twitch tugged at the corner of Thomas's mouth.

"She's a brave mouth on her, yer English lady," Jamie said.

Not all English, Fia thought. Part Scot, born and bred here. The part that wanted to refute Jamie's assertion, though why this should be was a mystery. She'd never aligned herself either in thought or deed or word with any people. She'd always been Carr's daughter. But here, now . . . Her eyes traveled along the black face of the cliffs, toward where she imagined Wanton's Blush would be. She wanted to see where it had stood.

"Aye. Brave but never before foolish. If she's wise she'll use caution when wielding that tongue of hers, lest she cuts herself with her own clever wordplay," Thomas said.

She knew what he meant. It seemed that here, too, what she was and who she was could be summed up in the words "Carr's daughter," for clearly Thomas was warning her not to reveal her relationship with the hated "Demon Earl."

And hated with good cause in these Scottish hinterlands. Any Scot within twenty miles of McClairen's Isle had had something taken, stolen, or extorted from him by her father. Many had paid for their defiance of him with their lives.

"I'm not stupid," she assured him under her breath.

"Good." He raised his voice. "Jamie, throw that trunk and bag into the back of the cart. I'll drive our guest to the manor."

"The manor?" Jamie's bushy brows rose. "But you've yet to see—"

"It will wait," Thomas said.

The giant did not argue. Something within recognized the authority in the younger man and answered with unquestioning obedience. Jamie gathered the luggage the sailors had dumped and tossed it into the back of the cart while Thomas held her, seemingly oblivious to that fact.

It pricked her pride. Men who held Fia Merrick in their arms were *never* oblivious to it.

"I can stand."

"The sand is soft and your shoes are thin, added to which you're about as weak as a kitten."

"I assure you"—she looked up at him through the thicket of her lashes—"I have enough strength for whatever you . . . require."

"Quit it," he said in the tone of one chastising an inappropriately precocious child.

She blinked.

He plopped her unceremoniously down on the narrow seat before squishing in next to her. "Jamie?"

The redheaded behemoth shook his head. "Nay. I've work to do here. I'll see ye here on the morrow." With that, he slapped the pony on the rump and stood back, his hand raised in farewell, a quizzical look on his blocky face.

Thomas guided the sturdy animal up a twining trail to the top of the headland and immediately turned from the sea, riding inland. Fia craned her head around but try as she might she was unable to see beyond the thick mantle of fog that closed in behind them. If McClairen's Isle was out there, it was hidden from Fia's sight. Soon only the scent of brine and the sound of the surf gave evidence of the sea's nearness, and with each passing moment both grew fainter.

Inland the heavy mantle of fog had lifted, though the sky still hunkered above. Fia breathed deeply of the clean, moisture-laden air. She turned her head often, the sights and sounds both familiar and surprising, like a child's favored music box lost and then found long after the child had grown.

Sweet, painful, each turn in the road brought with it the possibility of recognition. Near here she'd chanced upon her brother Raine and his lovely Favor, who'd escaped the company of a long-ago picnic. Favor had been mortified and red-cheeked, Raine angry and protective.

In that little copse of trees ten years ago she'd found a wee rabbit caught in a poacher's snare. She'd known that in releasing the creature some Scottish family might well have gone hungry that night, but it was so tiny a thing and its cries so pitiful. Gunna had helped her nurse it back to health. She released it . . . over there!

Too soon the memories vanished as the road they took moved beyond where she'd dared wander as a child. They entered territory dangerous for anyone related to Carr, especially his "favored daughter."

But unfamiliarity had its own charms, and Fia studied the changing landscape with interest, so taken with the unfolding vista that she decided to postpone the next step in her seduction of Thomas Donne. Besides, she was for once uncertain exactly what her next step would be. Touching him certainly hadn't brought him to his knees.

They traveled in silence for an hour before Thomas finally spoke. The sun had given up trying to penetrate the dark clouds overhead and quit the sky, and dusk began to wrap its dark mantle across the landscape.

"The name 'Merrick' is anathema on this coast," Thomas said in cautionary tones.

"You don't say."

"And there are those at the manor who'll remember the Earl of Carr's daughter's name, so don't even whisper 'Fia.' "

"I don't generally refer to myself in the third person," she said politely, winning a chagrined glance from him.

"Of course not. Foolish of me."

She seized the minor opening. "Not so foolish as deluding yourself."

He frowned and snapped the lead reins. "How so?"

"This noble rescue of your friend Barton—your reasons for it are self-deluding."

"You are entitled to that opinion," he said stiffly.

"Besides"—she allowed the sway of the cart to bounce her lightly against his hip and thigh—"did you ever consider that James might not *want* to be rescued?"

"I'm sure he doesn't," he admitted ruefully.

Her pulse quickened with this small success. "But that doesn't matter."

"No."

She laid her hand lightly on his thigh. The muscle beneath her palm jumped into iron hardness. "I think you do James a grave injustice. He is quite able to withstand temptation." She waited a minute, but he only stared straight ahead at the rutted road. "Are you?"

His gaze slew slowly sideways, his mouth curved. "Lady Fia, would you kindly *stop*? It's growing a bit embarrassing. For both of us, I should think."

She snatched her hand away as though burned and stared at him with round eyes.

His gaze returned to the road before he continued, "I appreciate that you consider my poor self a challenge to your womanly wiles. And that you are bent on teaching me a lesson in order to extract some sort of recompense for the indignity you consider yourself to have suffered at my hands. I even acknowledge that were I in your position I would likely do the same, but not by the same means. Simply put, m'dear, you are simply going to have to find another means to punish me."

She blinked, completely nonplussed.

"One of the hallmarks of maturity," he lectured comfortably, "is the ability to accept certain immutable facts and adjust one's expectations and goals accordingly. No matter how beautiful you are, how lovely your face or desirable your body, I will not be seduced by you."

"I wouldn't bet on that," she burst out.

He went on as though he hadn't heard her. "However, you *might* consider a knife in the rib cage. Though"—he inclined his head modestly—"I doubt you'll have any more success there. Besides, were I to die there'd be nothing standing between you and the local lads and they do so hate the English. No, best not kill me."

"I wouldn't dirty my hands."

"No? Since when have the Merricks been so fastidious?"

There it was again. The intimation that Thomas had knowledge of some terrible wrong committed by Carr. Well, *of course* Carr had committed terrible wrongs. Many, in fact. But Fia had the distinct impression Thomas spoke of a personal experience. Which was odd. She could not remember the name "Donne" amongst the secret hoard of blackmail papers she'd gone through in her father's library at Wanton's Blush. Still, she'd only had her hands on that packet of papers once, and she'd been looking for other information then.

"I suggest you ponder the question a while. Besides, 'twill give you something to do whilst I'm away."

"Away?" Such a scenario had never suggested itself to her, and she scowled heavily. "You're going to just leave me at this house of yours?"

"Only during the day. Come night I'll return. There's a project I've begun on my land. I'd like to complete as much of it as possible before I . . . before we return to London."

"And when will that be?"

"A few weeks," Thomas replied, making silent notes that he should return to the house only in the dead of night, when Fia would be tight in Morpheus's embrace. Better Morpheus's than his. Aye, let the poor god of dreams be the one to try to resist Fia when she was determined to be irresistible.

Thomas kept his eyes firmly ahead. That and distracting Fia by pretending disgust with her proposed seduction had been all that he'd had to counter his potent attraction to her. And pitiful weapons they were, too.

It wouldn't take her one full day to discover that all she'd need to do is persevere a bit and his defenses would collapse like the house of cards he knew them to be. For all his brave words and disregard for her charms, the last hours had played pure hell with his body and his mind.

The solution was simply *not* to spend a full day in her company.

Or he could just give in—and would that be so terrible? If she wished to invoke a penalty for his crime and it was one he was not only willing but near panting to pay, why not? He ground down on his teeth. Because what if once was not enough? Already she seemed to him like some exotic opiate, deadly, fascinating, addictive.

And she was Carr's daughter.

The realization ambushed him. He'd forgotten for a short time. How could that be?

"Whose house is that?" she asked, breaking his reverie.

They'd climbed a steep grade through a stand of pines and as they emerged Fia caught sight of a square manor house. The hard lines of its gray stone were softened by a tangle of creeping ivy overlaying narrow, mullioned windows. Lights glowed from the bottom level. As they approached, the front door swung open and a figure stood poised in the rectangle of yellow light.

"Who be there?" a young man demanded loudly.

" 'Tis I, Thomas!"

"Thomas who?" the young man answered, bringing a long, narrow shape to his shoulder and pointing it in their direction. The fool was pointing a rifle at them. Damn the boy!

Thomas glanced at Fia. He hadn't wanted to tell

her. Not yet. Mayhap not at all. But what did it matter? Her father would be reporting his identity to the authorities as soon as he realized that Thomas hadn't upheld his end of their "bargain." He stood up in the cart.

" 'Tis Thomas McClairen. Yer laird."

Chapter 16

Who did you say?" Fia asked.

Thomas snapped the reins, setting the tired horse trotting into the house's side yard.

"Thomas McClairen," he answered without looking at her.

"Colin McClairen's son?" she asked, stunned. Colin McClairen had been gone during the uprising of '45, having left his sons, John and Thomas, under the care of his older brother, Ian, the laird of the McClairen. He'd returned from afar to find Ian dead, killed at Culloden, his wife dead in childbirth, himself the new clan chief, and his sons hanged for treason.

Or so Fia had always been told. But now . . . She studied his averted profile, saw in the proud bearing and bold features the unbowed spirit of the Highlander.

She'd known him so long and never guessed. Yet it all made sense now. He'd come to McClairen's Isle incognito, seeking revenge, and revenge he'd nearly had upon her brother Ashton, if not Carr.

Fear began unrolling within her. Was she to be the next move in some decades-long chess match between him and her father?

"They didn't hang you," she whispered.

A smile like a lightning strike slashed across his face, brief and devastating. "No. My youth spared me my older brother's fate. Not that I'm surprised you didn't know. Why would you trouble to ask what happened to those whose lands and homes your father stole?"

"I thought they were all dead. All the McClairens," she said. Carr had claimed with awful relish that he'd eradicated every last McClairen from Scotland. But he'd overlooked at least one. . . . "But, if *you* are Thomas McClairen, that means that Favor is . . ."

"A McClairen, too. Aye."

"Raine knows."

"I suppose. I don't really know."

Had Raine had been spared a part in Thomas McClairen's revenge? Because he'd married Thomas's only living relative, his young sister?

Thomas jumped to the ground and went to the horse's head as Gordie came trotting down the steps. "Well, at least now you don't have to waste any more thought on how to avenge your abduction. Aye, there's a worthy revenge for a Merrick, m'love. As soon as you return to London you can inform the authorities that Thomas McClairen is back on English soil."

She bent a startled glance at him. *He* was wondering what revenge *she* was concocting? The fear that had been building began to fade. "You could always kill me," she said testingly.

His face folded into disgusted lines. "I'm not Carr."

No. He wasn't. The rest of her fear evaporated.

He *tch*'ed lightly, the bitterness of his expression startling her. "But if you want your revenge, lass, you'd best hurry before your father preempts you."

"Carr knows who you are, too?" Impossible. Carr would have had Thomas arrested years ago. There would have been no reason for Carr to spare Thomas, the virile scion of the once-proud clan Carr had set himself to destroy.

"Aye. He's held the knowledge for years, but he won't be holding it much longer."

"Why?"

"Does it matter?" Thomas asked flatly.

Yes. If Thomas hadn't brought her here as part of some scheme to hurt Carr and if Thomas was, indeed, only keeping her here until he felt James was safe from her influence, if Thomas had really meant his vow not to harm her, it could matter a great deal. To her.

But she'd no sooner recognized that essential truth than she also recognized how foolhardy it would be to reveal it to Thomas. One never placed one's . . . sentiments at another's disposal.

When she didn't reply, Thomas tied up the horse and went round to the back of the cart. There he removed her trunk and portmanteau, tossing first one then the other at the young man staring with gape-mouthed reverence at his laird.

The youngster stood a head shorter than Thomas. His sandy hair was matted and scraggly, his breeches stained, and his shirt torn at the cuff, but his face was clean enough. At least Fia could see a smattering of freckles covering his snub nose.

"Take these upstairs, Gordie. Lady MacFarlane will be staying in the corner bedroom."

"Aye, aye, m'lord. So Tim Gowan said when he come with Jamie's message." Gordie bobbed his head and with a grunt heaved the trunk to his narrow shoulders. He turned his head toward her—his laird's as yet unexamined guest—and his eyes widened. His smile grew into a grin. There was no mistaking the admiration in it. Perhaps Gordie wasn't as young as she'd first thought.

"Be sure ye don't slip in that puddle of drool as ye go, Gordie," Thomas said flatly. The boy's cheeks flamed in response and he shuffled away with his burden.

"Leave the boy alone, Fia."

"I have no intention of—"

"Spare me the denials. I'm warning you, Fia. The boy is just that, a boy."

"Hardly. He's probably near my own age," she answered.

Thomas snorted. "Years have little to do with age when one is speaking of you, Lady MacFarlane."

He was right, but hearing him put into words what she'd often thought herself was unexpectedly painful.

"I didn't mean to hurt you."

She looked up. He'd drawn near. His face was skewed in grave, troubled lines.

"Forgive me. That was inexcusable."

"But true?" She tried on a smile, felt it quaver, and let it dissolve.

He met her gaze squarely. "Yes." He sounded regretful, and that hurt even more.

"No matter," she said pertly, but when her flippancy did nothing to shake the pity from his expression, her puzzlement overcame her hurt. "You're a strange one, Thomas. You steal me away and then apologize to me—not for the abduction but because my past precluded a childhood."

"Someone should damn well apologize for it," he said fiercely.

Her breath caught. His gaze met hers and she had the distinct sense that he'd meant what he'd said, even though he regretted saying it. She wet her lips with the tip of her tongue, feeling awkward and uncertain, when both sensations were so foreign to her. He bewildered her. One minute the vitriol in his words was so sharp she could taste it, the next he championed her.

While she was pondering this and trying unsuccessfully to account for it, he came to the side of the cart and lifted her unceremoniously from the seat. For a brief moment longer than necessary he held her before depositing her on the ground.

"Come along," he said. Without waiting he strode around the corner of the house and up the front of steps, Fia trailing behind.

Inside the house kept the promise made by its austere exterior. Not that it wasn't well maintained. It was. It just wasn't very clean. Dust coated the few pieces of furniture in the entry hall and the flagstones were in dire need of sweeping. A cobweb occupied the space between the newel post and the first baluster mounting the stairway, its fat matriarch placidly spinning new spokes for her home.

"Here we are. It's . . ." Thomas took a look at her face, and frowned.

"It's dirty," Fia said. "You've brought me to a dirty house in the middle of nowhere."

It was decidedly not the right tack to take. Thomas immediately became defensive. "Well, I'm sorry if it's not some scented bower replete with a bed of rose petals and servants in silk turbans to fan you with ostrich plumes, or whatever they do at the sort of place the poor sots you bewitch take you."

A witch, was she? His imagination far outstripped any reality she'd ever known. Her reputed "lovers" were entirely a matter of other men's supposition—which, in all fairness, she'd encouraged. She supposed she should be accustomed to such . . . such *blather*. But in truth, she'd not expected it from this particular source.

But more, she didn't know what *to* expect from him. The uncertainty that had been born on discovering he was Thomas *McClairen* only exacerbated the situation. Was he an enemy? If so, her enemy or her father's? Was he protector of his friend? Avenger of his family? She did not know, and thus did not know how to react, and so reacted without thought, something she almost never did.

She hitched her chin higher, looked at him haughtily down her short, straight nose, and drawled, "I'm allergic to feathers. I prefer palm fronds. But rose petals are very nice."

It was, she knew, rather like poking a stick at a panther, and sure enough, flags of ruddy bronze scored his high cheekbones.

"There'll be no petals here, Lady MacFarlane, and as for the place being dirty—"

"Filthy," she sniffed, knowing the appellation to be unfair.

"*Filthy.* 'Twill give you something to do during the day."

Her hauteur vanished. "You can't possibly be serious," she breathed.

"Entirely," he replied with a return of his former insouciance. "I employ no permanent staff. I don't use the place often enough for that. Only a caretaker and his wife, who sweeps—"

"What? Once every other year?"

He ignored her. "*Sweeps*, changes the linen, and keeps the rooms aired out. I expect she can be persuaded to cook—with enough incentive. And"—he regarded her narrowly—"*if* you don't offend her."

"Offend *her*?" Fia said. "My dear sir, I am used to servants worrying about whether they offend *me*, not vice versa."

"Then," he said, his voice growing louder as he went, "I suggest now is as good a time as any for you to *start* worrying, because if you try those haughty lady-of-the-manor airs on a Scotswoman, you'll find yourself stirring your own gruel, you spoiled little witch!"

He was right. Over a decade and a half under Gunna's less than fawning care had taught Fia the character of the Highland Scot. Particularly Scottish women. Not that she was about to give Thomas the satisfaction of acknowledging such. "Humph."

He smiled. He couldn't possibly take that little grunt to mean anything other than scorn—certainly it hadn't meant she'd yielded to him one inch.

"There're brooms in the kitchen."

"Ah, good," she said sweetly.

His brows rose.

"I shall conjure up a spell directly and ride back to London. We spoiled witches do that sort of thing, you know."

He burst out laughing. She stared at him in amazement, which turned quickly to fascination. His eyes crinkled up at the corners, and the seams on either side of his wide mouth revealed those devastatingly attractive dimples again.

His smile was broad and rife with pleasure; his teeth were clean and straight. Delight filled his pale blue eyes, sparking them with silver.

Then slowly the laughter died in his throat. The room grew hushed, the air still with expectancy. With intimacy.

His brows drew together a fraction, but in puzzlement, not anger. The silver sparkle in his eyes banked to a darker luster. She could see the pulse beating at the base of his throat. Her lips trembled on the brink of opening—

"The bedroom is ready," Gordie announced from the top of the stairs.

Fia leapt back. How had she come to be standing so close to Thomas? He was frowning in earnest now, looking as confused as she felt.

"M'lord?"

"Yes, Gordie. Thank you. Lady MacFarlane?" He gestured for her to precede him up the stairs. When they were at the top, Gordie led her to the end of a narrow hallway. He opened the last paneled door and stood back, allowing her to enter ahead of them.

She looked around without enthusiasm. The room contained a bizarre and atrociously mismatched collection of furniture. A massive oak four-poster sat squarely in the center of the room, its drab dun-colored curtains tied back at the posts, exposing an improbable red counterpane. Beside it stood a delicate cherrywood dressing table with a pedestal mirror attached, a bench carved with griffin heads before it. A pair of lime green wingback chairs flanked a small fireplace, in which a peat fire burned.

She did not think she would be spending much of her time in here.

"I . . . I hope it meets with your approval, ma'am?" Gordie said shyly, twisting his hands together and shuffling, clearly embarrassed to have entered a lady's chambers.

"My approval?" she echoed. She was about to laugh and make some snide remark about being more likely to approve a nightmare when a splash of unlikely color caught her eye. She turned. Someone had picked a small bouquet of yellow flowers and set them on the windowsill. That someone, she was sure, was Gordie.

Why, he'd probably been given the responsibility of pulling together some sort of suite of furniture for her unexpected arrival. The room was his inspiration, and now, looking at it, she realized he'd gathered together what he must suppose to be the most beautiful and rare objects in the house—regardless of whether they suited one another. In another room—and with a different seat—the dressing table would have been lovely. And the Oriental screen in the corner was a work of art.

As were those yellow flowers. She turned back, smiling warmly.

"It's lovely. I am sure I shall be most comfortable here."

The boy released his breath and grinned with pleasure. "I'm happy ye like it, ma'am. Jamie had one of the lads ride here like the devil was on his trail to say as how ye was comin' with the laird. I done what I could in what time I had."

"If you knew I was comin', then why'd ye point yer rifle at us?" Thomas asked in exasperation.

"Well, how'd it look if ye rode up and I *wasn't* guardin' the house? Ye'd think me a poor sort of man then, wouldn't ye?" Gordie asked with impeccable logic. He turned back to Fia. "And did you see the flowers?" He pointed at the blooms.

"They're beautiful," she said sincerely. "No one's ever given me their like." Which was true. Roses and tulips she'd received by the dozens, but no one had ever given her a simple country flower.

"Cowslip they be, and the last of them at that," Gordie said proudly. "Late this year, they were, but I remembered where I'd seen some still bloomin', and whilst you and the laird were chattin' I slipped out and fetched 'em. I 'spect ye were wonderin' where I'd got to, eh?"

"Ah, yes. Yes, we were," Fia lied, her gaze slipping to where Thomas stood, unnaturally silent and watchful. "Weren't we?"

Whyever was he looking at her like that? She hadn't said a blasted provocative thing to the boy and yet his expression had gone grim again.

The man really should learn to relax and laugh more often. He had a lovely laugh. And then the irony of her, Fia Merrick, criticizing another for being too somber struck her and she grinned—as it was, in

Thomas's direction. He blinked, grimness metamorphosing into bewilderment.

"*Weren't we, milord?*"

"What?" he asked, coming out of whatever trance held him. "Ah. Yes. We were wondering where you were. Now we know. Come on, Gordie. I'm sure Lady MacFarlane would like to change clothes and prepare for dinner."

"Oh, aye, I bet she would," Gordie agreed promptly, in his artlessness reminding her of her own unclean and doubtless fragrant state.

She looked down. The lace edge of her bodice was grimy and a smear of dirt marked her bosom. Her once crisp brocade skirts hung like limp rags from the hoops of her petticoat. These, too, were dirty, stained with what, she had no intention of considering. As for her face and hair . . . She was very glad she hadn't looked into the mirror on the dressing table.

"I should like to bathe. How do I go about getting a hip bath?" she asked.

"Hip bath?" Gordie repeated uncertainly, leading Fia to suspect anew that the lad's acquaintance with bath, hip or otherwise, was limited.

"Fill that big pot standing over the hearth with water," Thomas told Gordie, "then heat it. As soon as it's hot, haul it up to milady's chambers."

"But what'll I do with it then?" Gordie asked.

Thomas huffed in annoyance. "I'll empty the rain barrel from the backyard and bring it here. Ye'll empty the water in that."

"You expect me to bathe *in a barrel*?" Fia asked.

He turned on her. "I don't care if you bathe or not. That's as good as ye'll get whilst in my home, lady, and ye ought to be thankful for that."

She returned his glare placidly. "Why is it, do you suppose, that since arriving here you've reverted to that extraordinary accent? It isn't even Scottish, really. Sort of a conglomeration of accents. Where were you transported to, anyway? The Colonies?"

"I . . . I don't know what you mean," he stated in clipped, impervious, and extremely British tones. He looked at Gordie, who was snickering behind his hand. "Get on with it!"

The lad bobbed his head and scooted through the open door and down the hall, leaving Thomas with Fia.

"Well?" she said, arching one brow.

He stalked out of the room.

"I'll get the bloody rain barrel. You stir the fire." Thomas tramped out into the dusk and rounded the corner of the house. He found the barrel and tipped a foot of brackish water out of it before hefting it to his shoulder. As he did so he glanced up. A light sprang to life in the corner room above. A second later Fia's dainty silhouette grew larger as she approached the window. She dipped down, and Thomas knew she was smelling the cowslip blooms.

The remnants of his anger faded as he watched— anger not at Gordie or Fia, but at Carr for his willful neglect and misuse of his only daughter.

No one had ever given her a simple flower, and Thomas wanted to know why the bloody hell not.

Even the most obtuse man alive could not have misread the surprised pleasure that had suffused Fia's usually enigmatic features, making them for one moment something more than ravishing, something uncomplicated and clean and honest, something breathtakingly *pretty*.

She moved away from the window and he readjusted the weight of the barrel on his shoulder, the side of his mouth drawing up in chagrin. He'd been standing beneath the girl's window mooning over her like a green lad. Worse, he was jealous of Gordie for being the first to give her cowslip. Not because the act had so obviously touched her, but because it had awoken a response in her he'd never thought to see: *kindness*.

There was no way around it. Fia had been kind to Gordie, tacitly agreeing that she—and he, he remembered with surprise—had wondered about the length of the lad's absence. And she hadn't balked a bit at staying in that nightmare of a room Gordie had arranged. In fact, he suspected Fia had guessed Gordie's involvement before he'd even admitted it. She'd shown compassion in dealing with the boy. His expression turned quizzical.

Kind? Sensitive? With naught in it for her?

This was dangerous. Fia, unaffectedly pleased and laughing, impulsive and charming and *kind*, was dangerous. Even more dangerous than the Fia who'd calculatedly purred well-rehearsed double entendres as she slithered against him. And *that* Fia had already been far dangerous enough.

He stopped at the kitchen door and kicked it open, his thoughts in a whirl. He'd an acute sense of having just sailed into uncharted waters. And he was certain there could be no going back.

Chapter 17

*H*aving caught a glimpse of herself in the dressing table's mirror, Fia disrobed as soon as Thomas left and was waiting in dirty chemise and limp petticoat when he returned, for once absolutely innocent of calculation. But if she'd for a moment forgotten her stated intent to seduce Thomas, he hadn't.

He took one look at her in her unprepossessing dishabille, scowled fiercely, and mumbled something about someone called MacNab taking care of her. Before she could frame a reply, he left.

She'd finished her bath—an undeniable luxury, despite the rain barrel—and was dressing in fresh clothes when a knock sounded at her door. She opened it to find a tray of food at her feet. Ravenous, she gulped down the food, expecting Thomas to appear at any moment. He didn't.

The next day, she waited in her room for him to come scratching. He didn't. She took both her midday and evening meals alone in the bedroom.

The third day, she wandered downstairs to an empty house, dressed in all the splendor she could contrive out of the few garments she'd brought with her. This, to be honest, was perhaps not so very "splendid" after all, for she'd found it impossible to lace her corset by herself to the degree necessary in order to produce the flamboyant figure that had so bedazzled men in London. And her filmy dressing wrap was not all that provocative, either, unless men found the sight of gooseflesh stimulating. She'd forgotten how chilly it was in the Highlands.

Still, the extra sleep she'd enjoyed had improved her looks. The texture of her skin was smoother, the whites of her eyes were as bright as porcelain, and the shadows at her temples and beneath her eyes had disappeared. She was definitely passable, and found it caused her no small amount of disappointment when Thomas did *not* appear at her bedchamber door begging for admittance.

By now she realized that not only was Thomas not returning for supper, he wasn't returning to the manor at all.

On the fourth day, she found Gordie piling rocks around the house. A few questions ascertained that Thomas had given him the task of rebuilding the kitchen garden wall—thus, Fia suspected, keeping the boy from her dire influence. On the subject of where exactly Thomas was, Gordie turned as mum as a post, mumbling, blushing, and finally darting away.

She'd no doubt that she could have gotten the information out of Gordie, but that would have landed the boy in trouble, and she was loath to drag the young man into . . . *whatever* this thing between her and Thomas was.

She turned east, toward where she supposed McClairen's Isle might be, but drawn to it though she was, she knew better than to try to walk that far a distance. She hadn't needed Thomas's warnings about highwaymen to scare her into staying where she'd been so summarily put. She'd lived in these lands. The face of poverty-inspired desperation was no stranger to her; her own father had been its author.

So she wandered back into Thomas's unsoaped, unwashed, unscoured, unrinsed, and unwiped house, idly watching Gordie's narrow sunburned back as he stacked stone upon stone around the place, until it finally drove her mad. Or to such madness as housekeeping was.

She removed corset and petticoat and donned a simple—and warm—dress and commenced to work, finding if not pleasure in the activity, at least the means to fall asleep at night without Thomas's image haunting her.

That evening Fia finally met the hitherto unseen Mrs. Grace MacNab—a woman whose talents in the kitchen more than made up for her lack of prowess with a broom. The elderly woman eyed Fia with monumental disinterest, muttered, "Good. Now I'll

not have to tote tha tray up tha stairs," and went back
to placidly stirring the pot of vegetables simmering on
the hearth.

It took Fia somewhere under an hour to determine
that Mrs. MacNab's conversational abilities ranked
somewhere below her housekeeping skills. But after
one bite of the dour Scotswoman's rich, savory stew,
Fia decided that if a dirty house was the price one paid
for Mrs. MacNab's stew, it was a bargain.

When Mrs. MacNab *did* speak, she was invariably
blunt, but she was also, with the exception of the
perennially blushing and tongue-tied Gordie, the only
person Fia saw. Thus, on her fifth evening at the manor,
Fia was already in the kitchen when Mrs. MacNab
arrived from wherever it was she lived.

"Ah! You're early. Good. I'm famished," Fia said,
when the kitchen door swung open and Mrs. Mac-
Nab entered, a load of fresh vegetables piled in her
plump arms.

"Did na' eat yer dinner, then?" Mrs. MacNab asked,
scrutinizing her closely as she dumped the produce on
the table. "Are ye sick? Fer if ye are, I'd best send
Gordie ta fetch the laird."

"No," Fia hastened to assure her. "I am fine. I just
have a healthy appetite."

"So I've noticed," Mrs. MacNab agreed, shaking
out a large, moth-eaten square of linen and tying it
around her ample middle. "Well, if yer sure?"

"I am!" She could imagine nothing more mortify-
ing than having Thomas Donne brought to her under
false pretenses.

"Should I bring yer food into the dining room when it's done?" Mrs. MacNab asked.

"No," Fia said quickly, fearful of being excluded from yet another living creature's company. She would never have thought herself so dependent on the simple solace one found in being in another's presence. It alarmed her a little. "I'll eat in here."

Besides, she told herself, there was really no reason to dirty the dining room. Particularly as that very morning she'd spent a good three hours there, with the windows flung wide as she beat the heavy draperies and then swept the resultant dust from the carpet.

She didn't fret over what ridiculous conclusions Thomas might make if he were to discover the means by which she'd taken to wasting the days. It was her experience that males seldom noted their surroundings unless they contributed directly to their discomfort.

"Suit yerself," Mrs. MacNab said, disappearing into the pantry.

"Do you mind if I wait in here while you make the meal?" Fia asked hesitantly. She could so easily be rejected.

Mrs. MacNab reappeared carrying cheese and what looked like some dried weeds, which she deposited on the table alongside the fresh vegetables. "Makes no mind to me, lass."

Mrs. MacNab then proceeded to chop, mince, hammer, pulverize, and otherwise lay waste to everything on the table before adding each ingredient in some arcane and complicated order to a skillet filled with sizzling butter. The fragrance nearly sent Fia into a swoon.

Throughout all, Mrs. MacNab said not a word. Knives flashed, wooden spoons whirled, and by the time she was done flour dusted the air and the floor and every other surface. But after one taste of the delicious savory custard flan that appeared from the skillet, Fia would gladly have cleaned the tiles on her knees for another bite.

At the end of her meal, Fia pushed herself away from the table and casually asked the question plaguing her. "Where is Captain . . . Thomas?"

Mrs. MacNab dumped the lump of dough she'd been stirring in a huge earthenware bowl onto the table's far end. She smacked the wad of dough, sending a puff of flour into the air. "Ye mean the McClairen."

Fia regarded the stout woman curiously. "You do realize that clans have been abolished and the chieftains divested of their authority?"

"Oh, aye," Mrs. MacNab responded placidly, rolling the dough with the heels of her hands. "So I hear tell. But tha' means nothing to us."

"Who is 'us'?"

"Clan McClairen," Mrs. MacNab answered with a touch of impatience. "Who else?"

"But I thought that C—" She caught back her words just in time. "I'd heard the McClairens were gone from these parts."

"Aye." Mrs. MacNab snorted, kneading away. " 'Gone' is one way ye might put it. And we were, too. But *he* found us." For the first time emotion underscored the woman's voice. "Found most of us in the Americas but some of us in the lowlands and a few, like me, were in Edinburgh."

She paused in the middle of her kneading. " 'Course, Jamie stayed here all along with old Muira and a few others that preferred to live like animals in the coves rather than run.

"But the rest of us, I'm shamed ta say, had scattered like cunny flushed from a warren after Carr informed on Ian McClairen and killed his McClairen bride."

Fia's head shot up. She forced herself to relax. To hear someone describe her mother's murder so prosaically . . . She waited for the inevitable inner recoil that always accompanied the thought of her mother's murder.

Was there a name for it? Like "patricide" or "matricide"? It seemed to her that there ought to be a specific term for the murder of a wife, and a specific name for the children of such a murderer. A brand of sorts to mirror the brand in her mind . . . and heart.

The pain and recoil came, but less insistently this time. The long-standing question still bubbled beneath the surface, demanding an answer she did not own—what had Carr's blood bequeathed her? What did having a murderer's blood in her veins make *her*?

Always before she'd heeded whatever inner protective devices had kept her from examining those questions too closely. Now she tentatively examined the very peripheries.

When she'd realized who Thomas was, she'd understood the bitterness that had rung in his voice when he'd spoken to Rhiannon Russell all those long years ago. Carr's crime had been not only against a defenseless woman, it had been against a member of Thomas's family—albeit a distant relation.

And if Janet had been Thomas's relative, then that meant that Thomas's people were, in some distant manner, her people. *Her people.*

The concept still surprised Fia. She had always considered herself uniquely alone—cut off from her brothers by her father and later cut off from her father by the truth. But suddenly she had . . . people. She stared at the homely, bovine Mrs. MacNab bent over her dough.

"Are *you* a McClairen?"

"Aye. I were in Edinburgh, working in a kitchen after me husband was killed at Culloden. The laird come down—oh, about five years ago now—and says he's come to fetch me home to the"—she looked up, cleared her throat, and went on—"isle. We was spread far and few but somehow the laird found all of us that was left. He paid up fer them that be in servitude and bought passage home fer them that was far away."

"And are there many?"

"La! Twenty-four of us. Twenty-three fer a while, but last spring Gavin's lady had a son." An unexpectedly tender smile appeared on Mrs. MacNab's face.

Thomas McClairen had found twenty-three people and gathered them back to this land. Why?

Fia pinched off a piece of bread dough and worked it absently between finger and thumb, puzzling out the increasingly complex enigma of Thomas McClairen. Ostensibly Thomas had brokered a handsome life for himself in the American colonies. He had wealth, the prestige of owning a successful shipping business, presumably a house, and most definitely friends to whom he was unswervingly loyal—like James Barton.

Yet here he was in Scotland, where he ran the risk of his identity being discovered and his life forfeited. A risk that would certainly turn into a reality, for Thomas had said that Carr knew his secret. *Why, then, did Thomas stay?*

It seemed to Fia of the utmost importance that she find out the answer to that question, and only Thomas could supply the answer.

Mrs. MacNab untied the apron from around her broad hips and settled it across the top of the mound of dough she'd fashioned. "There, now," she said with satisfaction. " 'Twill rise overnight and be ready fer bakin' on the morrow."

"Where's Thomas McClairen?"

Mrs. MacNab dusted her plump hands together, sending dried flakes of bread dough flying.

"Mrs. MacNab, please. Where is he? I need to speak to him."

"Aye, lassie, aye," Mrs. MacNab said, clucking gently. "No need to be so impatient. He's right there."

Startled, Fia swung around. Thomas stood behind her.

Her gaze drank up the sight of him. For a moment she could not suppress her pleasure, nor did she try.

His tanned face had been browned even more and the fine white lines at the corner of his eyes etched deeper. His proud, straight shoulders looked unnaturally straight, as though he needed to consciously keep them from slumping. A day's growth of beard darkened the hard angle of his jaw and amidst the dark stubble Fia could see a glint of silver.

He was in his thirties, she realized. At least a decade older than she and no longer a youth, no longer the suave figure who'd lounged in smoke-filled drawing rooms. He was a man used to hard labor and exhaustion and . . . and what else?

"Where were you?"

"I had business," he said, dragging a chair across from her out from under the kitchen table. "Do you have any more supper left, Mrs. MacNab?"

"Aye." Within minutes she'd produced not only a dish heaped with the flan Fia had enjoyed, but a cold joint of roasted beef glistening with crisp fat, a goose liver terrine, a loaf of bread, and a thick wedge of yellow cheese. She then filled a large earthenware pitcher with foaming ale, said, "I'll be back on the morrow. Mind the bread," and left.

"Mrs. MacNab," Thomas said around a mouthful of bread, "does not believe in standing on ceremony. And she shares the Highlanders' unaccountable conviction that she is as good as the next." The spark of amusement in his eyes was entrancing.

"Except you."

He chuckled. "Oh, no. No exceptions, I'm afraid.

In fact, I'm not at all sure her command wasn't directed at me."

"Mrs. MacNab," Fia said firmly, "worships the ground you walk on. I'm sure if you asked her to don a toga and dance around the stable at first light, she'd be happy to oblige."

He tore off a chunk of bread, stuffed it in his mouth, and swallowed. "Well, if she's convinced you of such patent flummery, I shall have to see about raising her wages. There's bound to be some advantage in having you believe that there exists at least someone who holds me in awe."

Her eyes widened. *Dear God, he was teasing her.*

She . . . she *loved* being teased!

Kay and Cora teased her sometimes, and the delight of it, the guilelessness, the fondness and charity of it never ceased to delight her. She sometimes shivered with pure pleasure that she could be treated with such beautiful, casual affability.

He was regarding her with mock speculation, waving the end of his baguette around to emphasize his words. "Whatever do you suppose that is?"

"I'm sure I haven't any idea," she murmured, trying to slow the beating of her heart.

"Neither do I. But look, I've been in your company a grand total of fifteen minutes and you haven't . . ." Whatever he'd been about to say he decided against and instead leaned over the table and flicked his finger across her cheek. "Do you realize you have flour on your face?"

Her hand flew to cover her cheek, and her eyes

grew rounder when she touched her skin and felt its heat and realized she was blushing. She, who'd been seen in public in the most outré of gowns without developing so much as a single degree rise of temperature, blushing over flour on her face. Or was she blushing over his playful touch and teasing smile?

She could not think of an appropriate reply. She did not want him to *stop* teasing her and she hadn't had the time to understand why and she never did things unrehearsed, without plenty of serious thought and consideration. And yet she didn't want him to *keep* teasing her because that way led to more possibilities unfolding upon more of possibilities—and possible consequences.

She would leave. She would go to her room and consider her course, consider what her goal here was and how she would achieve it. But her thoughts as well as her body felt unpleasant and unreal, as if she had somehow lost substance. She was *supposed* to be seducing him, she reminded herself, regarding him with troubled eyes.

But that was before she'd discovered who he was and that he'd good causes, the best of causes, for his enmity, and yet did not, *would not*, avenge himself on her, his enemy's daughter. In fact, she would wager her very life that he'd never even considered such a course. So, dear God, what was she doing here?

He wasn't even attending her, but sawing through the slab of meat in front of him. How can one seduce a man who's eating cooked beef?

She stood up.

"Please, sit down. I would count your company a favor," he said without raising his gaze from what was apparently a delicate operation.

She sat down. What choice did she have? she asked herself, striving desperately for a sense of injury. She was a prisoner in this house, kept away from people, from creature comforts. She was used to society, bright lights and . . .

It wouldn't wash. No matter how much she tried to convince herself otherwise. She was very used to her own company and very used to the tempo of country life. It was his company she missed. It was Thomas.

They were still enemies, made so by blood. He disapproved of her. He thought the worst of her. He'd brought her here because her very presence was a cankerous contagion from which purer beings must be spared.

He'd also held her head and stroked her back while she was sick. He'd covered her with his jacket and used his body to shelter her from the wind. He was angry about her childhood. And he teased her.

She gave up, capitulated utterly and completely, and sat down.

Thomas had tried to keep away. He'd lasted five days, each one tormented by the memory of her as he'd last seen her, standing in her undergarments, so damned and obviously innocent of the effects she'd had on his body. He'd returned determined not to let her know how anxious he'd been to come to her.

But this camaraderie was, in its own way, as enticing

as the allure of soft skin and sweet, clean hair. Though that was enticing enough.

Soft pink color tinted each of Fia's perfectly formed cheeks. A stray tendril of black hair curled along her throat and disappeared beneath the simple lace kerchief crossed over her décolletage and tucked beneath the edge of her bodice. Such practical, modest, country attire. Yet on her, ravishing.

He cast about for something to say. "I hope this stay in the country isn't too onerous for you."

She looked up. "Not at all. I love the country."

"Forgive me," he said. "I had been led to believe that your husband kept you from society."

Beneath her face's calm facade a shadow of scorn had arisen. "I'm not surprised. You've probably been led to believe a great many things about me that aren't necessarily true." There was no reproach in her voice, but he felt the rebuke nonetheless. She went on without waiting for him to reply.

"Gregory MacFarlane was never jealous of me, nor did he ever have cause for jealousy. I honored him and my marriage vows to the day of his death.

"In only one matter did I ever disobey him, and that was in the matter of our mutual residence. We had none. I would not go to London and he would not stay at Bramble House. Consequently, we lived much apart."

He believed her. She'd spoken every word without emotion or emphasis. She'd simply recited to him the facts of her marriage.

"I see. Why are you telling me all this?"

She shrugged. "I am not really sure. The truth, as far as my life is concerned, is a liquid thing. Perhaps I just wanted to tell you another rendition of it. My rendition."

"What else should I know?"

She studied him for a long moment and Thomas felt the consideration in her gaze. "Nothing," she finally said, "nothing more yet."

She relaxed and placed her elbows on the table, steepling her fingers before her lips and lifting one brow. "Might *I* ask a question now?"

" 'Twould seem fair."

"Where were you sent after you'd been sentenced for treason?"

He'd not foreseen this. He'd expected her to press him as to how long he would keep her, what he'd been doing while away from her. He'd never expected her to show interest in his past. "An island in the West Indies. I was a bond servant there. Until James Barton purchased my bond."

"I see," she said softly. And Thomas had the distinct impression that she did see, that she understood the history behind his few short words.

"This happened because you committed treason?" she asked.

"Because your father told Lord Cumberland that my brother and I had been couriers for the Jacobite conspiracy."

It did not surprise her and she did not question or deny it but only said, "And that is why you sought to hurt Ash by tricking Rhiannon into another's arms."

He wished she hadn't known about that. It had been a mean-spirited act, one that had lessened him.

"It wouldn't have mattered to Carr," she said. "You made the mistake of thinking he cared for his sons."

"I didn't seek to hurt Carr then. I sought to hurt *any* Merrick," he confessed, and then hastily sought to reassure her. "But no more," he said. "I swear it."

He held his hand palm up and extended it across the table, the gesture implicitly begging for her trust. She did not look down. Her gaze locked with his. A long moment passed. Then, as tentatively as dawn approaches the darkness, he felt her hand slip gently into his own.

Chapter 18

—after a month Kay apparently decided he'd had enough, for he stood up, glared at me, and announced to his tutor, 'Since she has all the answers, why doesn't she do the bloody assignment?' "

Thomas laughed. They had stopped beneath a hawthorn tree. The sunlight piercing the feathery foliage above cast a shimmering mosaic of light and shadow over Fia's upturned face.

"And did you?" he asked.

Fia cast him an impish look. True, a month ago he probably would not have been able to identify it as such, but they'd spent so much time in each other's company that he'd begun to discern the subtleties of her expressions.

It was rather like peering over the edge of a boat

into deep water. One had to look past the reflected sky to see the glories hidden beneath the surface. It was an immensely addictive endeavor. He lo— He delighted in watching Fia.

"Did you?" he prompted again, and won a brief, self-deprecating smile.

She leaned her back against the tree and crossed her arms. "No. Mr. Elton began giving me private lessons and thus stopped me from interrupting Kay's with my disastrously uninformed queries. We were both much happier for it. Kay," she said confidingly, "is quite competitive, you know." At his look of speculation, she nodded sagely. "And he crows something terrible when he wins."

The darling! Somehow he managed to refrain from telling her that Kay had said pretty much the same thing about her. He'd disbelieved the lad then, but no longer. He believed quite a bit he would never have credited.

"Didn't your—didn't you have instructors when you were a child?" By tacit agreement they both had excluded the name "Carr" from their vocabulary, as well as "James Barton." "Or perhaps you didn't attend those you had very well?" he teased.

Fia loved to be teased. Her eyes fair gleamed with pleasure with the smallest bit of badinage . . . as they did now.

"We had none," she said lightly. "Though I think Ash received a sporadic education at the hands of the local vicar. And Raine was at Eton until he was expelled."

"But you were not educated."

The faintest of colors washed up her throat. If he hadn't been looking for it, he wouldn't have noted it.

"I knew how to read and write, though not what to read. Remember, I was being groomed for a different role." She picked her words carefully.

"When I arrived at Bramble House I was wiser than a woman thrice my years but I was also as ignorant as a turnip. I remember eavesdropping on Kay's lesson one of my first days there. I couldn't believe the magnitude of what I did not know." Her voice grew hushed. "And I undertook learning it all."

She glanced at him and a spark of amusement lit her eyes. "And before you comment, I realize that I have not in all ways been successful."

It was true. Every now and again in the course of one of their conversations, he would make some remark that would cause her to stop him. She would make him repeat himself and then, with the skill and tenacity of the most seasoned barrister, query him until she'd exhausted whatever knowledge he had on the matter. The gaps in her learning were broad and unpredictable and her thirst for the knowledge to fill those gaps was immeasurable.

"I am a gentleman, I would never point out a lady's shortcomings."

Her arms dropped to her sides. "Yes," she said, taking a step forward, bringing her closer to him, "you are a gentleman."

He smiled at her and, before he realized what he was doing, lifted a tress of her hair and tucked it behind her ear. It was silky and warm where the sun had toasted it.

"Are you disappointed?" he asked.

In answer, she turned her head as though to catch the touch of his knuckles against her cheek. He must be imagining it. He'd taken to investing her expressions with his own yearning.

Yearning. What a pallid term for this feeling. He leaned toward her a little, hoping she would lift her face to his. She didn't.

"Do you know what the word 'platonic' means?" he asked.

She stepped away, concentrating. "I believe it is a form of . . . affection, defined by the Greek philosopher Plato."

"Exactly. And what type of affection is it?"

She met his gaze, shadows advancing to cloud the blameless blue of her eyes. "The affection of deep friendship."

He would never presume she might view him as a friend . . . he wasn't even sure he wanted her to. It might preclude something else. But the darkness eclipsing her bright eyes made him immediately aware of the ridiculousness of suggesting to her that *any* relationship exist between them—most especially *something else*.

He'd *kidnapped* her, for God's sake! He was keeping her here so that she might not bring harm to his best friend. Or so he'd once told himself. He was no longer sure what he was doing or why he kept her. He only knew it had very little to do with James Barton anymore.

She, on the other hand, was simply making the best of an untenable situation. He should be thankful that since they'd taken dinner together in the kitchen a week ago she'd not once alluded to, or evinced the slightest inclination of, seducing him.

More's the damn pity.

Instead, he'd begun . . . begun . . . *wooing* her. Yes. Trying to coax out one of her rare smiles, make her laugh, make her speak without first considering her words. She was still standing, waiting patiently for . . . for what?

The answer was loweringly obvious—for them to continue their walk.

"Is something amiss?" she asked.

Once more, his humor saved the situation. "Forgive me," he said, pulling himself together. "I swallowed something unpalatable."

"All's well now, I trust?" she inquired innocently.

"Everything is fine."

"Perhaps you'd like to return to the manor?"

"By no means. Please, let us continue." He offered her his arm, and after a brief hesitation she took it and fell into pace beside him.

"You speak fondly of your stepchildren. You've mentioned Kay several times."

She seemed to find the return to more mundane subjects a relief. "Yes. I like him very well."

"Tell me about him."

As usual when he asked something of a private nature, her chin rose a small degree as though she was bracing herself. Would he betray her trust? How much would he absorb before he used what she told him against her? she would be asking herself. He knew because he asked himself the same question each time she asked him to reveal something of himself. Yet she had not backed down from his queries. And neither had he.

It was heady and dangerous, this conversation they enjoyed, both of them wanting so much to believe in the other that they ignored the deep-seated suspicion neither had been able to purge. And only lately Thomas had become aware of an unforeseen consequence of their verbal intercourse: It was immensely arousing.

There was, he now suspected, a very good reason the biblical cant for coitus was "knowledge."

"I shall never forgive myself for Pip's having been wounded," she said instead of answering his question about Kay. He'd noted that the evenness of her voice was often in direct contrast to the depths of the emotions she guarded.

He no longer blamed her for Pip. He'd learned too much since. Some she'd told him, some he'd guessed, filling in the areas she was loath to speak about.

Fia had met Pip and been touched by his boyish playfulness. With no template to follow, she'd treated Pip as she'd treated the only other boy of her acquaintance, a boy who patently had no romantic interest in her, her stepson, Kay. She'd not foreseen that Pip would misconstrue her easy camaraderie for something else. And when she'd discovered it, it had been too late.

"I am sorry," he said.

She did not ask for what, but her fingers tightened briefly on his sleeve. They walked silently for a while, the scent of flinty, wet rock and pine needles rising with each step.

"Does young Kay miss his father?" he asked.

"Gregory? Some, but then Gregory wasn't with us much."

"And do you miss your husband?" He had no idea why he asked.

She stopped abruptly, turned, and considered him a long minute before saying, "Gregory MacFarlane was a dull-witted man with no greater aspiration than to be approved of by rakes, roues, and rotters. He treated his children with benign neglect and me with alarmed tolerance, which is better than most parents treat their children and far better than I expected. I neither loved nor hated him, respected nor despised him, which made our marriage a most unremarkable one."

"Why did you marry him?" It was an unfair question; she might not even know why Carr had wed her to MacFarlane.

"I married him for his house," she said, and walked away.

"Certainly there was more to it than that," he insisted, catching up and stopping her with a hand on her arm. "Carr wouldn't have need of a farmhouse in the lowlands."

"Carr?" she echoed. "What has Carr to do with this?"

"I assumed he'd . . . persuaded you to wed MacFarlane."

"Why would you think such a thing?" she asked.

He watched her in growing consternation. "Because," he said gently, "as you yourself acknowledged, Carr had groomed you from an early age—"

"Be damned to Carr," she suddenly whispered in a violent undertone. "Be damned to Carr's plans. I married MacFarlane to escape Carr and his plot and machinations. Because once MacFarlane died I thought I'd be free from ever being molded and prodded and manipulated by anyone again. I thought I'd be independent."

"But how could you believe that?" he asked. "What with MacFarlane's having a son—"

"I didn't *know* MacFarlane had any children when I married him," she said tensely before her expression softened. "I had no idea."

The vehemence in her voice made no sense. If Fia loathed Carr so much, then why was she so often in his company? Carr paraded Fia before the ton as a horse trader might a prime mare. He scowled, something in his unconsidered analogy fitting more closely than it ought.

Beside him, Fia's thoughts moved on kinder currents. Kay and Cora. How she'd resented them her first few weeks at Bramble House. But the resentment had faded, the emptiness it left filled with startling rapidity by something else, some unnamed and hitherto unexperienced emotion. For a long time she'd struggled to put a name to that thing, amazed that it should find a home in her hard heart.

Oh, she loved Gunna well and she owned a late-blooming affection toward her brothers, but to find that she loved two Scottish brats! Incredible.

How deeply she'd grown to love them she hadn't known until Gregory's death and Carr's appearance. She'd do anything to protect them. Her gaze slew toward where Thomas regarded her with a pensive, suspicious air.

Abruptly thoughts of Kay and Cora and Carr vanished. She could not stand to see that expression on his face. She swept rapidly past him. Why should the motives for her marriage matter to him? Other women married for property, or social advancement. In fact, the majority did. Why, then, had her admission sounded so distasteful?

She bit her lip hard, her ears attuned for the sound of his footsteps following. None. He'd stayed where she'd left him. She chanced a backward glance, saw him regarding her in puzzlement.

Had she been mistaken? Had that not been distaste and mistrust on his face? She'd never before had so much trouble divining a man's feelings. Of course, those feelings were generally obvious, because they were primal. One needed to have no more than a decent set of eyes directed at a certain part of a man's anatomy in order to ascertain them.

That being the case, 'twas obvious Thomas felt

something for her. But she wanted to be something more than the object of a man's salacious fantasies. Although to be the object of *Thomas's* salacious fantasies . . . She swallowed.

Sometimes at night, she'd think of him the way men thought about her—or so they'd whispered to her often enough. Her muscles would flex, arcing toward some spectral lover. The skin of her breasts and thighs would feel too taut, and she would ache with a need that had never been satisfied—indeed, a need she'd barely been aware she owned. A need Thomas could fulfill. If only he would.

God, what was she thinking? Her thoughts, her emotions, her motives in allowing herself to be abducted, her goals here, everything was in turmoil. Nothing was as she'd planned. By all that was sacred, she was *smitten* with Thomas McClairen. Like the veriest girl! And she had no idea, none, what to do about it.

A touch on her shoulder brought her swinging around. Thomas stood behind her, regarding her intently.

"What?" she asked breathlessly.

"Do you love Bramble House so much? Is it that important to you?"

"Love it?" she echoed in confusion. Her world had been set atilt and was spinning madly. "I don't know. Wanton's Blush was my home, even though I knew I would never have her, I would never be able to . . ."

"To what?" he asked, searching her face.

"To set her to rights."

"Rights?"

"Aye. She always put me in mind of a queen in exile, forced to hide her regal nature behind a courtesan's skirts."

"Yes," he murmured. He swallowed and the contraction of his throat set a wave of longing through her. His gaze was fixed on her mouth, his own lips relaxed, almost open. What would happen if she leaned closer? What would he do? What if he did nothing?

She forced herself to break eye contact, and to pick up their conversation.

"I found pictures of the castle as she was before Carr possessed her. She had an almost magical quality. But perhaps that was due to the artist's talents." She smiled wryly. "I used to pretend I was Lizabet, first lady of the castle, waiting for Dougal to come back and make things right."

"Dougal McClairen?"

"Aye," she agreed. She wanted to touch his face again, as she had the night of the masque. He was not so smoothly shaven now; his skin would have a different texture. "But when I grew older, I knew I was not Lizabet, and Dougal would not be coming. So I found another place to call home."

"And another Dougal?" he asked.

"No," she said firmly. "I knew better by then."

"You found your home at Bramble House."

"I found a *place* at Bramble House," she corrected. "But it will never be Wanton's Blush."

He hesitated a moment and then said, "Would you like to see it?"

"What?"

"The castle."

"There's naught to see. Carr said it had all burned down."

"Not all of it." He took her hand. "Come with me."

Chapter 19

$\mathcal{T}$he late afternoon air carried a warm southern breeze with it. Thomas, riding beside Fia, scarce understood the impulse that had led him there. He'd never considered taking Fia to the castle, but then he'd never considered that the castle meant anything to her.

After the days of companionable discourse they'd come full circle. The last few hours' ride, their conversation had been stilted, their avoidance of each other's eyes obvious. But as they drew nearer the coast and small things had begun to look familiar to her, Fia relaxed, her anticipation overcoming her shyness. Thomas's own unease vanished and he drank in the subtle signs of her delight playing across her lovely face.

'Twas like watching a master violinist play an intricate yet seemingly simple cantata. One needed to attend the nuances. He knew the scent of the sea comforted her, for she inhaled often and deeply. The softening in her eyes proclaimed that she favored the rowan over the hawthorn. Hares must plague the Bramble House kitchen garden, as testified by the slight flattening of her lips when a rabbit darted across the path.

They were near now. They wove between a stand of pine, and crested a flinty knoll as the trees gave way to the open. There, beneath them, lay the surging sea, McClairen's Isle, and Maiden's Blush.

The setting sun was quitting the sky in all due pageantry. Purples and mauves, crimson and orchid stained the horizon, bathing the castle walls in a soft, phosphorescent light so that from this vantage Maiden's Blush looked like a half-formed fairy castle.

About her base, small figures moved slowly—workmen leaving with an air of reluctance, as though begrudging the need for sleep and food that kept them from their tasks. For the castle was being painstakingly and lovingly restored. Not to Carr's mad standard of extravagance, but to her former beauty and dignity.

"You're rebuilding her," Fia gasped beside him.

He nodded, his eyes filled with the spectacle below. "Aye," he said softly. "As she was meant to be . . . only better."

"But why?" she asked incredulously. "Wanton's Blush—"

"*Maiden's Blush*," he corrected. "She was Wanton's Blush when your father held her, but now I own her and Maiden's Blush she'll stay for the rest of her days or until the last McClairen dies." He glanced at her out of the corner of his eye, his odd mood both black and triumphant. "If a man like Carr cannot kill us, who else could?"

"But how have you accomplished this?" Fia asked, her awed gaze fixed on the sight below. The north wing was complete and work was being shifted to the short central portion. Thick wooden scaffolding enveloped what was left of the facade.

"Carr didn't want it after it burned," Thomas said. "I did, and he'd no objections to selling the island to me—or rather, to my agent."

Fia stared. Carr had never told her. He'd sold her home without a single word. She flinched involuntarily, amazed there was anything left in her that Carr's heartlessness could hurt.

It was better this way. Thomas was achieving what she'd always dreamed of doing, making Maiden's Blush whole, healing her, ripping off her garish trappings, and revealing her proud and ancient lines. It *was* for the best. But, oh! How she would have loved to see the completion of the dream!

A gentle fingertip tilted her chin. Thomas had moved his horse closer.

"Tears?"

"No."

"Then the sun's reflection on the sea must hurt your eyes," he said, offering her an explanation, chivalrously respecting her private sorrow.

"Yes," she agreed.

He smiled, his eyes filled with tenderness, and rubbed his thumb across her lips. Instinctively she clasped his hand. A quizzical expression entered his face. She hesitated, then turned his hand over and brushed her lips across his knuckles.

His grip clenched painfully about her hand. If she saw the least bit of pity in him she would lose nerve. So she closed her eyes, coward that she was, and brought the back of his hand to her cheek and laid it there.

He made a sound. A curse? A prayer? She could not tell. Then suddenly there was motion all around her as the hot withers of Thomas's horse bumped her leg and hooves danced on the ground. Her horse shied sideways. Thomas yanked his hand free of hers and dragged her into his embrace.

Her eyes flew open. He dipped and caught her legs behind the knees with one arm, lifting her across his lap, while with the other hand he grasped a great hank of her hair and gently pulled her head back.

For one brief second their eyes met, and then he was kissing her, kissing her like he would never stop. Deep kisses; gentle kisses; wet, passionate, open-mouthed kisses such as she had never known. His hunger ignited a matching one in her. She laced her fingers behind his head, wanting his dizzying, thought-obscuring kisses never to end.

They did, of course. He finally drew back, and lifted his face to the sky. So she sought other venues to explore. She kissed the strong, dark column of his throat. Salty. Unique. He shivered.

She licked his throat. The shiver became a shudder, but he still did not lower his head.

She was a seasoned seductress, a heartless, irresistible jade. Men everywhere, including this one, proclaimed it. Then why could she not seduce Thomas McClairen into giving her more kisses!

"Thomas," she began.

He looked down at her, stilling whatever she might have said. His eyes blazed with desire, unadulterated, barely controlled. A ripple of apprehension raced through her.

"Is this some new form of witchery?" he demanded hoarsely. "A torment dreamed up in that complicated little mind of yours? Because it is unnecessary. There is nothing you can do to make me want you more and to make that wanting more unbearable."

"But you are bigger, far stronger than I."

He gazed at her ruefully. "I am weaker than a day-old kitten where you are concerned, madam. I am undone by you. I could no more force myself on you than I could fly."

"Even if I tempted you, teased you, brought you within an inch of what you want?" She did not know what evil impulse drove her.

He shook his head. "Would you have blood, Fia? Blood I would gladly give, if you would but cease these games and leave me in peace."

"I cannot."

"Then we are transfixed here, for I cannot leave you." His smile was infinitely sad.

Her heart pounded. She stood poised on the precipice.

"What do you want?" she asked softly.

He answered at once. "I want you to bid me to stay," he commanded. "But bid me stay knowing that I will have you beneath me on your back."

He said not a word about affection, but she was a woman, not a maiden. Her marriage bed had had no affection in it. She knew now its presence because she'd known well its absence. He needn't say the words for them to be true.

"Please," she managed to say, "stay."

Triumph blazed in his expression and his lips parted on an exultant smile. He swung his leg over the saddle and slid to the ground without releasing her.

He carried her back above the crest of the knoll, striding to where the grasses grew sweet and lush and thick to the edge of the pine copse. Only then did he release her, as he worked at divesting her of her skirts while her own hands hastily unlaced her bodice, as though they expected some clock to suddenly strike the hour and break this spell of enchantment.

Her skirts fell; her bodice was withdrawn; her shoes slipped from her feet. Thomas stepped back.

Uncertainly, Fia's gaze followed him as she became self-conscious and awkward. Why was he looking at her like that? She was supposed to be the bloody enigmatic one, not him!

"Are we going to . . . lie together now?" she asked, startling Thomas.

Her words were prim, uncertain, as if she didn't have a name for what she wanted of him. Her straight shoulders were drawn back, her chin tilted in that heartbreakingly valiant manner. But she didn't know what to do with her hands or arms. They hung stiffly at her sides, her palms turned out in an attitude of unconscious supplication. And her eyes were huge pools of fevered impatience and . . . trepidation.

A slow dawning suspicion took hold of his imagination. Could it be? "Fia," he said, "how many lovers have you had?"

She was lovely, so vulnerable. She shivered, standing there in her undress, the tip of one breast peeking through the lace trim of her chemise.

"Fia?"

She took a deep breath; the nipple quivered deliciously.

"I've had one husband," she declared. "I've never known a lover."

The gift of what she offered staggered him. "Let me be your lover, Fia."

"I would," she said faintly, "but I doubt I can walk."

He laughed at this frank confession, delighted with her honesty. In a trice, he swept her up in his arms—all softness and silkiness, lithe and elegant and tense. He nuzzled her throat, nipped at her collarbone, and licked the soft indentation at the base of her throat.

Then he dropped easily to his knees, sliding his arms from under her and shedding his jacket so that she might lie back upon it.

"God, I love your hair," he muttered, lifting a handful of the silken mass and letting it filter down over his forearm. He wanted this to be slow. He wanted to play with her, touch her, and have her touch him.

"What's wrong?" she asked, feeling his body tremble.

"Nothing," he assured her, whatever eloquence he could claim dammed up by desire. "I want you. I want you and it's hard not to just . . . take you."

His coarseness sent a wave of color up her throat and face. He bracketed her face between his forearms and leaned over her, conscious of how small she was beneath him, how delicate.

"I won't."

"But I want you to."

The admission was less timid now; she'd begun to believe in the depth of his want. God knows, she should, he thought humorlessly. His cock prodded her hip with something less than subtlety.

He rucked up her petticoats, finding her legs still sheathed in their expensive clocked silk stockings. He sat up, took hold of her ankles, and pulled her toward him until her legs lay across his lap. Her eyes grew round with wonder.

He grinned wickedly at her. "You've lovely legs, Lady Fia. As pretty a pair as I've seen grace a filly."

Her pupils sparkled. Her lips parted on an "Oh!" of delight. How Fia loved to be teased!

"Seems a shame to cover them," he said. "Why would a soul do that, do you suppose?"

"Perhaps there are warts beneath those stockings, sir," she said a bit breathlessly, lying back down, her legs sprawled across Thomas's lap.

"I think yer lying, Lady Fia," Thomas intoned, his burr a whiskey-rich brew, sensual and intoxicating. "I think yer legs are as flawless as the rest of you, and I mean to find out."

Still holding her gaze, he grasped her knee in one hand while with the other he slowly untied the berib-boned garter. His fingers skated behind her knee to the sensitive skin there. She started at the feel. Thomas's wolfish grin grew hotter.

Slowly, incrementally, he rolled the silk stocking down, his finger sliding in a long, leisurely journey down her calf. His eyes glowed. A little muscle jumped at the corner of his wicked, "eat-you-up" grin.

"What penalty do you suppose I should extract if this leg is as fine as the rest of you?" he asked.

She couldn't answer. Her voice wouldn't work. Her breath jumped in her throat. She raised herself to her elbows to see his dark, strong fingers on her thighs. The sight was indescribably erotic, and awareness pulsed in the tips of her breasts and between her legs.

"Well?" His eyes looked darker. "It's perfect."

"Must be on the other leg."

His smile bespoke his disbelief, but he grasped her other leg and with a flick of his fingers undid the garter. His palm stroked the back of her calf, moving slowly up past the back of her knee. Climbed higher. And higher. Her eyelids slid half closed. She shivered. Higher his hand traveled, skating to the very top of her thighs. Her head lolled between her shoulders. There was more. She could sense it, just . . . Ah, yes! He cupped her bottom.

She panted a little, closing her eyes to better concentrate on his touch, the heat of his hand, the roughness of his callused fingertips, the breadth of his palm.

"Lie back."

His voice was very near. He'd looped one long, muscular arm behind her back, easing her down. "Lie back, Fia love."

Fia love. How many maidens had tumbled back, legs sprawled wide, at the sound of similar words? Nonetheless, she heeded the sweet, hushed urgency of his voice. She was weak and drifting, hot and tense all at once. *Lie back, Fia love.*

His hand curved around her bottom, his fingers limning the cleft and moving lower, easing between her lax thighs and grazing the small triangle of black between her legs. She jerked, startled by the electric sensation accompanying that seemingly casual contact.

He brushed her mons again, this time lingering in the task, tracing little swirling patterns with his index finger, first on her pelvic bone, then lower, then lower still, until his fingertip caressed the most sensitive part of her, gliding smoothly, shatteringly over the small nub.

Dear Lord! She clasped his shoulders, needing

some anchor to keep her from being swept away by a tidal wave of sensation. He held her with his free hand while working his sensual magic with the other, whispering unintelligibly, sounds both yearning and encouraging.

"Yes. Yes," she answered, agreement, consent, and encouragement all expressed in that breathless, urgent word. "Yes."

Her hips rose, intuitively seeking him. One knee fell to the side, opening her completely to his ministrations.

"Easy, Fia."

His finger entered her.

She arched upright like a taut bow, her fingers digging into him. She'd not known. She'd heard but never realized, counted herself lucky to be amongst those women who were not at the mercy of sexual appetite. *Fool!*

His finger worked deeper. Her head spun, the earth whirled, and her eyes opened, seeking him, finding his gray-blue gaze riveted on her face, a sheen of moisture making his skin gleam like oiled bronze.

She understood. He wanted her. Wanted more of her than this. She did, too. She wanted the thick presence of him deep within her.

"Please," she whispered.

"What?" he asked, his voice rough, his gaze searching. "What do you want? Tell me."

"I want you in me."

He rolled away from her, his hands already at the closings on his breeches. She grasped his heavy wrist, stopping him. "I want you inside me and I want . . . I want you to be naked."

She waited, her breath staggering in her throat at her boldness. Would he think her cheap, sluttish—

In one swift graceful movement, he rose to his feet, stripping off his linen shirt as he went. He flung it carelessly aside, standing on the heel of his boot, jerking it off, and kicking it aside. He did the same to the other, and then straightened, fumbling with the closures on his breeches.

He was so male. His chest was broad and deep, covered with fine, dark hair that tapered where it grew lower on his belly. His arms were long and lean with sharply defined musculature, the skin smooth and clear.

He turned slightly, peeling off his breeches. His buttocks were as hard and well defined as the rest of him, his hips narrow, his legs long. Her gaze moved up to his face.

He was watching her with fascinating intensity, like he would devour her, or envelop her, but somehow consume her. He stepped out of the breeches and pushed his smallclothes off his narrow hips.

Her gaze traveled down a flat belly rippling with muscle to where his member sprang thick and swollen, angling proudly erect. He was big there, too. Thick.

A flutter of trepidation warred with mounting urgency. His gaze followed her own. A half smile lifted the corner of his mouth, revealing that unexpected and spellbinding dimple. A cocky thing, that smile, a hint of purring masculine self-assurance in it.

"I'll not hurt you."

"I know." And she did. He would *not* hurt her, unless he left her like this, on the brink of some arcane feminine experience she'd never before suspected and now needed above all things to know.

He knelt next to her and gently pulled the lace edges of her chemise apart. He sat back on his haunches, his eyes glowing.

"Beautiful."

She'd never understood the masculine preoccupation with breasts, but now she was glad of it. Glad he approved of her own so openly, so heartily. He made her feel utterly feminine, oddly vulnerable, yet completely powerful.

She'd known she was beautiful but she had never *felt* beautiful, not until Thomas McClairen had called her such.

He bent his head and placed his lips on her nipple. He kissed it, wet it with the tip of his tongue, sipped it into the warm interior of his mouth and . . . and did *things*. Marvelous things. Unspeakably stimulating things; rolling it between his lips, lathing its silky smooth perimeter until it glistened, nuzzling the deep curve of her nether breast and nipping it, and then going on to give her other breast similar attention.

She purred with the pleasure of it, grasping handfuls of his silky hair and holding his dark head to her. He pulled her nipple deep into his mouth, sucking hard and rhythmically.

Her heels dug into the ground as she lifted her hips, demanding, begging, seeking what she wanted.

Him.

In her.

His hand slid down her ribs and clasped her hip. Gently, he pushed her against the ground and rolled one heavy leg across her. She felt it between them, his cock, warm and incredibly hard, like chamois-sheathed steel, tantalizing in its proximity to her mons.

He kissed her mouth, burnishing her lips with his own as he'd done before, coaxing them apart. She knew now what he wanted. At once she opened her mouth, raking her fingers through the rich, thick waves of his hair before sending her hands flowing down his back, savoring the jump and bunch of his muscles beneath her palms, the smooth-hard texture of his skin. And all the while he kept giving her those deep, plundering kisses.

He shifted his hips, moving fully on top of her. His weight felt good. His body dense and masterful, her own lush and accommodating. His hand drifted down her side and then between them. He grasped his hard shaft and slowly, teasingly moved the swollen head between her sleek folds, over that little amazing bump. She cried out, and he drank the sound, moving closer, deeper, until . . .

"Fia," he muttered, and with a deep, controlled thrust pushed himself inside of her. She bucked. His body trembled, and he released her mouth, dragging his lips across her cheek and resting his forehead on the ground next to her.

"I am striving for some portion of control here, Fia," he whispered thickly. "I beg you to help me. Don't move."

Her eyes flew wide at his words, at his presence in her, at the feel of him lying on her. *Not move?*

Impossible!

She wriggled. His shaft jerked in response, drawing a gasp from her. *Aye! More of this. More.*

He pulled himself out and then slowly pushed back in. She followed his withdrawal, wanting more.

"Nay," he whispered harshly. "Wait." He withdrew on a long, slow hiss of pleasure. "Meet me now. Come to me, love."

He thrust as she raised her hips. A cry of discovery broke from her throat.

"Again."

And again. Each thrust and counterthrust taught her the rhythm of this ancient dance. Each fiber of her body sang with discovery, with involvement. His thrusts grew deeper, more powerful, and more elemental.

"Yes," she sobbed. "Please." For there was more. Just beyond this point, beckoning, urging, promising. There was more.

He grasped her leg, hooking her knee above his hip, increasing the depth and tempo of his possession. His jaw tensed, the hard muscles of his chest bulged, corded over with veins. His skin grew flushed with exertion.

Her eyes closed. Sparks careened against the velvety

blackness; the sensations spiraled around her, in her, taking her, owning her. . . . A pleasure so intense it felt like pain thrummed through her. He whispered, his rock-hard body straining above her and in her.

With her.

She lost herself, instinct overriding the dense armor of her self-protection. "Please, Thomas! Please!"

His arms surrounded her, lifted her. His mouth fell on the side of her neck, sucking gently in counterpoint to his hard thrust. "Let go, Fia," he murmured. "Let go."

Warmth flooded her. Electric waves of sensation coiled tighter and tighter, until all that was left was an urgent essence of need.

"Make it yours. Take it now."

With his words, desire exploded into fireworks of pleasure, rolling through her body like thunder, expanding as it went. Wave upon wave rippled outward, coursing, streaming molten satisfaction, emptying even as it filled.

"Thomas," she gasped in amazement. "Thomas!"

He did not answer, could not answer. Her body molded beneath his, accepting and giving back in kind his rising passion. He rode the thick, bucking waves of it, blocking out everything except the two of them, the cries she no longer tried to control, the beauty of her climax.

Then her thighs tensed, her fingers dug into his biceps, and another cry broke from her, one of pure repleteness, as deep within he felt her tighten around his cock.

His own crisis was upon him then. He planted his hands on either side of her and rose, leveraging his hips hard against her, driving himself fully into her, and shouted his release to the sky.

picture, as clear without thought for it as for a face in his open eyes.

The night came too upon him then—as it appeared in bits of time. And later, when they'd finished the wine and shared the...

Chapter 20

*F*ia touched Thomas's face, her fingertips a sigh across his mouth. Her eyes were lucent but sad, like moonlight.

"I never knew it could be like that," she said.

He turned his head, pressing a kiss to her palm, and read in her soft smile her regret and her withdrawal. He knew what she would say before he heard her words, and yet when she said them each one drove like a spike through his heart.

"It can't happen again."

"No?"

"It would . . . it would only end up hurting more when it was over."

A small part of him wanted to deny it, to ask why it needed to end. Why something that had felt so right, so perfect, must be "over"?

But honesty kept him silent. She was right. She saw his acquiescence in his face, and before he could read her thoughts, she dipped her head and turned her back as she began lacing up her chemise. Her neck looked vulnerable.

If this had been a fairy-tale romance, they would have fallen asleep in each other's arms and woken to a flight of swans casting shadows over their faces. They would have turned to each other and whispered sweet pledges and vows, risen from their pine bed, and ridden off into the setting sun.

But this was not a fairy-tale romance.

He looked away, reminding himself with bitter force that they did not exist separate from their pasts, their lives, their futures. What they did mattered to others as well as to themselves. He'd only to turn his gaze eastward, toward McClairen's Isle and all the people he'd brought here, to understand just how little time he could waste on his own pain, no matter that the wound felt mortal.

Even if things were different . . . He was still an outlaw in this land. Soon he would need to flee England, most probably forever if he valued his neck. Which he did.

And Fia? Fia was still Carr's daughter, and a week of gentle concourse and a few hours of passion did not change who she was. He knew Fia well enough to entrust his life to her, but he did not know her well enough to entrust others' lives to her. But that didn't stem the longing he felt for her.

If they were to make love again—for surely there

was more of love than rutting in what they had done together—it would only turn "longing" into "yearning." Perhaps a lifetime's worth.

Damn, he thought. For a man who'd only sought to erase all things Merrick from his life, he'd made a bloody mess of it.

He pulled his boots on and stood up, wanting to touch her but afraid, because it would only stoke the attraction that simmered so close to the surface. " 'Tis too soon dark to return to the manor, and the path is too faint to follow. We'll have to stay at Maiden's Blush this night."

She turned, her smooth countenance at variance with her all-too-readable eyes.

"Don't worry," he said. "I'll not press myself on you. There are rooms already finished within the castle walls, some with rudimentary furnishings. You'll stay in one and I'll stay elsewhere." Under the stars, he thought, though he did not tell her. He dare not consider being so near what he wanted so badly. He was only a man, after all.

She nodded and waited while he found their mounts and returned with them. With commendable restraint, he lifted her into the saddle and swung atop his own horse.

The path led to the thin, flinty land-bridge connecting the headland to the island. They crossed just as twilight's shadows dissolved into night's dark mantle. Overhead, nighthawks spiraled and wheeled in the indigo sky, as below, insects chirruped from the grasses. Torchlight flickered across the newly reconstructed terrace, where a few masons still chipped away at blocks of stone.

Fia recognized one of them as the giant, Jamie, who'd greeted them on the beach. He lifted his massive head at the sound of their approach and, recognizing Thomas, came to greet them.

"Sooo." Jamie released the word slowly, his bright gaze flickering knowingly between Thomas and Fia. " 'Bout time."

"Shut up, Jamie," Thomas said with more ire than the giant's friendly if suggestive words warranted. "Have one of the men take the horses. Lady MacFarlane will be staying the night."

The big man opened his mouth but one look at Thomas's hard face made him rethink the wisdom of whatever he'd been about to utter. He called out over his shoulder for one of his men.

Thomas dismounted, and without waiting for Fia's consent, clasped her waist, lifting her to the ground. He dropped his hands and stood back, all of this accomplished without a glance at her.

Pain lodged in Fia's heart, but no bitterness, no regret. It was not distaste that kept Thomas's gaze averted and his touch impersonal. On the contrary, it was desire, foolish, hopeless, hurtful desire. She knew because it filled her, too.

All the long ride down from the mountain, she'd watched his straight back, his broad shoulders, the way his hips moved with well-oiled ease to accommodate the movement of the horse beneath him. It had set pulses of desire shooting through her, the memories only moments old of his hips moving against her, his chest covering her, his arms wrapped around her.

She should count herself fortunate that he'd realized the folly of surrendering to desire as had she.

She'd never had a lover because she'd never *wanted* one. And now that she'd had one, she wanted more. She wanted Thomas. Not for just a few hours, but all the hours she could imagine. She wanted tomorrow and tomorrow and all the tomorrows after that. But wanting would gain her nothing. Except Thomas's death.

If Carr ever discovered what she'd done, he'd have Thomas arrested and hanged, and his head on Temple Bar within a fortnight. She could not live with that.

She should be grateful. Six years ago she'd given up all her fantasies about Thomas, and now, amazingly, she'd been allowed a taste of those dreams and they had been more wonderful than all her imaginings had conceived. She should be grateful, content with what she'd been allowed. But she was not, she wanted more, because she was greedy and selfish. Like Carr.

But unlike Carr, she needn't be ruled by her rapacity. She would not make Thomas pay the price of her greed.

She forced herself to look around at her surroundings, and as she did, wonder washed over her, releasing her from her painful conclusions.

She started forward, drawn by what she saw. It took her breath away. She tilted her head back, barely conscious that she was smiling in recognition of . . . Maiden's Blush.

" 'Tis said," she heard Thomas murmur behind her, "that Dougal McClairen first saw Lizabet McIntere at her father's keep when she was but thirteen years old. 'Twas the only time Dougal saw the girl, but 'twas enough.

"Dougal left McIntere's house, knowing the old brute planned to align his family with a wealthier one by marrying off Lizabet. That didn't matter to Dougal. He swore to have her. He came here to this island and he built this castle, knowing it would be impenetrable and impervious to siege.

"It took him four years, and when he was done he gathered together seventy well-armed Highlanders and went awooing. Luckily, Lizabet hadn't yet wed— though Dougal swore it wouldn't have mattered to him if she had—and after one look at Dougal's men, McIntere agreed to the marriage.

"Dougal brought Lizabet to this island, to his unnamed castle. . . ." Thomas's voice roughened and faded.

"And they stopped at the crest of that hill, near sunset," Fia continued in a hushed voice, for she knew the story well, had heard it from childhood, recited in Gunna's broad burr. Her gaze traveled with loving appreciation over the rough, silvery stone, the glinting, deeply recessed windows and high turreted towers. "And Dougal made a solemn oath. Once in his castle's walls Lizabet would remain forever innocent of any man's touch save his own.

"And Lizabet blushed, and the Highlanders that were with them, who heard the vow and saw the lady's cheeks, looked at the great gray fortress, and it seemed to them that in the setting sun it, too, blushed at its master's ardency. And so, forever thereafter, the castle has been called Maiden's Blush."

She turned and found Thomas's gaze upon her and she thought that no matter how ardently Dougal looked upon his bride, his expression could not have matched the intensity of Thomas McClairen's gray-blue gaze.

"Until Carr," Jamie said, breaking the odd, still moment. He stood a ways back, smiling bitterly.

Thomas looked away. "Aye," he said under his breath, "until Carr."

Her father had bought the castle by betraying the McClairens' Jacobite sympathies to the Crown, and then, to close the net, secretly testified against his own benefactor, Ian McClairen, and thus secured the execution of the castle's laird and rightful owner.

Having received the castle as payment for his treachery, Carr had gone about the business of prostituting the great gray dame. He'd tarted her up, adding bizarre excrescences to her silhouette and hiding her beneath a garish veneer.

But now . . . her stately towers no longer cringed beneath a tiara of unlikely gables and flying buttresses. Crenellation lined her summits like a simple circlet on an ancient ruler's brow. Gray stone melded with gray stone. All of it fit together; all of it was of a piece.

"It's magnificent, Thomas," Fia said quietly. "However have you managed? However could you afford it?"

"The privateering trade has been very good to me," he said with a tiny smile.

She turned. "But I thought that you owned a merchant shipping company."

He shrugged. "Sometimes one overlaps the other."

"I see." And she did. The dangers of sailing in pirate-infested seas were grave enough, but the dangers entailed in chasing down and engaging enemy ships would be immense. She disliked that he'd risked so much and, obviously, so often.

"I am very good at what I do, Fia," he said, his gray-blue eyes unwavering. "And 'tisn't only my efforts that finance what you see here. Jamie Craigg and a dozen others here have hazarded the sea-plying trade, too."

"I see. Yes." Heat pricked the back of her eyes. She looked away. She had no right to feel so angry with him, even less to feel frightened for him. A single instance of lovemaking invested her with no such privileges. He would see it as possessive, perhaps take a distaste of her.

She composed herself, looking up at the formidable building that had demanded so much of Thomas, her pleasure in it tempered by her knowledge. "How did you know what to do?" she asked, striving to keep her thoughts away from the dangers he'd faced and would face again.

"We rely much on the memories of those who lived in the castle before Carr," he answered.

"And are those many?"

"Nay. Too few, and their memories too weak," Jamie

said, deep furrows in his broad, ruddy brow. "I meant to talk to you on this very matter, Tommy." He gnawed his lip. "We've run into a wee spot of difficulty."

"Aye?" Thomas said, his attention finally arrested.

"There's no one here can recall the private rooms of the central hall," Jamie said. "We have the north and south wings to rights because there are those here who lived in suites in those parts of the castle. But while they took meals in the main hall, they rarely went beyond it to the chambers behind."

" 'Sblood," Thomas cursed softly. "Surely we can make an educated guess?"

Jamie looked doubtful. "The foundations give scant clues as to the arrangement of those rooms."

"Mayhap I might be of some assistance," Fia said. She knew those rooms by heart, and not only the division of the rooms that Carr had imposed upon the castle, but the original layout as well.

Thomas turned to her, a warning expression on his face. She regarded him evenly. She would not betray her identity. She knew better than he the danger that being Carr's child could bring.

Jamie was watching her curiously.

"I was a guest at Wanton's Blush," she said simply. "Indeed, I spent an entire season here one year."

Jamie's speculative expression increased and too late Fia realized that six years ago, when the castle had burned, she had been a child—at least in most people's estimation. It would be unlikely for her to have been Carr's guest. Quickly she salvaged the situation.

"I should say my *father* was invited to visit here,"

she said. "As my mother died when I was small, I accompanied him. Lord Carr allowed me the use of his library. A vast one it was, too. There were folios there, sheaves and sheaves of watercolor pictures of the castle, done by a young McClairen lass. Many of them were interior studies of the central portion of the castle. I assumed from the number and detail of the pictures that the central portion of the castle is where my unknown artist lived."

"Is this true, lass?" Jamie breathed, staring at her as though she was manna sent from on high.

"Yes," she said.

"And you remember these pictures?"

"Very well. I copied them," she said, and at Jamie's incredulous look smiled. "There was not much else to do for a girl of my age."

"Ah!" Jamie breathed, and his big, blunt face split into a wide grin. He clapped Thomas on the shoulder. "So *this* is why you brought the girl here! I never thought you'd be one to mix pleasure and work, though I warrant after one look at this girl, I'd not have blamed you if you had."

"Shut up, Jamie," Thomas said once more, disapproval and anxiety mixing in his expression. Jamie took no umbrage at Thomas's tone. His problem had been solved, and expeditiously, too.

"Can you begin to draw some sketches for us tomorrow, Lady MacFarlane?"

"Of course. I'll work on them at the manor, too."

"*Manor?*" Jamie declared indignantly. "Now, there's a pretty waste of time. I'll tell you what, I'll have a room here at the castle all cozied up for ye before noon. No need to be exhausting yerself riding back and forth. And if ye're here ye can quicker tell us if we misstep, eh?" He turned to Thomas. " 'Tis best if the lass stays here, Thomas."

To be at Maiden's Blush with Thomas? To speak with him, to have only to look outside her door or a window and know there was the possibility she might see him? Like a siren song, the idea bewitched her. She could not turn her back on the possibility of owning a few more days of the fantasy.

She stepped up to Thomas, lifting her face to his dark, scowling one. "Aye, Thomas," she said. " 'Tis best if I stay."

A little flame flickered in the depths of his eyes. His hand moved a fraction of an inch toward her, and stilled.

"She can stay," he said.

Chapter 21

The traffic leading to London's dockyards was impassable. James Barton stuck his head out the carriage window and shouted up at the driver. "I'm getting out here and walking."

"Foine fer yer ta say, now as ye have me tangled in this broil and no fare fer me trouble. 'Tain't goin' to be easy work turnin' round," the driver said sourly, and spat.

James tossed him several coins and clambered down out of the carriage. It was only a few miles to where the *Sea Witch* was moored. He'd promised Thomas he would take the Cape route, and that he would, two days hence. In fact, today he was making a preliminary inspection of his ship preparatory to sailing.

Besides, 'twould help pass the time, especially since

he'd decided it wouldn't do for him to call on pretty Sarah Leighton three afternoons in a row. He'd been spending too much time in Miss Leighton's company since Fia had disappeared and Thomas had gone chasing off in a half-crippled vessel, to God knows where.

The day he'd taken Miss Leighton and Pip from St. James Park he'd been impressed by her gentility and concern for her brother. The next day he'd returned the shawl she'd left in his carriage, and she'd invited him in to thank him properly for his aid. From there one thing had led to another until he'd found himself in danger of monopolizing her time.

"Barton!"

James wheeled around, looking for the source of that imperious voice.

"Here, sir!" On the street where traffic had come to a standstill, a silver-topped walking stick emerged from the window of a black-lacquered carriage and struck the door. Within the interior James could just make out two figures, one cadaverously thin, the other wearing a puffed and piled wig atop a handsome countenance. Lord Carr.

"Don't stand there gawking, sir," the voice commanded. "Come here."

It had been exactly what he and Fia had wanted, for Carr to seek James out and demand to be made a part of his insurance swindle. James would agree only if Carr signed over Bramble House, which he, in turn, would deed to Fia. But now that the moment was here James felt a tingle of fear.

Of Carr. James Barton had always confronted danger

head on but he'd never before had the sensation of willingly putting himself in the presence of true evil. He did so now as he reluctantly unlatched the door.

"Get in. Get in, I say, Barton."

For Fia, James thought, and entered the carriage.

Inside, Carr sat across the narrow confines from Lord Tunbridge, long rumored to be Carr's familiar and his agent of ruination. Carr motioned for James to take the seat beside Tunbridge, and James did so. Tunbridge did not glance his way but sat as still as an automaton awaiting Carr's hand to wind it up.

Carr regarded James from behind hooded lids. His long, elegant fingers relaxed over the knob of the walking cane. "Been a long time, eh, Barton?"

"Indeed, sir," James replied.

Carr's mobile mouth curved. "Imagine you've been expectin' me, what with Fia's tiresome machinations and all."

James could not keep the surprise from registering on his face. Carr saw it and chuckled. "I fear Fia grew simpleminded while living on that Scottish farm. Of course I know what she's up to. She's my get, ain't she?"

James swallowed; the evil he knew resided in this man had revealed itself. It was in his voice, the viscous, near sexual exultance of his triumph.

Carr's smile abruptly dissolved. His gaze lifted past James's face to stare out the window. "That's right, Janet!" he said. "I knew as soon as Fia told me about Barton's affection for the country what she was after, just like I know what you want!"

Startled, James looked around. A crush of working-class people moved slowly along the sidewalk, past their vehicle. Within the churning crowd he thought he glimpsed a lady's fine skirts and a fashionable hat.

"What're you lookin' at, sir?" Carr demanded. "I'm speaking to you!"

Confounded anew, James turned back. Beside him Tunbridge remained fixed and unseeing, but his aquiline nostrils spread in a subtle expression of derision.

An evil glint had entered Carr's brilliant sapphire eyes. Was this some sort of game Carr played with him? James wondered in disgust.

He was a simple, forthright man, but in the few short moments James had spent in Carr's company, he realized the magnitude of Carr's madness and the lengths to which he would go to win. He should have realized it before. *They* should have realized it.

How could Fia and he ever hope to win against the likes of Carr? Had Carr not killed Fia's mother and the two other wives that followed? *And most probably others, as well.*

The thought made James tense. Carr saw his reaction, relished it.

"The reason I stopped you, sir," Carr said, "is this. I have a message for my darling Fia. Please convey to her that your little scheme has floundered rather badly, almost as badly as, say, the *Alba Star* will shortly."

James stared. "I don't take your meaning, sir."

Carr laughed with delight. "I can see that you don't! Let me apprise you, Barton, that you may re-count it to Fia. I should like to tell her myself but I am this moment embarking on a trip to the continent and thus must forgo that singular pleasure.

"To begin with"—he laced his hands atop the knob of his walking stick and leaned forward—"I like this little insurance hoax of yours and I commend you on its previous successes." Carr nodded pleasantly.

Good, thought James, Carr had bought in to the rumors Fia and he had so carefully spread. Perhaps there was a chance after all.

"But Fia should have realized I would never seek to become part of your little couplet."

James's hopes wavered.

"Any man I associate with in such a venture is a man I own." He settled back and sighed. "I don't own you, sir. Yet. It is a situation that I shall look into remedying."

Before James could reply, Carr waved his cane gently in the air. "I *do*, however, own your partner, Thomas . . . Donne, I believe he calls himself? And him I've made my partner."

The air in the small, shadowed carriage suddenly seemed dense. A cold finger touched the base of James's spine. His fear for Thomas increased even as his hopes for his and Fia's plans collapsed. Carr in league with Thomas? It made no sense! Why would Thomas not have told him? How did Carr *own* Thomas?

There was no possible way to salvage any of Fia's plan, but at least he could try to protect Thomas.

"What sort of blackmail have you on Thomas?" he demanded.

"You mean you don't know? *Tch-tch*. And here I'd been led to believe you were such good friends," Carr returned blandly.

"I don't care what Thomas did, or rather what you say he did!" James said angrily.

"Don't you?" Carr asked. "That's good, because if Thomas didn't see fit to tell you about his past, it certainly wouldn't be my place to do so, don't you think?"

"You miserable bastard," James ground out.

Carr's bright eyes went flat. "Careful," he warned.

There was nothing James could do. Even if he were to offer himself or his ship in Thomas's stead, it would do no good. Carr was not the sort of man to honor a pact.

"Do your damnedest, Carr," James said, his outrage thickening his voice. "You have pathetic horrors like this creature"—he jerked his head in Tunbridge's direction—"willing to do your bidding no matter how filthy the work is. Between the two of you, you *may* even be able to ruin my shipping business."

This time 'twas James who leaned forward, his blunt face bright with blood. "*Try*. I'm leaving in two days for the Cape. Even a creature like you might find it a challenge to work your evil that far afield. And I tell you this, when I leave I shall be glad not to have to share the same air with you!"

Without another utterance, James jerked down on the door handle and kicked the plush-lined door open. He jumped from the carriage to the ground, shoving his way angrily through the crowd.

Inside the carriage Tunbridge watched him go. "Shall I challenge him to a duel?"

"Duel?" Carr blinked. "No," he said after a moment's consideration. "No duel. I'll deal with him later. Right now I am more interested in what he said. It disturbs me."

"And what was that?" Tunbridge asked dutifully, though no interest colored his voice. Nothing much colored Tunbridge's voice anymore.

"Barton said he would be leaving for the Cape."

"Yes?"

"I could have sworn that was the route Thomas Donne was to have sailed. Which leaves me to wonder"—his gaze wandered toward the window—"just where and what he is up to.

"And did you note Barton's surprise when I told him to convey my message to Fia? I swear he has not the vaguest notion where she is, which seems rather odd for two people supposedly in league, does it not?"

"Not particularly," Tunbridge said after a moment. "You and I have been 'in league' for years—or so most people would assume. Yet I rarely know what you are doing or where or with whom. Perhaps the apple has not fallen so far from the tree," he suggested bitterly, "and she feels no need to confide in her toadies, either."

The idea found merit with Carr, for he pursed his lips thoughtfully. "You may be right. And I did tell her to be circumspect. But I dislike these little discrepancies." He rubbed the bridge of his nose. "Still, I have plans in France. A certain alliance to secure. I would dislike even more having to postpone that. So . . ."

"So I will stay here and try to determine if Fia and Donne are partnered?"

"Yes. Look for anything that suggests that Fia has plotted at a deeper level than I assumed, and I have been—" He could not finish his sentence, the word "duped" in association with himself was simply too onerous to consider. Of course Fia had not plotted with Donne from the beginning. The notion was preposterous.

"And if I *do* find evidence?" Tunbridge asked.

"Then you have my permission to make them suffer. Both of them."

A little flicker of interest arose in Tunbridge's sunken eyes. "Aye?"

"Suffer, but not *die*," Carr clarified. "Do nothing to drive Donne away. Should they have plotted against me, I want to be the one to inform the authorities that Thomas Donne is in reality Thomas McClairen, transported for crimes against the Crown. I want to be the one that sends him to the gallows." His smile was like a wound. "Indeed, I insist on it."

Tunbridge left Carr at the quay where the ship sailing for Le Havre was berthed. He did not bother bidding his master adieu and he received no further words of any kind from Carr, though occasionally Carr would lean forward, peer out the window, and address his dead wife.

The man was mad, Tunbridge allowed, calling for

the driver to take him to where the *Alba Star* had been berthed. But as was the way of madmen, Carr was also canny and unnaturally perceptive and certainly more dangerous, because these days he was influenced only by his own whims.

Tunbridge knew well how swift and irrevocable Carr's whimsy could be—he'd been the instrument of those whims on more than one occasion. Twice he'd been an instrument of death. He very well might be again.

He thought all this without any perceptible heightening of emotion, not dread or disgust or exultance or even fear. Most of his emotions had bled from him years ago. More than anything else these days, he felt odd that he didn't feel odd. He'd arrived at that place where a man is a curiosity to himself and only vaguely alarmed by the realization.

Once on the pier, Tunbridge spent a half hour questioning, threatening, and bribing until he'd secured the information that Thomas Donne had left port fifteen days ago and that a lady had been seen embarking a short time before the ship set sail. Whether or not that "lady" had disembarked, Tunbridge was unable to ascertain.

He returned to the waiting carriage and gave the driver instructions to Fia's town house. During the ride he tried with little success to keep his thoughts from Fia Merrick and her probable liaison with yet another man.

Once he'd loved Fia with all the passionate intensity he nowadays managed to invoke only on the killing fields. He'd wanted her above all things and had been young enough, or perhaps still human enough, to believe he could have her.

Not only Carr, but also the beautiful Fia herself had disabused him of that notion. Both had been cruel, but his interview with Fia had been by far the worse. She'd looked at him without a shred of interest, her bright blue eyes as reflective and blank as silvered glass. She'd not even offered him the slight salve of hostility. Only utter disinterest and a simple, irrevocable "no."

She hadn't bothered to explain, or blame, or revile his black nature or his infamy. She hadn't even bothered to laugh. Just "no." He'd been a thing to her.

He *was* a thing. Carr had made him such slowly, degree by degree, sucking him dry of his humanity. If only he'd had the balls to take his chances with the magistrates twenty years ago when he'd killed a tavern maid in a drunken fit. But he hadn't. He'd run away, certain his secret was safe. But—a grim smile twisted his lips—one was never safe from one's actions. Carr had been there that night. Oh, he'd not witnessed the murder himself, but he'd found a witness who'd signed a sworn statement attesting to his guilt. He had been under Carr's thumb ever since.

Tunbridge jerked his head up, his gaze locked unseeingly outside the carriage. *Oh, well.*

There was nothing he could do for it now and at least he could soothe himself with the notion that Fia was no less a "thing" than he. He'd seen her. He'd watched all these years since she'd refused him, and he knew that no man, particularly that Scots fool she'd

wed, had ever brought her a moment's honest joy. She
was as incapable of it as Carr. As Tunbridge himself.

And it made him glad.

He relaxed, pondering the bit of information Carr
had uncharacteristically let slip. So, Thomas Donne
was a McClairen. It surprised Tunbridge that Carr
should have held this piece of information so long without making use of it. *If* he hadn't made use of it.

The carriage drew to a halt, and with a start Tunbridge realized that an hour had passed since he'd left
the dockyards. The door swung open and the driver
pulled out the steps and stood back as Tunbridge
emerged.

He climbed the steps to the town house and rapped
on the lacquered front door. It opened upon the auto-
cratic countenance of a butler, who bowed and said,
"A good afternoon to you, sir, but I regret that my
mistress is not presently at home."

"Oh, that's quite all right," Tunbridge said, stepping inside. "For 'tis you I've come to see."

Tunbridge left the town house twenty minutes later,
having the information he'd sought. The stately butler
had taken quite a bit of persuading. It would take him
a long time to regain his self-esteem and forget that
ultimately his fear had outstripped his loyalties. It was
a lesson, Tunbridge knew, that could . . . damage a
man if repeated too often. Not that it was any of
Tunbridge's concern.

The butler had confirmed that Fia had left the
town house the same day that Thomas Donne, born
McClairen, had sailed. The suggestive indications

that Fia was bestowing on another man that which
Tunbridge had once so fervently sought sent an unac-
customed wave of vitriol coursing through his thin
body. His hatred piled atop his grievances, and under-
lying both yawned a chasm of unarticulated loss.

Oh, yes, Lord Carr, he thought grimly as he drove
away, *I will most certainly punish them both.*

Chapter 22

What I'd like ta know, and some of the other women, too"—Mrs. MacNab set the small kettle of braised mutton at her feet and planted her big, raw-boned hands on her wide hips—"is what yer doin' with yon young widow?" She jerked her head toward where Fia sat at a worktable near the castle walls, head bent in concentration over her most current sketch.

Thomas, in the act of reaching for their lunch, straightened. "What?"

"Tha young widow MacFarlane," Mrs. MacNab clucked impatiently. "Ye dinna take advantage of the lass whilst at the manor. I can swear ta tha' and I have, too, when the conversation warranted.

"And they say ye sleep out under the stars with the rest of the men come night," she went on, "though anyone with eyes in thar heads can see by the way ye look at her yer near to burnin' with want."

"That obvious, eh?" Thomas said, finding his voice.

"Aye," Mrs. MacNab returned dryly. "And anythin' tha' obvious cannot be kept long held in without somethin' bein' done about it; and tha's what I'd like to know, what ye mean to do about it."

Damn the woman. How was he supposed to answer that when he didn't know himself? From the look in Mrs. MacNab's eyes, she wouldn't leave until she had an answer, and he wanted her to leave so that he could take this kettle to Fia and she would stop working and devote all her attention to him.

How spoiled he'd become in eight short days. For if he denied himself the pleasure he'd found in Fia's arms, he certainly didn't deny himself the one he'd found in her company. 'Twas no wonder she'd charmed the McClairen ladies—and men. She worked diligently and uncomplainingly. She did not presume upon her relationship with him, but offered herself on her own merit. And whilst she clearly did not consider herself one of them, neither did she place herself above them.

"Well?" Mrs. MacNab demanded.

"Are you asking me what my intentions toward Lady MacFarlane are, Mrs. MacNab?"

"Aye. Because we"—she cast a quick look behind her, where five McClairen women stood in an anxious little band—"we've grown fond of the gel and we wouldna like ta think our laird would use her harshly or disrespectfully, fer all tha' she was once English."

Once English. That's how they thought of Fia, as one of their own who'd somehow been mistakenly born to an Englishman, like a changeling. And that she was, Thomas thought. How much so, they would never know.

What would happen if his clan knew the woman in their midst was the Earl of Carr's daughter? Mayhap they'd still be as smitten as he. On the other hand, they might well stone both of them. Though he was their chieftain by virtue of his bloodlines, in truth Thomas knew little of the people he'd worked so hard to unite.

His "leadership," if it could be called such, had been mostly in absentia. He presumed that their loyalty was not to him but to what he represented.

In the meantime, what could he say to Mrs. MacNab? "I promise you, Mrs. MacNab, that I will not use Lady MacFarlane harshly, nor will I disrespect her."

"But . . ."

She was not satisfied. Well, neither was he.

"You have my word, Mrs. MacNab," he said in a tone of voice that made his crew jump and his enemies quail.

"Yes, m'lord," she said, then bobbed a curtsy and scuttled back to her brood of ladies.

Thomas retrieved the kettle, banishing Mrs. MacNab and her concerns from his mind. The day was bonny and bright and Fia sat a few dozen yards away at the large battered table Jamie had set beneath the overarching branches of an alder, her brow furrowed in concentration. She didn't look up as he approached.

"What was this room used for?" Thomas asked, leaning over her shoulder and pointing. The scent of her freshly washed hair rose and inveigled his senses.

"This?" She didn't turn.

"Aye." He bent, cautious as a thief, and brushed his jaw lightly against the silky spiraling tendrils. Crisp. Cool. He wanted to wrap his hand in the luxuriance of it.

"There is where Carr fattened up the children for roasting."

So lost in his vivid imaginings was he that for a half moment Thomas didn't react. "What?"

She swiveled in her chair, her cheek in her palm, her elbow on the table, and regarded him with one arched brow. "The children. We fattened them up for roasting."

At the expression on his face she burst out laughing and his confusion instantly became desire. Lud, she was lovely when she laughed!

"At least that's what one of your men told me this morning. That Carr bought stolen children from the gypsies and fattened them up to serve to his evil friends."

"What did you say back?" he asked worriedly.

Her delight dimmed. "I didn't tell him a thing, of course. You may take as gospel that I feel no need, or the slightest inclination, to defend my father from any charges, no matter how horrifying or, in this case, ridiculous.

"And should you have any curiosity about that matter," she continued, "Wanton's Blush was ne'er a Medmenham Abbey—though I am certain it would have become one had my father's tastes leaned in that direction."

Her gaze never wavered, yet he sensed the deep hurt masked by her insouciance. He didn't know how to respond. His feelings for her were raw and complicated; the anger that flooded him each time he thought of Carr grew greater each day. As did his desire, to protect her, to be with her, to love her. Which he could not do.

"We're a sad lot, aren't we?" she said softly, seeming to divine his thoughts.

"Aye." He smiled ruefully. "Most pathetic."

She rose and stretched her arms as she looked about. The workmen were breaking off to take their midday meal. "Will you take me in?" she asked suddenly.

"Where?"

"The fattening-up room, of course," she said, a shadow of her former roguishness in her tone. "I'm a bit stiff. I could use a little walk. And I've yet to go into that part of the castle. Jamie says 'tisn't safe. So will you take me in?"

How could he refuse her when she smiled so winsomely?

"Your wish . . ." He bowed like a courtier and with a flourish ushered her ahead of him, trailing behind as she moved eagerly toward the castle entrance.

As they drew closer the scent of charred wood became stronger. He took her hand and helped her cross some of the rubble yet to be cleared from the doorway. He watched her, reading in her avid scrutiny amazement, sorrow, and interest.

Overhead, black timbers emerged like the stumps of rotting teeth from the half-tumbled ceiling. Daylight poured through the open roof. Whole sections of walls had crumbled in the heat, leaving standing only chimneys to mark the various apartments and suites they'd once served. The grand staircase curved twenty feet above them and then abruptly ended, suspended in mid-space.

"We think the fire began in one of the east-facing apartments," he said.

"No one lived in those rooms," she answered. "They were used for storage, and the blaze was set on purpose, which any number of men or women would have had cause and opportunity to do. I am glad they did, for if they hadn't, Carr would have held on to the castle until he'd squeezed the last drop of blood from her." When she turned, her eyes were shining with approval.

"You are doing a wonderful thing here, Thomas. I am awed. And"—her gaze fell—"I am so . . . I am pleased you have allowed me to be part of it. Thank you."

"Don't," he said, her humility distressing him. "You are doing us an invaluable service. 'Tis I who owe you my thanks." He gestured toward the outside. "We all do."

A faint pink colored her cheeks and she looked up at him from under her lashes. For a long moment they regarded each other, and Thomas was visited with a distinct sensation of time running out, of matters outside this island rushing headlong toward some culmination that would tear them forever apart.

How could he lose her? But how could he keep her?

There was too much history between them, other people's history, and for all that he'd spent so much time with her these last weeks, there was still so much he did not know. She was like the bud of some never-before-seen flower slowly, petal by petal, unfolding.

He needed to be careful, he adjured himself, not for his own sake but for the sake of the others who'd returned here . . . many illegally. So much, so many, depended on him.

Unless . . . What if he was to leave Scotland? If Fia was to come with him?

"I won't be staying in Scotland much longer," he said.

She nodded, unsurprised. "How much longer?"

"I don't know. There are people who will send word as soon as I am in danger, as soon as Carr reveals my identity to the Crown. I can't imagine he will be duped by my absence much longer," he said.

She frowned. "Why would Carr choose now of all times to expose you?"

There was no reason not to tell her now. She'd learn soon enough. "Your father came to me several weeks ago, just before I abducted you," he said, watching her carefully. "He had a proposition." He smiled bitterly. "Or rather, he had a threat. He wanted me to purchase some merchandise for him, a great deal of expensive merchandise, which he would then insure and hire me to ship to"—he lifted his hand and let drop—"nowhere."

"Oh, no," she whispered in a stricken voice. "Oh, please. Tell me he didn't come to you to— Dear God."

"I see you understand," he said curtly. He'd known she was involved, but this incontrovertible proof that she'd connived at James's corruption still cut. Even hearing her all but admit it, he still couldn't quite believe she was capable of such a thing. She would have pressured James into such a scheme only if she'd been desperate. "Carr wanted me to take James's place in an insurance fraud. If I refused he threatened to inform the necessary authorities of my identity."

She covered her eyes with her hand. Her fingers trembled. Abruptly he became conscious that she was hearing the ruination of her plans.

"I couldn't let James take such a risk," he said. "There is no blemish against his name, as there is against mine. So I agreed to Carr's demands. I never intended to carry through the plan, though. I just wanted to buy time until James was well away from the country."

"And away from me," she said.

"And you," he agreed.

She took a deep, shuddering breath. A tear fell from the corner of one eye. One tear for all her plans and hopes. And that was all. Gently, he brushed it away.

"James was never going to scuttle the ship, you know," she said.

Relief swept through him. "No?"

"We wanted Carr to think he would, so we spread rumors. Rumors Carr could neither prove nor disprove. Because by the time the company supposedly involved issued a repudiation, Carr would have had to either take the bait or let pass potentially huge profits."

"You and James put forth those rumors?"

"Yes," she answered. "But in truth James was going to purchase and then deliver Carr's merchandise according to their contract."

In exchange for what? Bramble House. Kay's inheritance. The relief he'd so shortly felt slipped away.

He did not blame her for having wanted Bramble House. It represented to her home, security, and freedom from Carr. But part of him regretted her willingness to take her stepson's home from him—even though he did not doubt for a moment that she would do well by the lad.

"Carr couldn't very well go to the authorities and complain that his merchandise *had* arrived, could he? And he had no other leverage over James." She raked her hair back from her temples, her mouth set in an angry line. "I should have known Carr would never deal with a man he could not blackmail. But I was sure he would consider it only a matter of time before he *did* have something on James."

"He might have agreed to your plan, if he hadn't had a far easier victim to blackmail in me," Thomas said.

She shook her head. "I didn't know. I thought it might work. I'd hoped so. . . ."

"Fia . . ."

She gave him a tremulous smile. "It's all over, then. There's nothing more to do."

She wouldn't need Bramble House if she came with him. The thought slipped beneath his guard, taunting him with potential.

"But Thomas," she said, a new worry causing her brow to furrow, "it's all over for you, too. Because you are correct, Carr will come after you as soon as he discovers he's been deceived.

"I am so sorry, Thomas. Sorry for your involvement. Sorry we did not know . . ." Whatever she'd been about to say, she thought better of and instead looked around her. "Oh, Thomas. However can you leave the castle unfinished?" she asked.

"I'll find a way back home now and again," he said, aware that in this they were kindred, in losing what they wanted and finding they would still make do. "The coast is filled with secret harbors and Scotsmen with no particular liking of the excise men."

She nodded sadly and began moving slowly from the rubble-strewn corridor into the renovated portion of the castle, peeking in here, pausing to study something there. He followed, content to watch her explore, note, and approve the various changes he'd had made to the original plan. After a while they found themselves in the new north end, where their footsteps echoed on the newly polished flagstones.

She entered what had once been a receiving room but now was used as a dining hall of sorts. A long battered trestle stood against a bank of tall windows overlooking the sea.

Fia moved to a window and pressed her palm against the glass. The sun shimmered around her, bathing her in warm honeyed light. "It's marvelous, isn't it?"

"I am glad you approve."

She smiled. He looked out at the sea. The sun had dropped past its zenith. He should get back to Jamie and the others. There was so much more he wanted to complete before he left. There was so much undone. He feared he did not have time to make a satisfactory end.

"We never ate," Fia said, following his gaze.

"No, we didn't." He forced himself to give up the absurd notion tantalizing him. How could he ask her to go with him? He had nothing. Everything he owned he'd invested in this place, in these people. She wanted autonomy and freedom, and all he could offer her was the life of a convicted traitor.

"We should be getting back."

"Yes." She moved within arm's reach, foolish wench. He could not resist touching her. What harm would it do? One brief caress. He brushed her delicate jaw-line with his fingertips, lifting her face into the sun. The light attached itself like gold leaf to the curve of her cheek, sparkled in her eyes, and glistened on her lips.

"We've been here so long I fear I've compromised your reputation." He smiled and let his hand drop.

"Yes." She ducked her head and began to turn, to leave him— He reached out and clasped her wrist, stopping her. For one heart-shattering moment she stood frozen in place, her gaze as naked and helpless as he knew his own to be.

And then she was in his arms, wrapping her own around his neck and pulling his head down to meet her lips. He swept her up against his chest, all the hunger and anguish and need erupting in a confla-gration that burned all conscious thought to cinders. His mouth swooped hungrily down on hers; he pulled her higher, tighter, as though seeking to draw her into him, to make her part of him so that she could never leave him, never go away. "Oh, Fia! Sweet Fia!" he muttered. "Kiss me. Dear Lord, kiss me."

She lifted her hands, holding his jaw between her palms, and pressed her open mouth to receive his tongue. She wanted him as much as he wanted her and he needed to feel himself buried deep within her.

He lifted her easily, his mouth still seeking hers in passionate, deep, wet kisses, and walked her forward, dangling in his arms, until he felt the table stop them. He clasped her to him with one arm as he swept his other arm across the table's surface. Bowls and platters and mugs flew off its surface, clattering to the floor. One hand cupping the back of her head, he rained kisses on her mouth, her eyes, her throat, and lay her down on the tabletop.

He began to rise, but she clutched handfuls of his shirt. "Don't. Don't leave me for an instant."

Her words shattered his self-restraint.

Pulling her slight body up against his chest, he planted one knee on the table, and scooted her to the center of the table and straddled her. He followed her, pinning her beneath his body.

She tore at his shirt, her movement impeded by his weight, so he rolled over, carrying her atop him, his hands bunching her skirts up around her waist. He cupped her bottom, sweet handfuls of luscious female flesh, and settled her against him, nudging his cock high against her. She gasped.

Silently, he cursed his clumsy eagerness. "I'm sorry." Her lips were bright and wet with his kisses, soft and pliant and— He pulled her down. "The hell I'm sorry."

She pushed him away, her hand flat on his chest. Her breath was ragged, her hair tumbling in glorious disarray. "No."

"No," he repeated numbly. His head fell against the table with a bang. His hands dropped to his side. "No." He closed his eyes, swearing violently in a soft, harsh underbreath, but he made no attempt to touch her.

Bemused, uncertain what had happened, why he'd suddenly stopped . . . *everything*, Fia waited for him to open his eyes. When he didn't she bent over him in concern. Her unbound hair brushed his face and throat and she reached down to flick it away. Her wrist was suddenly clamped in a viselike grip, startling her. His eyes were still closed tight, his features racked by some powerful experience.

"What?" she whispered, aroused and confused and a little afraid. "What is it?"

"If 'no' it's to be, then for the love of God, Fia, get off me!"

He didn't understand. She hadn't framed the words right. Desire had made her stupid. "No. I meant, 'No, let *me* kiss *you*.' "

The violence vanished from his visage. A smile began at the corners of his mouth. "Oh," he said faintly, and then, "By all means, milady, have at it."

Given permission, a thrill ran through her. She might do what she wanted, explore and touch and caress each magnificent inch of him. He'd said so. But she wanted most of all to see him.

She had never known sex could be something so powerful, so wondrous. For once, her upbringing stood her in good stead. For, never having heard allegations against the sexual act from other girls or a mother's strait-laced views on women who enjoyed the bed, and never knowing a woman who evinced the slightest shock at any sexual exploit, Fia came to the act free of either expectation or fear.

Thus she reveled in the sensations Thomas taught her. She was innocent and healthy and passionate in her abandonment in a way no other woman of her age and class could ever be, meeting his desire with a matching one, aggressively seeking her own fulfillment, and in doing so spurring Thomas's ardor to untold heights.

She grasped the loosened sides of his shirt and wrenched it open. His chest was broad, hard, and chiseled like Scottish rock. Her gaze roved hungrily over every inch of it. Big, masculine, and powerful, he lay beneath her, quiescent, at least for the moment, and except for the heavy, thick presence between her legs.

Tentatively she caressed the silky hair covering his chest. He made a sound deep in his throat. His lips parted in a grimace of carnal pleasure.

"You're beautiful, Thomas McClairen." He laughed until she stroked him again, lower down over the rippling contours of his belly, where the furring narrowed to a dark channel that disappeared beneath her skirts. Then he growled.

He grasped her hips and pulled her tighter to him so that his erection lay fully against her, separated only by the material of his trousers. He angled his hips upward, deepening the contact and bucking lightly.

Sparks of pleasure flickered around the periphery of her vision. Her head swam with the promise she now knew was there to be fulfilled. She braced herself as he pitched his hips again, feeling him moving along the cleft of her body.

She shifted with the next buck of his body, seating him deeper yet, dampening the soft wool of his trousers with moisture from her body, stroking him with her body, stroking herself with his. Beneath her palms, his skin was afire, his muscles bunched and shifted. She closed her eyes, arching her back, seeking more of the delicious, amazing sensation.

"If your plan is to kill me, yer on yer way to doin' a fair job of it, lady." The whiskey-smooth burr stroked her with heady empowerment. She looked down at him. His face was dusky, his chest moving in powerful rhythm to his ragged breath. But there was a glint in his eye, a shred of teasing that was not all in jest, and to this she answered.

"Oh, I don't want you dead, Thomas McClairen. I've other plans for you."

"Then by all that's sacred, lady, I pray ye deliver me quickly before I succumb from want."

"I'll deliver you," she promised, and fumbled with inelegant haste, loosening his trouser closings and slipping her hand beneath the material. Her hand closed about him. He was hot and smooth, downy skin slipping over a hard, thick shaft—

"Nay," he said, reading her slight hesitation and grasping her wrist. "Learn me. Touch me."

There was no lightness in him now, only a dark and heated want that hung heavy in the air, enveloping her with need. She moved her hand experimentally. His hips jerked, his teeth clenched, his eyes narrowed to pewter-colored slits. She pushed her hand down. The warm thin layer of heated flesh moved silkily over the hard rod it contained. She pulled—

He bolted upright, in one movement his forearm snaking beneath her bottom, while his other hand wrapped around the back of her neck and pulled her mouth to his. He kissed her, deeply and richly, as he tugged her knees wider. He shifted and lifted her. A small movement, a quick guiding touch, and he thrust deep inside of her.

She cried out, startled by the fullness in her. Immediately he stilled, his breath laboring. He rested his forehead against hers. His breath fanned her collarbone. "Are you all right?" he panted. "Is it too—"

"No! No. It's not . . . you feel . . . I can feel so much of you," she tried to explain.

"Too much?" he queried breathlessly and slowly began to withdraw.

"No! I would . . ." Her courage almost failed her. She fumbled for a way to make him understand. "I would like—"

"Thank God, lass," he interrupted her, his mouth once more on hers. He thrust upward, the hardness of him filling her, destroying thought, making her cry out. "Because I would 'like,' too."

She twined her arms around his heated torso and felt his sweat-slick muscles flex as he thrust again, vigorous and potent. Shudders surged through her, a wave of intense, driving need started at their jointure, spreading out, building with each thrust of hips, flowing molten and creamy and rich and . . . Oh!

"Now show me what it is you want, Fia," he rumbled into her ear, "and I'll do it or die trying."

So she did.

Chapter 23

A booming crash outside brought Thomas bolt upright from where he'd lain kissing Fia in a nest of skirt,
bodice, and petticoats. With a curse, Thomas uncoiled
from the bed of his and Fia's clothing they'd made on
the floor and strode to the window, throwing open the
casement.

"What the bloody hell is going on!"

"The scaffolding on the east facade fell!" a man
shouted up as he and another man ran toward the
front of the castle.

"Bloody hell." Thomas glanced out at the sky as he
swept up his trousers. They'd been in the castle three
hours? Impossible.

He turned to Fia. She'd sat up, a ruffled petticoat

covering her breasts, her lips swollen with his kisses, her hair mussed, her expression dazed.

"What's wrong?" she asked.

"The scaffolding collapsed."

"Was anyone hurt?" Her gaze sharpened with alarm.

"I don't know." He dragged on his trousers and then his boots. "I have to go and find out." He picked up his shirt and pulled it on, stuffing the ends into his breeches. "I'll be back as soon as I can." He bent, tipping her chin up, and only after his lips had met hers in a soft, lingering kiss did he realize how natural, how easily the idea of returning to her was.

Even though they'd spent an afternoon making passionate, intemperate love, devouring each moment with unparalleled rapacity, he wanted more. He shouldn't have taken her like this, here, but there had been no gainsaying the desire that drove him, or their hunger for each other's touch. Her desire for him still amazed him. Still, he wouldn't ask her to wait. There was no telling how long he'd be.

"I have to go," he said.

She smiled. "I'll wait for you."

The offer was a gift. Still, he shook his head regretfully. "I don't know what has happened or how severe the matter, or how long it will take to rectify."

"Aye." She wasn't piqued, as one would expect of a lover whose offer had been turned down; instead, her somber eyes held understanding and approval. "Aye."

He could find no words for what he wanted to say,

so he said nothing, leaving her and heading down the corridor. From there he ducked beneath an archway and emerged on the north end of the castle. Already a few men were returning, their looks of disgust and relief telling its own tale.

He caught the sleeve of a stonemason. "No one's been injured?"

"Nay," the man said. "Though Arthur and Niall have a few scrapes fer their troubles."

"What happened?"

"I'll tell ye what happened." Jamie Craigg came around the corner of the castle carrying a rolled sheaf of paper in his fist. "Arthur and young Niall decided to save a bit o' time and dinna lash the scaffolding proper to the castle wall, and whilst they were on it, it tipped over."

"Ah, I see." He began to move past Jamie, his first impulse being to return to Fia. But Jamie caught his arm in his great paw.

"Easy, Thomas, me lad. There's a few things need tending to before ye tend to yer lady." His smile was knowing and pointed, and Thomas flushed.

"If you're implying—"

"I'm implying tha' yer shirt is ripped down its front seam and half of it hangin' out of yer breeches and there's a mark on the base of yer throat that I've not worn since me weddin' night—and a bloody shame I count it, too."

Thomas scowled, stuffing his shirt into his trousers. "Mind yer tongue, Jamie."

"I mean to," Jamie said with a long, appraising look

at his laird. He began unrolling the long cylinder of papers in his hand. "But before you go back to . . . wherever it is yer goin', would ye have a look at some plans I've sketched from Lady Fia's drawings?"

Thomas froze. No one knew Fia's Christian name. 'Twas uncommon and too readily associated with her father. "What did you say?"

Jamie's glance shifted from side to side. No one else was near them; the men had all gone back to their work. "I only saw her a few times, Tommy, and that was years ago, but a man who's seen Fia Merrick does not forget her."

Thomas gripped the giant's huge forearm, turning him to face him proper. "Ye'll no harm her, Jamie. Ye'll not tell any of the others, either. And I warn ye, my life stands between her and any harm that might come to her."

Jamie's deep blue eyes met and held Thomas's paler blue ones. He gave a little snort of offense and jerked his arm to free himself from Thomas's hold. Thomas's grip did not break, and instead Jamie found himself jerked closer to his laird. "I mean it, Jamie."

"Aye, ye young hothead," Jamie snorted. "I see ye do, but you've no need to act the dragon to tha lassie's maid. I mean the gel no harm, and neither would these others if they knew who she was, which"—he took advantage of Thomas's amazement to snatch his arm free—"they don't and won't lest ye say different." He rubbed his arm with a slightly aggrieved air. "Though I think ye do them a disservice in keepin' it from them."

"I don't understand," Thomas said through stiff lips.

"Ach!" Jamie's disgust was patent. "We done much, we McClairens, before ye returned us here. Some of what we did, we did fer vengeance, and it brought us no joy. 'Struth, it nearly cost us our souls."

Seeing Thomas's confusion, he went on, his eyes sliding away from Thomas's. "Yer own sister, Favor, almost paid the dearest price of all, just so we could say as how we were avenged on the Earl of Carr. We made a plan, ye see, and had her raised in France, groomin' her fer that plan. We were goin' to marry her off to Carr, Tommy—"

At Thomas's violent start, Jamie grabbed his shoulders. "Please! Listen to me. We couldna tell ye, Tommy! We knew ye would never agree to it but we'd twisted it all up in our minds, what we wanted and what we needed and what we'd do to get it. We'd convinced ourselves that the price of one young girl's innocence was not too much to pay fer justice.

"Were it not fer Raine Merrick we would have done it, too, wed her to Carr and then murdered him so she would inherit his lands. But Raine stopped us in time and saved us from injuring ourselves in a way that all of Carr's plottin' and schemin' and treachery could never have achieved."

He bit his lip, his gaze moving away from Thomas's amazed one, shame coloring his ruddy face a darker hue. "I'm not proud of my part in it. I only thank God we never achieved what we set out to do." He nodded, his lower lip thrust out. "So, don't be surprised if ye don't meet the sort of reaction yer clearly expectin' if ye tell the rest about Lady Fia. We've no taste fer vengeance anymore and we've no time to waste chasin' after retribution." His gaze returned to Maiden's Blush. "We've a castle to build."

His gaze dropped to meet Thomas's. "And ye've yer own life to begin. Ye've spent all yer adulthood workin' fer this, fer us. Ye found us and ye brought us here, but now it's up to us.

"And while ye'll always be our laird, ye must let us atone in our own way fer what we nearly allowed ourselves to become, and we'll no challenge ye on what ye must do, either," he finished tellingly.

Thomas stared at him in stunned silence. He'd had no idea. Favor had never told him of this part of her and Raine's courtship.

Jamie rerolled his drawings. "I suspect we can look over these plans some other time, eh?" He thumped the roll against his leg, and with a last glance walked toward the front of the castle. At the corner he stopped. "She's the prettiest thing I've ever seen. But her character reminds me powerfully of her brother Raine. A good man, he is."

It was as close to a blessing as Jamie could give. Possibility broke and dawned within Thomas's imagination, shining, brilliant, and attainable.

Jamie was right. It was long past the time that he allowed Carr to have such power over him. Carr might chase him from Scotland and make him an exile from his home, but he didn't need to allow Carr to make him an exile from his heart. From Fia.

He would ask her if she would come with him when he left.

As his wife.

Fia stretched as indolently as a cream-fed kitten. Three times Thomas and she had luxuriated in the aftermath of their lovemaking and three times he'd catapulted her toward that summit of sexual desire. . . . Her face warmed with her thoughts.

She did not want someone coming in by chance and finding her on a pile of petticoats. For though society claimed her to be both a temptress and a strumpet, Fia was modest and, when circumstances allowed, nearly shy. So, she dressed quickly and then went to the table and sat down.

Soon, however, the images of what Thomas had done to her on that table chased her from there, and she wandered from the room and along the corridor, marveling at the beauty and serenity Thomas had wrested from the ruins. Drawn inexorably, she found herself back at the central part of the castle, facing the charred, stained remnants of all that was left of Carr's rule.

She swallowed, gooseflesh rising on her arms. The ornately carved leg of a table emerged from beneath a pile of plaster. Over there, shards of a Chinese vase were scattered like the missing puzzle pieces of a child's game. Two sides of an ornate gilt picture frame lay tilted against what was left of a wall.

She picked her way carefully amidst the debris. This would have been the hall leading off the great

entry and this—she stepped over a blackened beam—
would have been Carr's study. Nothing was left. The
great desk was gone and if the velvet-covered chairs
and rich tapestry were there at all, 'twere ashes.

Only the fireplace still stood, more or less. One side
had fallen and the back was missing. Its costly marble
mantelpiece lay cracked on the floor. She approached
it warily, as one would a dead snake.

Within that mantel, Carr had secreted his blackmail papers. She knelt down, brushing off the thick
layer of ash. The second . . . no, the third tile from the
right. She slipped her fingernails beneath the flat pane
and tried to lift it. It didn't budge.

She looked around and spied a thin piece of blackened picture wire. She picked it up and twisted the
end into a hook and wedged it firmly beneath the tile,
prying it open. She peered into the black hole and
reached inside. Her fingers closed on a thick-banded
stack of papers, thin slivers of dry material peeling beneath her nails. Carefully she lifted it.

It was a packet of letters and correspondence, the
outermost ones charred by the infernolike heat, but
those between still intact.

Carr's blackmail material.

She'd always assumed that he'd retrieved all of it
the night of the fire. Indeed, he'd told her he had,
even showing her some of them. Now she understood
why; she'd been set up as a witness to their existence.

But he hadn't retrieved all the material. Right after
the fire, when he'd been told that Wanton's Blush had

burned to the ground, he'd come here and seen the unrecognizable and still-smoldering pile that had been his home. He must have assumed nothing could survive the fire.

And it shouldn't have. What chance confluence of factors had allowed this little hidden niche to remain relatively unscathed?

Gingerly she unfolded the top letter. It was dated nearly twenty years earlier. Her eyes scanned the contents in amazement. She finished and with unseeing eyes refolded the paper and finally, ultimately, the worth of what she held came to her.

Power.

The power to control and compel and force others to her will. *Carr* to her will. Power she could broker for whatever she wanted: jewels, gowns, castles, and land. She shuddered with the potential she held in her hand. She could have anything she wanted. She could have . . .

Bramble House.

"Fia?" She heard Thomas's voice distantly, and turned like a sleepwalker toward the sound. He stood in the doorway, a shaft of light falling on his dark-auburn head, a quizzical expression on his handsome face.

"Do you know what these are?" she asked, holding out the letters.

"No." He shook his head. "What are they?"

"Letters. Records. Deeds. Promissory notes. Titles. Mortages. Depositions. The source of Carr's power, the basis on which he has built his world. The lifeblood"— her voice dropped—"of his victims."

He did not reply but she barely noticed, her mind was unraveling skein after skein of possibilities, what she could do, what would happen. With what she held she could be free of Carr, completely and absolutely and forever. Her eyes closed, she swayed, nearly swooning with the possibility, the always before inconceivable here, now, suddenly attainable.

Or . . . she could turn the papers over to Carr in exchange for the house and a small sum of money with which to flee. With Thomas. No one would know.

"Fia?"

What did it matter to those others who'd so long labored under Carr's yoke? It would make no difference to their lives whether she held the proof against them or Carr did. They wouldn't even have to know. Only Carr would know that if he tried to take Bramble House she would release the papers back to their original owners and his empire would crumble.

She would just send word to him, perhaps one of the less damning papers, and everything she wanted would be at her disposal. Everything.

The sense of power surged through her, black and thrilling. She would have her freedom and more.

And she would purchase it with others' enslavement.

She swallowed, her exaltation ebbing. Angrily, she told herself that those fools Carr held in subjugation had placed themselves in his power, that they deserved their fates. They were adulterers and gamblers, cheats and frauds and charlatans. They were desperate.

As was she.

"I could have Bramble House," she whispered. She sighed, releasing the tantalizing possibility that had danced before her like St. Elmo's fire, and just as St. Elmo's fire was not a fire at all, her possibility was no possibility. It was a chimera. A trick. She'd nearly been seduced by the same drives her father served. She opened her eyes.

Thomas had come farther into the room. "Don't, Fia." His voice was urgent and low, his expression guarded.

"Don't?" she repeated uncertainly.

"You don't need them, Fia. Destroy them."

"I can't!" she exclaimed. Nothing would change if she destroyed them. Carr would still be able to—

"Fia, I beg you. You don't need to use these things to gain you Bramble House. You can't be so desperate for it that you would take your father's place in subjugating these poor fools. It's vile to even consider it! And it's not necessary!"

She stared at him, saw his horror and felt its echo within herself. He was right to be horrified, she had been close to doing what her father had done. Never mind her motives.

"Don't. Please don't," she whispered.

"I'll give you Bramble House, Fia," he said.

"You will give me Bramble House," she repeated numbly. He came and took her hand. She hadn't the strength to resist. She felt as though every last bit of her vitality had drained away and that all that was left was a shell.

"Yes," he said, his eyes somber. "When your father came to me, he threatened to expose me unless I do what he demanded. He also told me about Bramble House and how he'd cheated MacFarlane of it and how you'd hoped to get it through James Barton. He laughed about it, Fia, and then he told me about Kay."

"Kay. Yes," she said tonelessly.

"I couldn't stand the thought of Carr stealing yet another boy's birthright, so I told him I would agree to his proposition only on the condition that he sign Bramble House over to me. He didn't want the house. It only meant something to him because you wanted it and Carr thought—he was certain—it would never come to your hands through me."

"You didn't tell me," she said. But of course he didn't. He didn't trust her. And with good cause.

"I wanted it to go to the boy. But if you will just burn those papers, I swear it is yours."

She pulled her hand from his. He let it go easily. So easily. She turned, seeking that flawless serene mask. Her eyes closed, she bit hard on her lip to keep from sobbing. Where was her bloody, bloody mask?

"We can't burn the papers," she finally managed to say. She'd dared to dream that it would end like some fairy tale, that she and her tall, dark captain would sail away and live happily forever after.

"Oh, Fia." Two such simple syllables invested with such disappointment. A death toll.

"I never wanted Bramble House for myself," she said. "It was always our intention to have James sign the house over to Kay."

"It was?"

"Yes," she said, turning back to him.

He regarded her closely, surprise and then hope and finally joy reflected in his expression. "Oh, Fia!" He started eagerly toward her.

She stepped back. "You can, of course, verify this with James Barton."

"James?" He stopped, puzzled. "I don't need—"

"I'd rather you would. I want you to know that I never began this for my own profit or comfort. That I would not submit James to something so dangerous lest I could think of no other way to obtain Bramble House for Kay."

"Of course not."

She could not contain a bitter smile in response.

He saw then, understood. "Fia, please, just because I did not guess what your plans were does not mean I do not . . ." He stared at her, feeling her withdrawal, and reacted with shaken alarm. "Please, Fia. I love you."

She flinched, but there was no return of warmth to her lovely, cool features.

The ground seemed to open beneath Thomas. A black abyss yawned at his feet and he was teetering, off balance with no handholds in sight. "Fia, please. You can't condemn me for misjudging you. You can't throw away what we have, what we are together, because I doubted your motives." Fear brought anger to his voice. "You said you wanted the house. You never implied you wanted it for anyone other than yourself. Don't condemn me for ignorance, Fia, I beg you!"

"I don't condemn you at all," she said, vanishing inside herself.

"The hell you don't! I am being tried and convicted for thinking what any man in my place would think. How could I not? *You are Carr's daughter*, for the love of God!"

Her eyelids fluttered, as if his words dealt a final, fatal blow to something essential inside of her, something fragile that she had thought to protect and discovered too late was still exposed. "You are right," she murmured. "How could you think otherwise?"

He grabbed her shoulders and there was no reluctance in his touch, only desperation. He would have told her again he loved her but she'd dismissed the same avowal moments before. He would not bleat piteously, begging for an emotion she might not own.

He shook her lightly but she'd left as surely as if she'd walked from the room. She was gone and he'd done this thing. "For what reason are you punishing me? What have I said, what have I done that is so unforgivable?"

Her sorrow matched his pain. She touched his cheek gently.

"I am not punishing you, I am saving us both a great deal more pain."

"What could be more painful than this?" he shouted.

"You've done nothing that is unforgivable. It is I who am unforgivable. Not because of anything I've done." Her smile was rueful. "At least not yet. But because of what I am. You yourself said it. I am Carr's daughter. How can you ever trust me?"

"Dear God, Fia!" Desperately he sought the right words. "I don't give a damn if you are Carr's daughter."

"But you do," she avowed with such conviction that her certainty shook him. "You always will. You might forget for a while, you might pretend I am someone else, but every time a doubt shadows your thoughts you will wonder."

"No." He shook his head. "No."

"Yes," she answered. "And you are right to say that, because I say it myself. I've wondered and waited since childhood for the taint of his blood to show up in me, for his black murderer's spirit to reveal itself in me. Because I *am* Carr's daughter, Thomas. I always will be, and you will never be able to forget it. Nor should you. I can't. I won't.

"Even here. Even this afternoon. You were right to wonder what I would do with those letters. My first thoughts were not to destroy them, as yours were, but to keep them, to use them to set myself free from him. So you see, I can't . . ." At last her voice broke, just a small crack immediately mastered. "I can't sentence you to a life of watching and waiting, too. Because I can tell you with absolute assuredness that I am *not* a good woman, Thomas.

"I hunted down an elderly widower and connived for him to marry me, all for his house and land and money, and when I found out he had children, heirs, I hated them for inconveniencing me with their existence."

"Fia, anyone in your—"

"No!" Her voice rose now. She shrugged her way out of his grip. "Not anyone else did! Only me! Carr's daughter."

He moved forward and she shrank back, trembling like a roe in a net, her eyes large and unseeing and blank as the sapphire gems they so resembled. "Please, take me back."

"To the manor? Yes," he agreed in relief. If he could just—

"No. Back to London."

"A few days—"

"Please. Now. Today. Please. I don't think I can stand to be here any longer."

"Give me two days," he pleaded.

She looked as though she would break apart if he touched her. She wrapped her arms around her torso, hugging herself tightly. "I am begging you, Thomas. Take me back to London. You promised when you took me from that house that you would return me unharmed."

Her words pierced him to the heart. "Fia . . ." He held out his hand. She ignored it.

"If you do not return me at once, you will have broken your promise to me." Her voice quavered. "And whatever we know of each other, Thomas, I know you to be a gentleman whose word is his bond."

He would break his word a thousand times over if he thought by keeping her with him he could take back the last quarter hour. But he could not hurt her by keeping her against her will.

He turned. The abyss he'd felt at his feet disappeared and in his mind's eye the landscape smoothed into one vast, unending nightscape desert, empty and silent and cold. He began walking.

"We'll leave come nightfall."

Chapter 24

 $\mathcal{A}$ sulphurous glow poured from the front door of the exclusive address and streamed over the wet cobbles where two men waited. A moment later a gentleman emerged and pattered down the stairs to the street.

"Tunbridge isn't in the club," Johnston announced on making Thomas Donne's side. "And I doubt he'll come later. It's almost three o'clock in the morning, Thomas."

Thomas nodded grimly and began walking. Both Johnston and Robbie hastened to match his stride. "This is madness," Robbie said. "He's gone to ground, I tell you. He hasn't been seen in public since just after you and . . . since your arrival two weeks ago!"

Thomas stopped. His face was dark at any rate, and

now, even more so, cloaked in shadows. Only his gaze appeared alive, a mercury-bright glimmer. Instinctively, Johnston backed away.

Thomas looked like some awful angel of doom. It seemed grim determination was all he needed to sustain his body.

He'd put that implacable resolve to one use: placing himself between society and its burgeoning condemnation of Lady Fia MacFarlane. A condemnation that Tunbridge had begun, along with a sustained and vicious rumor campaign.

"Tunbridge," Thomas said tightly, "is most certainly in town. He could not very well be spreading his vitriol from afar. Someone is shielding him and I will find out who, and then I will find him." The very softness of his voice caused his friends to shiver.

"But Thomas," Johnston reasoned, "even if you find Tunbridge and silent his cursed mouth forever, I fear we both know it is too late."

"No," Thomas snapped. "It is not. Especially if Fi— Lady Fia could be convinced to retract her preposterous statement that she willingly went away with me."

Johnston's gaze fell. "I've tried. She'll not see me. In truth, she will not see anyone. She has become a recluse, further confusing the matter and titillating the gossips. Society believes her story, you see, not yours."

Thomas let forth a stream of violent epithets, but Johnston went doggedly on. "It's just that, with her reputation," he said carefully, "what she claims seems so much more probable than your story, Thomas, that you kidnapped her against her will." His gaze darted to Robbie in appeal.

"You must allow, Thomas," Robbie said, "it makes no sense for a wronged woman to protect her kidnapper."

"I don't give a bloody damn what makes sense! That's what happened, and I'll challenge any man who says differently."

"We know," Robbie finally put in. "How many duels have you challenged others to since your return? Five? Six? And how many of those were you obliged to carry out? One. You are fortunate the fellow called it quits before either of you was seriously injured. For, just in case it escaped your notice, dueling is against the law!"

When this produced no reaction from Thomas, Robbie continued in frustration, "You're pushing your luck, Thomas. Soon someone with more skill than you will repeat what everyone is repeating anyway and you'll die for it and it will all be for naught because it will only add to the rumors surrounding her. *You're not helping her, Thomas.*"

At this Thomas swung around, his cloak fluttering as he strode away. With a quick look of helplessness at each other, Johnston and Robbie hurried after him, catching up as he crossed the street.

"Where are we going?" Johnston asked in bewilderment. He barely knew Thomas anymore, the man was so changed. His face was as still and hard as the bronze engravings of the martyred warrior in St. Peter's catacombs. His voice was harsh.

"Hyde Park. A Captain Pierpont is meeting me

there tomorrow at dusk and I've a whim to see it at dawn."

A premonition caused Johnston's spine to tingle. "Dear God, Thomas. Pierpont is a most skilled marksman."

"So am I."

Robbie shook his head. 'Twas suicide. But perhaps that is what Thomas want— No. He'd too much courage to seek his own death. "I will be your second, of course."

Once more Thomas stopped. This time the anger that filled his gaze lifted, and suddenly he looked spent beyond what he could pay. "I've never asked anything of you in this. I don't now. Go home, Robbie. Take Johnston here with you. I don't want—"

A hand gripped Thomas's shoulder and spun him around.

"Oh, Lord, no," Johnston murmured. Pip Leighton had backed several paces away from Thomas. He wore a sword at his side and his hand clenched the hilt as he glowered at Thomas.

" 'Sblood, boy!" Thomas thundered. "You'll get yourself killed that way."

In answer, Pip raised his hand and lashed it across Thomas's cheek. "That's for what you've done to her, you cur!"

The red welt on Thomas's face brightened, yet he regarded the boy stonily. "Go home, Pip."

The boy's lips curled back over his teeth, and with purposeful slowness he lifted his hand again and brought the back of it smashing into Thomas's other cheek. His head snapped back under the impact. Still he didn't move.

"Go home, Pip. I won't fight you, boy."

"Boy?" Pip shouted angrily, drawing his sword on a hiss of steel and holding its point a foot from Thomas's throat. "Boy, am I? Well I'd rather be a boy than the man who seduced and destroyed her!"

Thomas's eyes narrowed to silver gleams. When he spoke his voice was low and throbbing. "You cannot begin to loathe me as much as I loathe myself for my part in her distress."

The thin veneer of hatred crumbled, exposing the hurt and confusion beneath. " 'Distress' is too easy a word for what you've done to her!" Pip said, his voice cracking. "You should see her, and *then* you might feel some portion of what you've done!"

"You've seen her?" Thomas asked, suddenly eager.

The boy clenched his teeth on a renewed surge of hatred. "Aye! I have. And spoke to her, though I received little back. There's no life in her, in her eyes or her voice. There's nothing. She's empty. You've destroyed her." Thomas moved closer. The tip of Pip's sword brushed his chest. "And now I'll destroy you."

"Now then, Pip, me lad," Johnston said, finding his voice.

Pip prodded Thomas's chest, his eyes riveted on Thomas's face. "Don't come any closer, Johnston."

Johnston raised both hands palm up, smiling. "Only if you allow, Pip. But I know you won't kill an unarmed man. Think of the scandal 'twould bring on your family."

It was the right note to hit. The fury faded from Pip's countenance, replaced by abashed frustration. "Of course not. Draw your sword, Donne!"

"No."

"Bloody hell," Robbie muttered, searching for some way out of this fix.

"Damn you! Draw your sword! I love her, can't you understand that?" The boy's voice broke on a sob. "Damn you, damn you. You will *not* deny me the privilege of fighting for her honor. Even you must have that much conscience, that much decency."

" 'Sblood!" Johnston said under his breath to Thomas, his gaze unwavering on the young man's red face. "You'll have to fight him. He's at the end of his rope, poor lad. He could not live with the knowledge that you didn't consider his challenge worth answering."

"What are you saying?" Pip demanded hotly. "I am not some schoolboy to be 'handled,' Johnston! I thought you were my friend!"

"He *is* your friend, you young fool!" Thomas said, grabbing hold of the sharp blade-tip in one hand, pulling it aside, and launching his other fist into Pip's jaw. A look of surprised pain sprang to Pip's face and then he crumpled to the ground.

"Now he'll not have to fret over his precious dignity. See that he gets home, eh?" Thomas stepped over the lad's inert form, leaving Johnston and Robbie standing staring after him.

"But where are you going?" Robbie called.

"I am going to see Fia, and this time, by God, she *will* see me."

She wasn't sleeping. It seemed sleep was simply one more thing that she had always considered necessary but was not. She sat in the armchair she'd pulled next to the window and waited for the dawn. It would come, she told herself. The unreasonable fear that it would not and that she would forever be in this dark room alone made her fingers tremble on the page of the book she held.

She answered the boudoir door on the first knock. Porter admitted himself.

"I am so sorry, milady. But there is—"

The door behind him opened and Thomas filled the shadowed frame with his tall, broad figure. His eyes met hers. "Send him away," he said.

Porter's jaw tightened perceptibly. "I shall get the footmen at once, milady, and we shall—"

"No," Fia said. "No. It's all right, Porter. You may go now."

"But—"

"Please, Porter."

Unhappily, Porter bowed and exited the room. Thomas closed the door behind him. Her heartbeat fluttered in her chest and her lungs tightened painfully. He looked awful. His eyes were stark in his face. He'd not shaved. The stubble lining the hard angle of his jaw glinted with silver in the soft low light of her table lamp. His hair was unkempt, his neckcloth loose and disheveled. She'd known he'd come, that eventually he would simply sweep away whatever obstacles stood between them. He couldn't do any less. Because of what and who he was. He felt she'd been wronged and that he was to blame, and Thomas—noble, angry Thomas—could never tolerate another's paying for his actions.

She thought she'd prepared herself for the sight of him, but nothing could prepare her for the hunger his appearance awoke.

But, Lord! he was beautiful. So large and intense and strong. She yearned to go to him, to be shielded in his arms by that strength, a strength of spirit as well as body.

But who would shield Thomas from her, from what she might one day do? Because even as she knew Thomas could do no less than come to her because of who he was, she knew who she was, too. Carr's daughter. Someday she might not choose the higher course. Someday she might be willing to sacrifice others for her own ends.

"Fia." His voice nearly undid her with its yearning.

"Yes?" She forced herself to ask calmly.

"You look awful."

She smiled. Sometimes Thomas forgot his gentlemanly manners and reverted to those of a blunt merchant-ship captain. She found the discrepancy most appeal— She stopped herself. A month ago she would have countered with an ironic rejoinder but now . . . She didn't have the heart for it.

"I am fine."

"Truly?" He came one step farther into the room, his gaze warily scouring her face. "You are not unwell?"

"Despite the evidence of your eyes, I am well."

"Good. I could not—I needed to assure myself. I am sorry for the intrusion." He inclined his head in a bow.

He was leaving? No! Not yet. It had been but two weeks since the *Alba Star* had brought them back to London. Two weeks since the hired coach had driven her away from the silent, taciturn man whom she'd caught only glimpses of during the short journey back.

"I have had word from a friend in France. My father has left there and should be arriving in London by the week's end."

"Yes?" he asked.

"You must leave London, Thomas," she said. "He's only waiting to return to inform the authorities of you so that he can be here to gloat."

"Let him."

"Thomas . . ." She held out her hand beseechingly. But the sight seemed to offend him, for he closed his eyes.

"I won't leave you here alone to face the consequences of my actions," he said.

"*Our* actions. I could have stopped it at any time."

"No." He shook his head. "I would have found a way. You were right, you see, I wanted you. It had nothing to do with my honorable concerns and my righteous anger. I wanted you and I would have found a way to justify it to myself. I know that now. I am not as good at honesty as you, Fia." He stood rigidly, as though held by steel bands.

"Don't, Thomas." She could not bear to see him hurt like this. "Please."

"No. Don't worry. I won't badger you." He took a deep breath and released it slowly. The lamp guttered; the light flickered over his visage. "If you would just retract your claim to have gone with me willingly, I would leave you in peace and . . . and go."

"I can't do that, Thomas. You'd be arrested forthwith . . . for abduction . . . possibly for rape."

"I promise, I will not be arrested," he said smoothly. "I vow it."

"But you once promised you would not shed blood on my account and you've proved that a lie. Yes, Pip told me. He said you sustained no deep harm." Her tone made it a question.

"None at all."

"But that is a lie, too. For I know there was blood on your shirt. So how can I accept your word on this?"

"I don't know," he said numbly, and she saw that she had wounded him by calling him a liar. She hadn't meant to do that.

"Stop these duels, Thomas, I beseech you. It's a profitless endeavor. It won't stop one tongue from wagging, nor one gaze from being raised in speculation."

"I can't do that, Fia. I have nothing I can give you that you will accept, but I can force you to accept the defense of your name."

She could stand no more. She felt her composure begin to shatter inside, a small breaking of glass that would result into a million fragments. He must not see it. It would cause him too much pain.

"Please," she managed. "Please go, now."

"But Fia . . ." He moved a few steps closer, and she turned her head, holding up a hand to stay him. It did not stop him. He reached up and gently swept his fingertips along the curve of her jaw. "Fia—"

"No." It had all been said. She could not even stand imagining what he would look like, the sound of his voice, the expression in his eyes if she ever failed in her fight against the nature Carr had bequeathed her.

She'd come so close to embracing her bloodlines. She'd *wanted* to keep Carr's blackmail material. She loved the rush of power she'd felt holding them, knowing she could destroy Carr with them. She'd even found the justification to keep them, nearly fooled herself that her motive—to return Bramble House to Kay—was worth the damage to her soul. Next time she might not be so strong.

Next time she might fail.

She closed her eyes, the heat of imminent tears burning behind her lids.

"Go, Thomas. I beg you."

His caress lingered. She thought she felt his hand tremble. Then his touch was gone. She dared not look. She dared not move. She heard the door open and close. And she sank to the floor, her body racked by silent sobs.

Thomas descended the stairs without a flicker of emotion betrayed on his harsh countenance. At the foot of the stairs Porter waited in silent censure to let him out.

Whatever Porter saw on Thomas's face caused the butler to stare in amazement. He'd never seen such . . .

Thomas threw his cloak over his shoulders.

For the rest of his life Porter would wonder what made him ask, but ask he did. "If Lady Fia desires to . . . contact you, sir, where might she send a note?"

Thomas laughed, and the sound raised the hairs on the nape of Porter's neck.

"I will be taking all my future correspondence at Hyde Park, I believe," he said with dark humor.

"But—"

He smiled. "Don't worry. I was only making a little joke. And she won't want to contact me."

And with that, he left.

Chapter 25

 $\mathcal{L}$ ate the next morning the post delivered a batch of packages that had been mailed some days before.

The first arrived at the modest home of a successful banker, who looked up when his butler delivered it. He was relieved by the interruption; the column he'd been poring over would not tally. He would have to make additional cuts to the household expenses and he didn't know how to tell his wife, who sat darning his shirt before an open window.

Fall was in the air, bringing to the banker's mind other autumns, particularly one fifteen years ago which the banker would have done anything to erase but which quarterly he was forced to relive. It had been the autumn when he'd embarked on a pointless, ego-stroking affair.

Looking now at the figures beneath his hand, he wondered if he should have confessed the affair to his wife, but then . . . His wife was his closest friend, his most cherished companion, and truly the center of his world. He would not hazard her love for anything.

As these thoughts crossed his mind, the banker slit open the seal on the small package and dumped out the contents. It looked to be an ancient letter, yellowed and darkened so that the address was barely—

With a sharp glance at his wife, he opened the letter. He recognized it at once even though he had not seen it in nearly fifteen years. It was the letter he'd written that woman—the letter she'd sold to Carr and that he had used all these years to extort money from the banker.

He frowned, peered into the package that had contained it. Nothing. No note. Nothing.

He sat back, the overwhelming sense of freedom dizzying. Then slowly, piece by piece, his fingers shaking, he rent the letter into tiny, tiny strips.

In a neat, fashionable house in Berkeley Square, Sir Gerald Swan stared down at a document bearing his signature, the package that had contained it at his feet. He'd never dared hope to see that document again, let alone hold it in his hand.

He'd been a young member of Parliament avid to see his policies adopted when he'd been approached by one of his party's power brokers. The man had offered Gerald his support if Gerald would sign his name to a document that would ensure a very profitable contract was won by a very disreputable company. He'd done so. There'd been a scandal soon after but since the document bearing his name had never come to light, he'd remained free from the stigma that had attached itself to many of his fellow members.

Carr had somehow come into possession of the document. And ever since, Gerald had been paying to keep it from the public with little favors. Now, for whatever reason, it was back in his hand. He would no longer need to compromise himself.

When, a short while later, Gerald's butler arrived to investigate the scent of burning paper, he found his master smiling blissfully at a pile of ashes at his feet in the front hall.

"Lord Carr is due back from France this afternoon," Gerald said. "I was to send my carriage to the pier to meet him."

"Yes, sir?"

"Cancel that order."

"Should I send a message explaining you will not be able to accommodate the earl?"

Swan considered a moment before saying, quite lightly, "No. No explanation is necessary, and should the earl inquire after me, I am not at home to him. Now or ever."

In Mayfair a young woman brought a letter dated seven years ago to her husband's hand. Her eyes were wide in her face, her expression bemused.

"What is this, Anne?"

"Bart"—she held out the paper—"I believe it is the affidavit the midwife signed testifying that our Reginald was born before our marriage."

Her husband took the proffered paper and stared at it long moments before folding it carefully. When his gaze returned to his wife's, it was filled with amazed relief.

"I don't know why he would return it now," she said, her voice troubled, her eyes dazed. For so long they'd hidden their firstborn's illegitimacy. Bart had been a young soldier and they'd made a baby and then he'd had to go away and she'd gone away, too.

As soon as he'd returned they'd wed, but it was too late to make their son legitimate and therefore next in line for her father's title. The midwife had since died, but somehow Lord Carr had gotten his hands on her written testimony. Lately Carr had been impressing upon them his willingness to disclose the truth if he was not allowed a certain portion of their son's anticipated inheritance.

"Carr must know my father is ill and it's only a matter of time before Reginald inherits his title," she whispered.

Her husband rose and embraced her softly. "I don't think Carr sent it, my darling."

"Then who?" she asked.

"I don't know, but thank God for him."

In the front hall of a small, mean lodging house in Cheapside, Lord Tunbridge accepted the package after paying the bearer an additional shilling to keep him from revealing Tunbridge's whereabouts. He looked from side to side down the rain-soaked streets before closing the door and returning to his room.

There he opened the unmarked package, upended it, and shook. A thin letter, one edge blackened as though it had been held too close to a fire, drifted to the floor, followed by a small card.

He picked up the card first.

Lord Tunbridge,

I have not read the enclosed missive but from the envelope assume it to be yours. I never meant to hurt you.

Lady Fia MacFarlane

His eyes narrowed to suspicious slits. What new torment was this? He studied the envelope. It was utterly unfamiliar. He tore it open and read, and as he read the sneer left his face, shock replacing it, and then near cretinous bafflement.

A dockyard surgeon had written it some twenty years earlier. In it the surgeon apologized for bothering Lord Carr but had heard from various sources that Carr was most interested in what had happened to a young woman named Nell Baxter who had come afoul of a knife in an altercation with a hotheaded young aristocrat named Tunbridge. The good earl might then be pleased to know that the wench had not succumbed as a result of her wounds. Indeed, the surgeon had doctored the girl himself and seen to her recovery, only to witness her tragic death the following week when she was hit on the head with a steel signpost in a tavern brawl. The surgeon thought that, in light of the earl's earlier interest, he might be inclined to reward the surgeon for his original heroic efforts on the girl's behalf.

Tunbridge read the letter five times. When he looked up from the last time, he was sitting in the middle of the floor. He'd spent a lifetime covering up a crime he'd never committed and committing sins thrice over as cardinal to do so. He shook his head and began laughing, and he could not stop.

Lord Carr walked into his sumptuous mansion, swinging his cane in mild irritation. The trip to the continent had not been as profitable as he'd desired, Janet had begun a campaign of appearing at his window laughing, and Swan had not sent his carriage as he'd been instructed.

Swan would pay for that little oversight.

His good humor restored, Carr shed his cloak into the waiting hands of a footman and motioned for another to bring him his mail.

"Milord." The footman bowed and presented him with a silver tray on which a meager little pile of envelopes lay.

"The rest is in my study, I presume," Carr said coldly. The little bastard had best learn that when Lord Carr wanted his mail, he didn't give a damn how much trouble he put his lackeys through to fetch it.

"No, milord. This is the sum of it."

There had to be some sort of mistake. Perhaps the mail service had been disrupted in his absence or his correspondence was being forwarded to his country estate.

He snatched up the little pile and began sorting through it. Five invitations to events long past, and the rest bills.

There had to be some explanation. And he intended to find out what it was.

It was not until the same mechanical impulse that prompted Fia to brush her hair and wash her teeth led her, still in nightrail and dressing gown, downstairs to look numbly through the mail that she received the official-looking letter from an unfamiliar agency in . . . Edinburgh?

A twinge of curiosity pierced her numbness and she opened the letter. It was from a lawyer who was trying to ascertain the whereabouts of her brother Ashton Douglas Merrick regarding a new addition to his holdings in Scotland.

Fia frowned in consternation. Ashton owned nothing in Scotland. He'd used all the money he'd accumulated to buy his estate in Cornwall. . . . Her brow smoothed with insight.

That Thomas had purchased Maiden's Blush through an intermediary, she'd known, but now she realized that he'd named Ashton its legal owner. Of course. He'd protected the land from being forfeited to the Crown, as were all criminals' possessions, by never really owning it.

This way should Carr or anyone else ever expose him, it could stay safely out of English hands. But why Ash?

The answer came immediately. Because Thomas had hoped, had believed, that as Janet McClairen's oldest child, Ash would take care of the land—and the people he'd brought there. And because he was atoning for the wrong he'd done Ash.

"Oh, Thomas," she murmured.

"Milady." Porter stood uneasily before her.

"Yes?"

"I have been trying unsuccessfully to determine whether or not to inform you of a matter that—"

She smiled slightly. "Porter, you have guided as well as butlered for me for six years now and your instincts have never yet been wrong. What is it?"

"Captain Donne."

Her gaze fell. "If this is about last night, you needn't be concerned with the unseemliness of so late a visit. He won't be coming back," she said tonelessly.

"That is what I fear, madam." His tone brought Fia's gaze back to Porter's face. "Last night as Captain Donne was preparing to leave, I asked him where he could be found should you desire to contact him. He laughed and said he would be taking all his future correspondence at Hyde Park.

"Milady, Hyde Park is where the gentlemen fight their duels."

The blood rushed in her head, buzzing in her temples, the implication of Thomas's words clear.

"There's more."

"How so?" she demanded breathlessly.

He told her gravely of the two visitors that had arrived mere hours apart that very morning, and when he was done, her face was ghostly white and her eyes dark with horrifying premonitions.

"Send for the carriage at once," she said. "As you value my sanity, my *life*, do so at once!"

Chapter 26

$\mathcal{L}$ate that same afternoon, atop a knoll in one of Hyde Park's less frequented corners, a tall, elegant young man in somewhat foreign dress sat lounging at the base of a statue of King George II. He stretched his great long legs before him and leaned back against the sovereign's bronze foot, lacing his fingers over his own satin-vested belly.

He'd pulled the gilt-embroidered collar of his coat up, warding off the mist that waited for night to come before completing its metamorphosis into one of London's legendary fogs. He'd tipped his tricorn hat low on his brow and directed his attention to two gentlemen currently pacing off from each other a short ways below his vantage point.

As he waited, another figure approached on

horseback, a slender, lithe figure in a shabby coat and hat, black gauntlets, and black, well-worn riding boots. The foreign-appearing gentleman glanced up, noting the fine piece of horseflesh the man rode, and then returned his regard to the duelists currently shedding their coats.

"Which one is Donne?" the newcomer asked, peering into the mist at the phantomlike figures below.

"The taller fellow on the right," the large young man replied.

"My thanks." The slender, shabby gentleman dismounted and tethered his horse to George's outstretched hand, and took a seat on the opposite corner of the marble base, leaning forward, his arms resting on his knees.

"You have business with Donne?" the elegant young man asked after a moment, when it became clear that some sort of delay involving one of the duelists' pistols was going to go on rather long.

"Hm," the other man rejoined. "I hear this Frenchman, Pierpont, is an excellent shot. It would make things decidedly simpler if he wins, but if not, I intend to challenge Donne."

"Thank God," the other man breathed, bringing the newcomer's head swinging around in surprise. "Because—" He stopped because in turning to thank his benefactor, he found himself gazing into a most familiar and roughly handsome face.

For a long moment the two men regarded each other in silence. Finally a crooked grin curved the long, mobile mouth of the slender, shabby gentleman.

"Well, Raine?" he said.

An answering smile was born on the rough, chiseled features of the other. "Well, Ash?"

Ashton Merrick rose to his feet, strode to where his brother sat, and pulled him up and into a warm embrace. Raine returned it with one equally as warm. They then proceeded to pound each other affectionately on the back.

"Damn me, it's good to see you!" Raine said.

"Aye," Ash said, grinning as he held his brother from him at arm's length, his gaze traveling over his tall, elegant figure. " 'Tis grand to see you, too, Raine. 'Tis been too many years. Far too many. Since France.

"Letters are all very well and fine, but they can't . . ." For a moment emotion stopped Ash's voice, but he mastered himself and grinned. "They can't begin to describe the horrors you've allowed your tailor."

Raine laughed, a rich infectious sound, and cast a telling glance over the disreputable coat covering Ash's lean, elegant frame. "At least I *have* a tailor."

Ash answered with his own laugh. "Well, I'm but a humble horse-breeder, not some lofty consul to Italian princes. Besides, I came in a hurry."

"Aye." Raine sobered, his smile fading. "Why are you here?"

"A month back I received a letter from a man named James Barton—a friend of Fia's. Or so he claimed and so he must have been, because he warned me that Fia had become embroiled in some sort of situation with Carr and Thomas Donne. I know—I knew Thomas Donne. I came forthwith and arrived yesterday, only to discover Fia's name being bandied about in the coarsest manner. Because of Donne." His mouth flattened. "I followed his trail here."

Raine nodded. "You arrived yesterday? I, also. And I followed a similar route, coming at the urgings of this man Barton. I could do no less. I have always felt that I abandoned Fia when I left England. I could not do so twice."

"I understand," Ash responded grimly. "I have always felt that I betrayed you in not ransoming you from that French hellhole. After Rhiannon and I learned you had escaped, I tried for a long time to discover your whereabouts, but by then the war had closed what channels were open between England and France.

"I swear to you, I never did know you'd been recaptured. Not until your letter arrived telling me your story." Ash braced his hand on his brother's shoulder, his gaze level and somber. "Forgive me."

Raine smiled awkwardly. "There's nothing to forgive. If you had rescued me, my Favor wouldn't have had the pleasure and I would never have . . ." He shook his head ruefully. "As hard as it is to admit, I'd have stayed another decade in that place to ensure that things had turned out the way they have."

"Good—"

The sound of a pistol blast shattered their reunion.

Both men swung around. A thin wisp of smoke issued from Pierpont's pistol. Thomas Donne stood with his pistol still hanging at his side.

"*Mon dieu!*" shouted Pierpont as they watched. "If you mean to fire, by all that's holy, do so!"

Calmly, Thomas raised his arm and aimed. Nothing moved. No sound stirred the still, damp air.

"Damn, he's a cool one," Raine muttered.

"Aye," Ash returned, "he always was."

"Will you issue a public apology to Lady Fia?" Donne suddenly asked in a clear voice as cold as an arctic blast.

For a long moment Pierpont said nothing, and then in a voice choked with emotion, "*Oui! Je suis d'accord!*"

Thomas lowered his gun. Even at this distance, they could hear Pierpont's sigh of relief. The Frenchman hastened up the knoll toward the brothers, his second hurrying after him. When he reached them, he cast a quick look behind him, his face grim.

"Rethink your vanity, my friends," he advised tersely. "I tell you honestly, I am accounted a brave man, and I've faced many on the field of honor, but I've never faced a man like that."

"Really?" Ash said. "How so?"

"You look into his eyes and there is nothing. And a man who has nothing to protect, monsieur, is a very dangerous man indeed." He struggled to recoup his pride. "Besides, I was drunk when I made those unfortunate remarks about the Lady Fia. I am a gentleman. It is not for my own safety that I cede the contest, you understand, but for the lady's honor."

"It is certainly healthy to realize one's mistakes in time," Raine said, a warning edging his smile.

Pierpont eyed him cautiously. "Ah, yes. Well, er . . . Good luck to you."

As soon as he'd gone, Raine turned to his brother and bowed, his face grim. "After you."

Ash's mouth twined with distaste. "You were here first."

"Aye. But my wife has spoken fondly of Donne and I am loath to hurt her."

"But at one time he was my friend, and even if he was playacting, his imitation was better than any reality I'd known, or have since. At least until the end."

"How many children do you have, Ash?" Raine asked.

"Ah, yes. There's that, too." Ash nodded in understanding. "He's a formidable opponent, isn't he? And in answer, I've but one to your three." With a sigh he turned and walked down the little knoll.

If Thomas was surprised to see the friend he'd once betrayed, he gave scant indication. Other than a slow curl of his lip and an elegant bow such as he once used in London's drawing rooms, he displayed no emotion.

"I can't kill you, Ash," Thomas said after hearing Ash's cool challenge. "Besides being Fia's brother, you are entirely in the right in calling me out."

"And I'd rather not kill you," Ash said. "But you've rather done a job of destroying my sister's honor—however close she'd already come to achieving that herself, which, from what I hear, was very close indeed."

"Watch your tongue," Thomas cautioned harshly.

He looked down at the pair of dueling pistols Johnston silently offered him and waved them away. "Your
forte, as I recall, is blades. Bring us swords, please."

As Johnston hurried to get the épées, Ash shrugged
out of his coat. "Damned if I like this, Thomas. Has it
occurred to you to marry the girl?"

"It had occurred to me," Thomas replied stiffly.

"She's a very pretty thing, I recall. And while I realize she might not be one's first choice for a wife, from
her letters I suspect there are depths to her well
worth—"

"*Go to hell, Merrick!*" Thomas shouted. The violence in his sudden outburst startled Ash to such an
extent that he stopped in the midst of experimentally
swinging the épée he'd chosen and regarded his opponent with dawning incredulity.

"Begads! You offered and she declined," he breathed
in fascinated tones.

Thomas did not reply. Instead he gave Ash a cur-
sory salute. "*En garde!*"

With no recourse but to defend Fia's honor, Ash
returned the salute, and both men engaged. They
fought in silence, Ash on the attack, Thomas profi-
ciently parrying his thrusts. Both men's increasingly
harsh breath condensed in the chill air, the dew glistening on their hair as the wet grass beneath their feet
grew slick.

Some minutes passed before Ash realized that
Thomas fought from an entirely defensive posture, taking no advantage of his lunges to *riposte*. The *fleche* he
performed met no stop-thrust or counterattack, merely

mechanical blocking. Oh, Thomas masked his intent, but most of the exploratory finesses Ash attempted met with success. Twice he'd pierced Thomas's defense, drawing blood first from his shoulder and then from his wrist. With the realization of what Thomas hoped to achieve, anger flowed through Ash's lean body.

He was being set up as Thomas's executioner.

Furiously he drove inside, determined to hammer Thomas's hand guard with as much force as possible, striking the blade from the bastard's hand. Then . . . they would have a little talk.

Thomas countered perfunctorily, his apathy further inciting Ash's ire. Ash ground his teeth together, dodging beneath a slapdash lunge and—

"No!" A woman's voice rang in the mist-drenched silence. "No!"

Both men lowered their weapons and turned. A slight feminine figure raced down the knoll, her petticoats swirling about her feet, her black ringlets rippling behind her. In a trice she was down the hill and pitching herself at Donne's rigid figure, wrapping her slender bare arms around his torso and pressing her head against his chest.

"No!" She turned to Ash. "Stop this. I could not bear it were either of you to cause the death of the other."

It was Fia. Ash stared at her in disbelief. Perfect, composed, suave Fia. She'd not dressed completely, her gown was loosened, her hair a tumbled tangle, and her feet— By God! Her feet were bare.

"Go home, Fia," Ash heard Thomas say. He'd

made no move to touch Fia; his hands remained at his sides, the épée's point buried in the ground.

"No. Not until you stop this," Fia said, and to Ash, "You can't hurt him because of what he did, what he tried to do, so many years ago, Ash. He had cause. Just cause. He isn't Thomas Donne. He's Thomas McClairen. And he's bought McClairen's Isle and he's deeded it to you!"

Ash looked up at Thomas's impassive face. "Is this true?"

"What difference does it make?"

"A bold bit of difference, I'd say," came a furious rejoinder as Raine Merrick strode toward them through the thickening fog. "Because if old Ash here hadn't succeeded in killing you, *I* was going to have a go. And my wife, who will have much explaining to do when I return home"—his face was dusky with emotion—"might have had a few things to say about my killing her brother, you damned heathen Scot!"

"I don't suppose she would be any more pleased if I killed her husband," Thomas returned coldly, and would have stepped forward to meet Raine but for the fact that Fia held him so tightly, so tenaciously that he could not move without hurting her. He grasped her arms, determined to pull himself free, but when his efforts caused her to flinch, he gave up, the anger in his face turning to agonized frustration.

"Ah, little sister," Raine said softly. "How good of you to join us."

"Don't speak to her in that fashion," Thomas said. "Can't you see how this is hurting her?"

Both brothers looked at Fia. Ash frowned. Fia's ravishingly beautiful face was as smooth and unreadable as ever. If Thomas thought he read something in that enigmatic—

Ash tossed down his sword, wheeled around, and grabbed his larger, younger brother by the arm. "We're going now," he said loudly. "And you needn't fear we'll return to finish this nonsense."

"But Fia's honor!" protested Raine.

"Is already being well tended, you ass," Ash hissed as he half dragged Raine behind him.

Silence descended on the couple standing in a parody of a lovers' embrace.

"Please, Fia." His voice was thick with pleading. "Don't interfere like this again."

"I'll interfere every single time you put yourself in danger. Every time," she declared hotly.

His big, taut body trembled against her.

"Then what am I to do?" he asked faintly, in a voice unlike any Fia had ever heard from him. "You will not renounce me and you will not have me," he said. "And I find I must have one or the other."

She smiled softly at that, at the gruff insistence in his voice, at the hard, uncompromising slant of his brows. He'd wrested victory from enslavement, found and brought home his Scottish clan, and fought to regain their island; he'd never known lasting defeat.

But it was possible to live with it. It had to be.

"No," she said quietly. "You have only to turn away from this place and leave. I know it will hurt you to feel that you abandoned me, but you haven't. I forgive you for abducting me. Do you need society to forgive you as well? I wouldn't have thought so."

"You know that's not what I want," he said.

"Then it's society's absolution of me you seek, and there's no reason to do so, because I do not care for society's approval or condemnation. See? Once again your suit is unwarranted."

"But you will," he said tensely. "Someday you will want a home and family of your own and a man to share it."

How could she reply? Tell him that she would never want anyone but him?

"I know, Fia," he said slowly, his voice low and resonant, "that you think yourself lesser than others and I know I did that to you. I would cut my heart from my chest if it would take back my words."

She put her fingers over his lips, but he drew them away, holding them tightly in his fist.

"You never acted on any hateful thought or impulse. You married a rich man and when he died you loved his children so much that you were willing to sacrifice your future for them.

"You found the means to set yourself forever free of a monster and you gave it up, *had* given it up before I ever said a word. I know about the letters, Fia. Swan told Johnston, who told me. Just as I know you would never have used them to procure your own freedom."

"I might have," she denied.

"No." His gaze was clear, focused, absolutely certain. "You never acted on the darker impulses, but I did. I purposefully played the part of friend to your brother and then used that friendship to hurt him," he said, his voice ragged and low. "Yet you forgave me. You never even challenged me with it. Being Carr's daughter does not diminish who you are, Fia, it only testifies to how extraordinary you are."

She caught back a sob. She had never dared think of being Carr's daughter as anything other than a stigma, a poison that she carried. He couldn't mean it.

"It's easy to be good, Fia, if you are never tempted."

"I am no saint, Thomas."

She could not lift her gaze; her hands remained folded at her waist, her fingers curling round one another. She stared at his boots, vaguely aware that the wet grass had soaked them through, and then that her own feet were wet and cold.

"Please, Fia. I love you." His eyes were afire. "Do you love me?"

"Yes," she exclaimed, surprised into honesty by the stunning realization that he'd not known.

"Then be my wife!"

"Oh, Thomas, however you look at it, whatever you hope to see in it, I am still Carr's daughter." There it was, the inescapable truth, and yet it never had felt so much true as inescapable. She did not wait for his reply, for there was no reply to such an unassailable fact. She turned, forcing her numb legs to move, her gaze fixed unseeingly on the blank empty fog that surrounded her.

"Fia."

She kept walking.

"Fia!"

A few more steps and she would be lost in the soft, cool, faceless void.

"For God's sake, Fia. Please." His voice broke on the last words, bringing her spinning around. Pain and sleeplessness and hunger had taken its toll, but it was she ultimately who'd accomplished what no sadistic gaoler, no harsh transport ship's galley guard, no bond-master's whip had accomplished; she'd broken the spirit holding that great, tall body defiantly straight. He was on one knee, one palm flat against the earth, his head bowed as though he'd taken a blow.

He looked up. His eyes were like stones, and she hated herself for hurting him.

"What can I do, Fia? I swear to you that Carr's blood in you is no curse. I would give you my heart's blood, but you will not let me."

She approached him slowly, more fearful than she'd ever been of anything in her life, a small tentative hope unfurling its fragile wings. His ravaged gaze scoured her face, and what he read there ignited a fierce light to his dimmed eyes. He pushed himself to his feet and waited for her.

"Thomas, don't you know who I am?"

But this time Thomas answered with poignant certainty. "Why, you are yourself, Fia. No more, no less, and that is what you have always been and always will be. My love, my life, more than I ever dreamed was possible, and far more than I will ever be able to surrender. So either bury this blade in me, Fia, or be mine. Forever."

The tears started in her eyes and they would not stop; they fell from her gem-colored eyes and coursed unimpeded down her cheeks, wetting her lips and dropping from her chin.

Blinded, she reached out, stumbled, and before she'd taken her second step she was in his arms, his embrace like steel bands, his heart thundering against hers, and he was kissing her lips, her cheeks, her eyelids, her temples, and her mouth.

"Forever," she vowed.

Chapter 27

The flinty land-bridge connecting McClairen's Isle to the headland was in danger of being submerged by the rising tide. The hired chaise had gone only a third of the way across when the driver thought better of the proposition, no matter what the monetary incentive, and gave his passenger the option of turning back or going the rest of the way on foot.

Ronald Merrick, Earl of Carr, chose to go on. He emerged from the carriage and tossed the driver a coin and waited for the peasant to be gone.

He turned, one hand on his hip, the other poised on the silver knob of his walking cane, and regarded the great hulk of Maiden's Blush. Gray, monolithic, workers crawling over her surface like termites on a nest.

Lud, he loathed the place. Particularly as someone—presumably Thomas McClairen—was endeavoring to rebuild it in keeping with the deplorable style in which he'd originally found it. Perhaps, Carr thought, he would repossess it, particularly since he'd found it necessary to leave London for a while.

He began walking up the land-bridge, his countenance rippling with hatred, like worms beneath a thin silk glove. Not that he was destroyed. No! Not by a far cry. He still possessed damning evidence against many important and powerful people, and if since his return from France one or two—or perhaps more, why should he keep count?—had flown in the face of his wrath and exposed their little secrets themselves, well, not everyone develops balls so late in life.

He approached the base of the castle, careful to keep out of sight of the workers as he headed round back, toward the sea-facing facade, where he could enter the place unseen.

So what if his name was anathema and people who'd last month crept on their knees to petition him now crossed the street to avoid him? His malevolent gaze turned to the castle. He'd been told the wretched place had burned to ashes. All of it. Who would have foreseen that his second packet of materials would survive and be found by his darling youngest child?

Once more, hatred erupted like a boil on his features. With a deep steadying inhalation he brought himself under control. Fia and her paramour, Thomas McClairen, would pay, in spite of Tunbridge's efforts to thwart his revenge against the Scotsman.

Carr dug inside his jacket for the front page of the *London Times* newspaper, and reread the letter reproduced there.

> *I, James Wells, Lord Tunbridge, do hereby avow as my last act on earth the truth of the testimony provided herein. I, James Wells, Lord Tunbridge, in anticipating that Ronald Merrick, Earl of Carr, will denounce Thomas Donne and subsequently accuse him of being the traitor and deported criminal Thomas McClairen, offer incontrovertible proof that this man is not the aforementioned Thomas McClairen and that Lord Carr's enmity and spite have led him to make this accusation in the hopes of bringing about an innocent man's death.*
>
> *I know Thomas Donne is not Thomas McClairen because I, James Wells, killed Thomas McClairen in cold blood at the behest of Ronald Merrick on February the 20, 1752, in a tavern in Kingston, on the island of Jamaica. I did this for no reason other than to fulfill Lord Carr's command, because of his long-standing hatred of the McClairens, just as I have killed others at his behest, including his butler, Rankle.*
>
> *I can no longer live with my deeds and so now commit myself to God's mercy, swearing this and everything I have written herein to be true, as God is my judge. May He have mercy on my soul.*
>
> *James Wells, Lord Tunbridge*

Clever, Carr thought. Tunbridge actually had once been arrested in Kingston for the murder of "persons unknown." As to the rest . . . apparently Tunbridge had not placed much faith in his God's mercy, since he'd offered his eternal soul testifying to a lie just before severing his wrists.

But why? Carr lifted his hand, as though holding a silent exchange with another. Tunbridge must have hated McClairen for achieving what Tunbridge had spent years trying for, a way into Fia's bed.

"Because he hated you more than McClairen."

At the sound of that long-silent voice, Carr wheeled around, smiling.

"Ah, Janet. I knew you'd speak to me someday soon. Over your sulks, are you?"

Lud, she was lovely. Her dark eyes sparkled and her hair fell in rich, ebony waves. Her one-sided smile, so piquant, so enchanting, lit her white face. He truly had loved her.

She curtsyed, her lovely face alight with humor. "I might be."

"And perhaps you 'might be' right about Tunbridge," he said magnanimously.

"I know I am. Why are you here, Ronald?"

He waved his cane in the air. "I've come to kill McClairen."

"Ah," she exhaled. "Why?"

"Poor, simple Janet. Because if I kill McClairen others will see that I am still a man to fear, a man to obey, a force to be reckoned with."

She laughed, the ghostly trill like sunlight dancing on water, and beckoned him closer.

"I don't think so," she said as he approached. She

turned, floating above the flinty ground, as graceful as a feather on water. He followed her, mesmerized by her beauty, captivated as he'd been so many years ago by her freshness, her obvious adoration of him.

"Wait! What don't you think?"

She looked over her shoulder at him, gesturing for him to come with her. "I don't think that's the real reason you're here, Ronald."

How dare she question him!

"Really?" He invested the word with haughty intonation, but she only laughed again and moved on, and he hastened to follow her.

"I think you want to kill Thomas because as long as he lives, the McClairens will have won!" she whispered like a naughty child revealing a secret.

"They haven't won!"

"But they will." She finally stopped.

"Oh, yes, Ronald," an older feminine voice said.

He turned slowly. An old hag stood before him, bent beneath the weight of her gray dress, a black veil draped across half her face, leaving exposed a twisted and deformed countenance, a smashed nose, a drooping eye, a slack and malformed mouth.

"Who are you?" he demanded, angered that she should have interrupted his conversation with Janet.

"Gunna," she said.

He searched his memory. "You're Fia's nurse!"

"Aye."

He snorted. "Begad, does she keep such as you around still? Has she quite lost her faculties?" He laughed cruelly, glancing over his shoulder to see if

Janet appreciated his wit. Her gaze was fixed on the deformed creature in front of him, clear recognition in her pretty black eyes.

"No. But methinks you have," Gunna said. There was something wrong. The way she spoke . . . His eyes widened. Where was the creature's thick, near unintelligible burr? Why did she suddenly sound like Janet?

"Who are you?"

"I told you," she said. "Gunna."

"No." He shook his head, violently aware as he did so that Janet was mimicking him, her spectral head shaking in increasing agitation as she mouthed the words, "No, no, no."

Gunna's mouth pleated into some semblance of a smile. "But there was a time, a long time ago, when I was someone else. Someone who no longer exists."

"Who's that?" he demanded, a little river of fear running through his bowels.

"Janet McClairen," she said softly.

He jerked his head around and met Janet's impish smile. She shrugged expressively. "Impossible," he said. "I killed you. I pitched you from—" He stopped abruptly and looked about as if coming out of a daze. Only then did he realize where he was, where she'd led him.

He stood on the cliff path beyond the old kitchen garden, above the rocks where Janet had died. In horror he stared as the surf below bludgeoned the shoreline.

"You're dead," he whispered.

"No. I was hurt, oh . . . very badly. But I still had my mind. I clung to a piece of driftwood. The riptide carried me far down the shore, where some passing fishermen found and rescued me."

He looked up, incomprehension clouding his beautiful blue eyes. The hag lifted her hand and pulled at the scarf. It dropped, revealing a Janus face, a horrifying amalgamation all the more disturbing because the ruined half melded with the half that was still lovely, the high curve of the cheekbone taut and smooth, the dark-lashed eye as dark as ink.

"Impossible." He backed away from her in horror.

"Difficult," the creature corrected in Janet's voice. "Years went by while I recuperated. Remember the night you killed me how I swore I would do anything to protect my children from you? I meant that, Ronald.

"I came back. With your loathing of ugliness and your love of good value, it was easy enough to convince you to hire me to take care of my own children. All I needed to do was stay out of your way and I could care for them, love them, but most of all do what I could to counterbalance your poisonous tutelage."

"They know?" he asked.

The smile curving half her mouth disappeared. "No," she said. "I could never reveal who I'd been for fear that one of them would let something slip and you would simply kill me anew. So I stayed Gunna, the nurse. In a very real sense you did kill me, Ronald, for I could never tell them now. How could they understand, and what to say? For though I was nurse, companion, servant, and tutor, I never again was their mother."

His head whipped back to stare at the beautiful Janet. She was gone. "Janet!"

"To whom do you speak, Ronald?" the half hag asked quietly.

"To Janet. To you. To . . ." He stopped, his gaze widening with terror. For how can a man be haunted by a living woman? And yet haunted he surely was and had been for years. He'd only to look—

"You are mad, Ronald," the monster Janet said calmly. "How can my spirit haunt you when I still own it, no matter how hard you tried to separate me from it? How else to account for the phantom you see? You are mad, Ronald. Haunted by your own evil."

"No!" he shouted frantically. "Get away from me. You are the phantom! You aren't real. You're not Janet! Janet is beautiful. Janet loves me. Janet—"

"Is here."

The beautiful side of her mouth curved into that perfect, three-corner smile while the other side of her mouth slackened, a hideous, toothless maw. He backed away, his hands thrust out before him.

"Monster!"

He was still crying out in terror when he plummeted to the rocks below.

It took the workmen fifteen minutes to get down to the cliffs. They'd heard the cry and some had even seen a man's figure flailing wildly just before disappearing over the cliff's flinty lip.

"Lord have mercy on him, poor bastard," Jamie Craigg said, peering down at the rocks below.

"Ye can lower me down to him," offered the boy Gordie, already tying a rope around his waist.

"Good." Jamie nodded his agreement. "But there's no hurry, lad. No one could survive a fall to those rocks. Eh, Gunna?" He looked sadly at the old, twisted woman who'd followed the small crowd out.

"Nay," she said calmly. "No one ever has."

Epilogue

MAIDEN'S BLUSH
MCCLAIREN'S ISLE
CHRISTMAS, 1766

I don't hold out much hope for him," Ash Merrick said. He was sitting beside his wife, Rhiannon, speaking in a low, hushed voice to his brother, Raine. Outside the windows rattled as a fierce wind swept down from the north. But inside Maiden's Blush a huge fire roaring in the hearth chased away any encroaching chill.

The Merrick children had all been tempted, coerced, and bullied into bed, where they'd fallen immediately into slumber. Except for Ash's youngest. Gunna sat near the fire, clucking as she dried young Cora MacFarlane's tresses, and Kay was snuggled deep in a wingback chair, his perennial companion, a book, open in his lap.

nnon, involved as she was in nursing their firstborn daughter, paid little heed to her husband, Ash. Raine, however, nodded in agreement.

"Poor devil. I know I shouldn't feel sorry for him, but I do. I mean, it's not like *we* escaped unscathed. Why should he?"

"Exactly," Ash said.

"Ach!" Favor appeared behind Raine's chair, fresh from putting the last of their brood to bed. She leaned over his shoulder and bussed him on the cheek. "Misery loves company, is it?" she asked, a challenging light in her eye. "You are the most wretched, horrible pair. Why on earth would you wish on another that which you yourselves so patently and vocally hated?"

"Well," both men mumbled a bit sheepishly.

"I mean, really, Favor, me love," Raine defended himself, "consider the victim. He's not exactly without resources."

"For all he's done, he's still only a man, Raine Merrick. Just think of what he's up against," Favor countered, and to this unassailable argument there was simply no response.

At that moment a feminine voice, cool, calm, measured, and suave, could be heard coming toward them down the hallway.

"*Ashton*," the voice said, "has had *his* preliminary sketch done. *Raine* has sat for *his* preliminary sketch. And *I* have had mine."

Fia appeared, gliding into the room on nary a whisper, her beautiful face as enigmatic as ever, only the accent she gave certain words betraying a hint of temper. One slender and eloquent brow rose on her pure white forehead, investing the silence that followed with regal imperative.

"Not a chance in hell," Ash muttered. "Poor bounder."

"And a very nice family grouping it shall make." Thomas Donne, newly granted the hitherto unclaimed title Viscount McClairen for his invaluable service to the Crown in ridding her waters of maritime brigands, strode into the room after his wife. A tall, lean scoundrel, he looked hard as the life he'd led.

"I don't know." Rhiannon had apparently been attending after all, for she looked up from her daughter's face and studied Thomas closely. "I have a gold guinea says McClairen doesn't have his portrait painted."

"You're on," Ash said, and leaning close so that only Rhiannon could hear, whispered, "but when I win I'll collect in something more precious than gold, lady wife," bringing a blush to Rhiannon's cheeks.

"I don't want a family portrait," Fia said, turning suddenly and moving toward Thomas. He watched her warily. A small sway had begun at her hips and it was damned provocative. And she knew it.

He glanced hopefully at Ash and Raine, who returned his smile with blank expressions. Apparently his damned brothers-in-law weren't going to fall all over themselves coming to his rescue.

"Odd as it might sound," Fia said, her voice growing more sarcastic as she went on, "I want pictures in the new picture gallery. As the picture gallery is at this moment bare, it falls on us—mind you, I said *us*,

Thomas—to furnish new ones. I assume—mind you, I said *assume*, Thomas, because I could be in error—that as the laird of the McClairens you might like portraits of McClairens on the walls. But that . . ."

She closed her eyes for just an instant, gathering her temper, and when she opened them he found himself staring into the blue, shimmering clarity of her eyes. Their gazes locked, holding him spellbound. Her, too. He could not help himself. He reached out and gently cupped her cheek. Her lips opened but no words came out. She turned her head slightly, deepening the caress.

" 'But that' what?" Raine's voice cut in, pouring over them like cold water. The traitor!

Fia jerked back, her expression suspicious.

"But that will be impossible," she said tersely, "if the bloody laird of the bloody castle won't even allow my poor artist to do a simple sketch!"

She stomped her small, satin-covered foot on the floor. The display of temper immediately set Ash to grinning broadly. It still amazed him that their silent, enigmatic sister should—only with her husband and only in the security and warmth of her own home—be given to emotional displays.

But Thomas had jumped on the pronoun. "*Your* poor artist?" He stepped forward, possessiveness ringing in his voice. Fia stepped back. "*Yours*, Lady McClairen? How so . . . *yours*?"

She gulped as he loomed closer, and scurried back a step. " 'Twas just a phrase! You know I only love—" She was suddenly being swept up into Thomas's arms and he was smiling down at her wolfishly.

"Oh, drat you, Thomas! You did that on purpose!" Her lush, red mouth broke into a smile, and then she laughed, a full, heady laugh. "You do not play fair, sir!"

Rhiannon smiled at her husband. "Told you."

"He might have won the battle but she'll rise to fight another day," Ash said. "Look. She's already honing different tools. Ones I've seen before in my own household. Enough to recognize them, at any rate."

"Ah, yes!" Raine nodded sagely. "Most familiar."

For Fia had wrapped her arms around Thomas's broad neck and he was watching her with an entirely different sort of light burning in his eyes.

"Enough my bonny, my beauty, my love. Soon ye'll have a brand-new portrait to hang on the wall and I'll make sure there's plenty more to follow that," he murmured, nuzzling her throat.

But Favor's ears were quick and she looked up, her piquant face alight with wonder. "What's this?" she asked.

Thomas turned to the little group, his dark face bright with pride. "Fia's carrying our baby."

Gunna stopped, frozen in the midst of plaiting Cora's hair. " 'Tis true?" she asked, her eyes glittering with tears.

"Fia?" Kay asked, looking up round-eyed from his book. Cora just grinned, as did the others in the room.

"Aye," Fia said, suddenly shy. "Come early summer, he'll be born."

"*She*," Thomas corrected smoothly.

Raine looked over at Ash, the contempt of the expert for the novice clear on his face. "Has anyone told them how this works?" He looked back at the pair. "It isn't like giving a tavern order, you know. One generally takes what one gets."

"*She*," Thomas insisted, looking down at Fia. The glow in his eyes caused a pink blush to creep into her cheeks.

"And I suppose you also know what she will look like?" Ash asked sardonically.

"Aye," Thomas said softly, his gaze dwelling with loving fascination on Fia's upturned face. "She'll have hair as black as midnight velvet and shinier than a raven's wing. Her eyes will be as blue as the sea's deepest soul and her skin as white as the Dover cliffs." A smile broke upon his handsome, austere face. "And I will find her, like her mother . . . ravishing."

Dear Reader,

Thank you so much for journeying with me to McClairen's Isle. I hope that I have been able to convey to you just a wee bit o' the Scottish magic that so charmed me from the rugged northern highlands to the lush, green lowlands. It's heady stuff, indeed, and has kept my imagination firmly rooted on McClairen's Isle. I hope someday to return both in body and spirit to Scotland and see how things are going with the disreputable, passionate, but always fascinating, clan McClairen.

But for right now, there's a resourceful, mischievous, and delightful young woman three hundred miles south of Scotland who's demanding my attention. She's gotten herself into one helluva a fix and there's this gorgeous nobleman who's eager to disentangle her. For a price.

Obviously, they need my help . . .

As always, my very best to you,

Connie Brockway

Watch for Connie Brockway's next
thrilling romance . . .

The Bridal Season

ON SALE IN FALL 2001